P9-DWB-549

The
Snow White
Christmas
Cookie

THE
SNOW WHITE
CHRISTMAS
COOKIE

A Berger and Mitry Mystery

DAVID
HANDLER

MINOTAUR BOOKS

A THOMAS DUNNE BOOK

NEW YORK

A THOMAS DUNNE BOOK FOR MINOTAUR BOOKS.
An imprint of St. Martin's Publishing Group.

THE SNOW WHITE CHRISTMAS COOKIE. Copyright © 2012 by David Handler. All rights reserved. Printed in the United States of America. For information, address St. Martin's Press, 175 Fifth Avenue, New York, N.Y. 10010.

www.thomasdunnebooks.com
www.minotaurbooks.com

ISBN 978-1-250-00454-3 (hardcover)
ISBN 978-1-250-01734-5 (e-book)

First Edition: October 2012

10 9 8 7 6 5 4 3 2 1

For Ruth Cavin, who I'm convinced is still watching over me

THE
SNOW WHITE
CHRISTMAS
COOKIE

PROLOGUE

SHE WAS ALREADY TWENTY minutes late and it was making him totally crazy. The snow was coming down so heavily that he was starting to wonder if she was going to show up at all. Eighteen inches were expected by nightfall. The schools were closed. Again. The state government offices were closed. Again. The governor was ordering people to stay off of the highways. Again. It was the state's fourth shutdown blizzard in the past two weeks. Epic stuff. But she'd promised him she'd show up. He checked his cell phone one more time. No messages from her. So he just sat here in the deserted parking lot and waited, growing more and more desperate.

When he'd opened his eyes that morning and seen all of the snow he'd been plunged into total despair, thinking she would bail on him. But she'd called him to say she'd definitely be here, snow be damned, because she really, really needed to feel his arms around her. *She* needed *him*. Which he was okay with. Hell, more than okay. She was everything to him. Even though they were only able to meet like this maybe twice a week—just the two of them alone together—she was pretty much all that he lived for.

"What am I going to do about you?"

Those were the first words she said to him. This was back in October at the free flu-shot clinic at the Congregational Church. It was she who approached him. Was waiting outside on the steps for him after he got his shot.

"I-I don't know what you mean," he stammered. Because he was kind of shy around women. Especially such pretty ones.

"Yes, you do," she said with that bold self-assurance of hers. "You keep looking at me everywhere I go but you never talk to me. How do I get you to talk to me?"

"Seems to me we *are* talking."

She smiled at him, her eyes twinkling mischievously. "Hey, you're right. We are."

And, somehow, they ended up together here.

Honestly? He couldn't believe his luck, although he was a creature of luck and always had been. Pretty much everything that had ever happened to him in his whole life was about luck. But most of it had been bad luck—until she came along.

The first time they'd arranged to get together she arrived before he did, and when he walked in the door and saw the way she was looking at him he experienced such a powerful sexual rush that he thought his entire body was going to explode right there in the middle of the room. He'd never experienced anything like it before. Had never met anyone else like her. He couldn't believe how *calm* she was about sex. How completely free and easy she was about her body. She acted like it was the most normal thing in the world to walk around naked in front of him. Of course it helped that she was so beautiful, with smooth, flawless skin and abundant curves in all of the right places. Even more lushly built than he'd dared to imagine. She was vital, alive and gorgeous. Naturally she felt comfortable in her own skin.

He didn't. Naked, he felt exposed and vulnerable. He cringed at the sight of himself in the mirror. Always had. He wasn't someone who'd ever been lean, hard-bodied or tanned. Hadn't been one of those guys back in high school who liked to hang at the beach all summer long, playing volleyball with his muscular buds and their slim, bikini-clad girlfriends. Running into the surf, laughing and frolicking. Zipping around town in an open-topped Jeep with no shirt on. Those guys had been proud of their bodies. Not him, with his concave chest, soft tummy and that terrible acne all over his shoulders and back. He'd hated team sports. Hated anything that called for him to undress in front of the other guys. They called him Pizza Man because his zit-encrusted back looked so alarmingly like a bubbling hot pepperoni pie.

And you don't just forget something like that.

The stigma had stayed with him, same as those scars on his back had. He'd had his share of women over the years but he was never at ease when he was naked with them. And so they were never at ease around him. Not once, to the best of his knowledge, had he completely satisfied a woman. Whatever it was that made them gasp and moan and scream—they never, ever did that with him. Except for that one time in Atlantic City, and he was fairly certain that Ambrosia was faking it. She was a pro, after all. Honestly? He considered himself to be a total dud as a lover. Same as he was at everything else in life. Nothing more than a waste of skin. Pitted skin at that. That day he'd gone for his flu shot he was feeling about as low as he ever had. He could see no reason to get out of bed in the morning. No reason to do much of anything.

Until he met her. She changed everything. She took an interest in him. She liked him. And, from that first moment when she came walking out of the bathroom naked, she made it clear that she wanted him. Even though he could not imagine why.

He got so incredibly nervous when she started to undress him. If she'd made fun of him or put him down he would have gone straight home and killed himself. But it hadn't been like that at all. It had been *wonderful*. She was so gentle and kind. Her touch excited him beyond belief. She was delighted by how he responded to her. "Flattered" was the word she used. And then they were together right there on the sofa and she was alive under his touch, gasping and crying out his name and it was . . . incredible. *He* was incredible. Potent. Confident. In charge. He had no idea why it was so different with her, but it was.

For the very first time in his whole life he was the man he'd always wanted to be.

After their first time together, she was pretty much all he thought about, day and night. The scent of her. The way she felt in his arms, so silky smooth, supple and strong. The way he felt. He was a brand-new man when he was with her. A bold, strong man who could take on any situation and not feel overwhelmed. Not feel the need to drink or get high to keep it together. He *was* together, thanks to her.

He wasn't someone who had ever set long-term goals for himself. He'd just lived his life day to day, making his share of blunders along the way. But because of her, he was now thinking about tomorrow. Making plans. Making things happen. That's what a man did. Thought big and acted big. He still wasn't entirely certain where their relationship was heading. They hadn't talked about that yet. And she did have someone else in her life. But he knew exactly where he wanted it to go:

Hawaii.

He was going to surprise her with two plane tickets to Honolulu just as soon as he had enough money stashed away. Enough so that they could stay there in the warm sun together for as long as they wanted. Forever, if he had anything to say about it. And to hell with everyone else.

Hawaii.

Just the two of them on a deserted beach somewhere. Sipping

tall, cool drinks. Making long, slow love whenever, wherever they felt like it. It was like a dream. Except this was no dream.

I am making it happen.

That's what he said to himself as he sat in the empty parking lot waiting for her, his heater blasting, wipers barely keeping up with the snow that was falling in heaps on his windshield. A big orange town plow truck went rumbling by, the ground shaking as its blade scraped hard against the pavement.

And then he saw her car coming toward him through the snow. She parked next to him and got out. He could tell right away that she was upset about something. Although she insisted it was nothing.

"Are you sure? You look like you've been crying."

"I'm fine. I'm just so sick of all of this snow."

"Me, too," he said, picturing the two of them on a beach together in the sun. Her in a bikini. Him in a pair of trunks and nothing else, just like one of those tanned, muscular guys he knew back in high school.

The room was ice cold. She turned up the heat before they took off their hooded parkas. He wore a new plaid wool shirt and corduroy slacks. He never used to pay much attention to what he had on. Now he did.

"I'd like to play a game today," she said. "Is that okay?"

"Sure thing." He loved her games. "What kind?"

"I want you to punish me."

"Punish you?" This was something entirely new. "Why would I want to punish you?"

"Because I've been a bad girl."

"You have? What did you do?"

She shook her head. "That's not part of the game."

5

"Well, what am I supposed to do?"

"Whatever you feel like. I'll do whatever you say. Just make me pay, okay?"

"I don't understand."

She sighed impatiently. "Then I'll make it simple for you. Just this once pretend that *I'm* the 'fraidy cat."

"I'm not a 'fraidy cat," he shot back.

"It's just an expression." She studied him curiously. "You're awfully thin-skinned sometimes."

"Sorry."

"Don't apologize for yourself. I don't want you to be a yutz. I want you to make me pay, damn it!"

"Okay, here goes . . ." He felt himself growing taller, his chest puffing out a bit. "Stand there and close your eyes."

She obeyed him.

"And *don't* move. Not a single muscle." It was he who moved toward her. First, he unzipped her jeans and yanked them down so roughly that she let out a yelp. Then he put his hands up underneath her turtleneck sweater, grabbed hold of the sleeveless cotton thingy that she wore instead of a bra and ripped it from her body, tossing it aside.

She started breathing heavily, her breasts rising and falling. "Don't stop!" she whispered urgently. She was actually into this. Liked what he was doing. "Keep going!"

And so he did. He shoved her down onto the sofa so hard that she bounced a foot up into the air. Pulled off her slip-on snow boots. Yanked her jeans all of the way off and hurled them aside. His own chest was heaving now, and he was aroused beyond belief. Couldn't get out of his clothes fast enough. Naked, he took hold of her panties and tore them from her body, too. All she had on now was her turtleneck sweater. He pulled that over her head—only he was so rough about it that his knuckles struck her left eye, which instantly began to twitch and water.

"Oh, God, I'm sorry."

"*Don't* apologize! How many times do I have to tell you?"

"But I-I think I just gave you a black eye."

"It's okay. Really, it is."

Except it wasn't. Because she was crying now. Hell, she was sobbing uncontrollably. *Something* was really bothering her, he realized as he heard a siren off in the distance. Another car accident, no doubt. There'd been so many on these snowy roads.

"Maybe we'd better stop."

"No!" she pleaded, clutching at him with great urgency. "Just make me pay, will you?"

He kissed her hungrily. She kissed him back. And then they were together in each other's arms and he was buried deep inside of her. Never had he been so deep.

"Is *this* what you wanted from me?" she gasped in his ear.

"Yes," he groaned. "Oh, yes . . ." He'd never wanted anything or anyone as much as he wanted her right now. In fact, he was so consumed by pure animal desire that he was barely even aware that the siren kept getting louder and louder.

Not until he heard the screech outside.

Not until his whole world came crashing down upon him.

THE PREVIOUS EVENING

CHAPTER 1

"MASTER SERGEANT, HAVE I told you how incredibly hot you look tonight?"

"Exactly eight times so far," Des responded as she and the unlikely man in her life strolled arm in arm through the Dorset Street Historic District, taking in the wondrous sights.

Truly, there was no lovelier time of year in the historic New England village of Dorset than the Christmas season. Especially if enough snow had fallen for it to qualify as a genuine white Christmas. And this December had delivered an epic amount of snow. Three monster blizzards had already blanketed the village in forty inches of the white stuff, and Christmas day was still a whole week away. The gem of Connecticut's Gold Coast had been transformed into an idyllic winter wonderland, one part theme park, two parts Currier and Ives print. Giggling kids were riding their sleds right down the middle of Dorset Street. Families were out building giant snowmen in their front yards. Red-cheeked carolers went from door to door spreading Yuletide cheer as the eggnog flowed at house parties throughout the village. Horse-drawn sleighs took giddy revelers to and fro. Candles burned in the windows of the Historic District's colonial mansions to welcome them.

Yet another nor'easter was due to blow in by tomorrow morning. But tonight was frosty and clear, with a bright half-moon and stars twinkling in the sky. And so they strolled, swaddled in their winter coats, scarves and hats. Des Mitry, the Connecticut state resident trooper, a lithe, long-limbed, six-feet-one-inch woman of color. And Mitch Berger, the weight-challenged Jewish film critic from New York City whose only experience with violence before he'd met Des had consisted of the films of Mr. Sam Peckinpah.

"Well, I just may have to mention it a ninth time," he said. "I'm still in a state of awe."

"Mitch, I'm just wearing my new jeans."

"Your new *skinny* jeans. Do you have any idea how spectacular a double-bill this is—your booty and a pair of skinny jeans? Hell, you're lucky I don't throw you down in that snow bank over there."

"Yeah, good luck with that, wild man."

"Don't you know what a hottie you are?"

"I know I've never worn pants this tight in my life. They feel like dark-washed Saran Wrap. Are you sure they don't make me look like a skanky teenager?"

"Yeah," he said dreamily.

"Yeah *what*?" She came to a halt, shoving her heavy horn-rimmed glasses up her nose. "You'd tell me straight up if I looked silly, right?"

"Of course. But how can you even think that?"

"Because I'm not fifteen years old anymore."

"And I for one am glad. If you were we'd have zero to talk about plus I'd be a felon and . . . hold on a sec, you've got something on your face."

"What is it?"

He took her in his arms and kissed her. "Just me."

She touched his beaming face with her fingers. Never before had a man made her feel this happy. "Doughboy, are you *ever* going to act your age?"

"I wouldn't count on it."

"Good."

They were on their way to an eggnog party at old Rut Peck's house. Rut had served as Dorset's postmaster for thirty-seven years and seemed to be related to everybody in town. He definitely knew everybody. And he'd lived across from the firehouse in the same upended shoebox of a farmhouse on the corner of Dorset Street and Maple Lane ever since he was born. Until last summer, that is, when the eighty-two-year-old widower got lost driving to his dentist across the Connecticut River in Old Saybrook. When the police stopped him for running a red light two hours later he was sixty miles away in Bridgeport and not sure how he'd gotten there. A small stroke, his doctor determined. Rut wasn't allowed to drive after that. Nor did it seem like a good idea for him to be living alone. His cousins, Marge and Mary Jewett, the no-nonsense fifty-something sisters who ran Dorset's volunteer ambulance service, had moved him into a unit at Essex Meadows, an assisted-living facility, and put his house on the market. But because of the Great Recession he still hadn't gotten a single decent offer. When Marge and Mary asked the old postmaster what he wanted for Christmas this year, he told them he wanted to come home for an old-time eggnog party. And so they'd obliged him. His cleaning lady, Tina Champlain, who continued to keep the place tidy for prospective buyers, had set up a tree in the parlor and decorated it. There was a wreath on the front door and electric candles in every window. Tina's husband, Lem, had cleared all of the snow from the driveway and front walk.

Rut was waiting right there at the door to greet them, happy to be home again with so many friends. He was a short, stocky old fellow with tufty white hair and a nose that looked remarkably like a potato. His eyes were an impish blue behind his thick black-framed glasses. He wore hearing aids in both ears and a big red Christmas sweater that one of his many widowed lady friends must have knitted for him.

Inside, the parlor smelled of nutmeg and fresh spruce. A fire crackled in the potbellied wood stove. Dozens of bright-eyed people were chattering excitedly as they sipped eggnog and nibbled at the high-cholesterol circa-1957 hors d'oevres that Dorseteers seemed to love. Mitch could not get enough of them. After he'd shed his coat he headed right for them, salivating with fat-boy delight over the array of deviled eggs, cocktail weenies, and chicken livers wrapped in bacon. There was an entire sliced ham, cheeses, a basket of bread and rolls. There was wine and assorted soft drinks to go along with the eggnog which, judging by the decibel level of the revelers, was spiked with bourbon but good.

Rut was one of those rare people whose friendships cut across Dorset's class lines. Bob Paffin, the blue-blooded first selectman, was standing right there sipping eggnog alongside a full-blooded Swamp Yankee like Paulette Zander, Dorset's current postmaster, whose father, Gary, had maintained the village's septic tanks. Paulette was there with her live-in boyfriend, Hank Merrill, who was a postal carrier as well as assistant chief of Dorset's volunteer fire department. Actually, it looked as if half of the fire department was there.

Des was also happy to spot Bella Tillis, who until very recently had been her housemate and now lived practically next door to Rut's place at the Captain Chadwick House, the Historic District's choicest condominium colony. She'd moved in two weeks ago along with three of the six feral kittens she and Des had rescued from behind Laysville Hardware. Bella, a feisty seventy-eight-year-old bowling ball of a Jewish grandmother from Brooklyn, was

Des's next door neighbor in Woodbridge when Des's ex-husband, Brandon, had dumped her for another woman. Des wouldn't have survived without Bella. And part of her missed having Bella around. Although it was awfully nice to have the bungalow overlooking Uncas Lake to herself again. Des's studio was spread out all over the living room. Her heart-wrenching drawings of the murder victims she'd encountered were tacked up here, there, everywhere. She drew them in the early light of dawn, deconstructing the haunting memories line by line, shadow by shadow. It was how she dealt.

"How are you, girl?" Des asked, hugging Bella warmly.

"I've been groped by three different old coots already. I don't know if it's the eggnog or what. I do know that not one of them can finish what they started. But enough about me. Those jeans you're wearing . . ." Bella eyed her up and down. "Are they new?"

"Why are you asking?"

"Because they make you look like a runway model, that's why." Bella glanced over at Mitch, who was shoving a deviled egg into his pie hole as he stood chatting with Lew the Plumber. "Does that man know how lucky he is?"

"I try to remind him from time to time." Des reached over and squeezed her hand. "I miss you, Bella."

"Tie that bull outside, as we used to say on Nostrand Avenue. You two need the house to yourselves. Now you can cavort around naked whenever, wherever you feel like it."

Des smiled at her. "And, God knows, we cavort a lot." Usually, two or three nights a week at Mitch's antique caretaker's cottage out on Big Sister Island. And another two nights a week at her place. They had no particular schedule. They were comfortable with where they were. Or weren't—which was ready to live together full time. Plus he had to be in New York a lot for screenings and still had his apartment there. It wasn't a conventional arrangement, but nothing about them was conventional.

Tina Champlain came over to them toting platters of deviled eggs and cocktail weenies.

"You're Rut's guest tonight," Des reminded her. "You don't have to serve."

"Yeah, I do," Tina responded. "If I don't, your boy will eat all of them."

It wasn't just Mitch. Deviled eggs and cocktail weenies were catnip to the male of the species. Tina's husband, Lem, was already hovering close to her.

Tina and Lem made for one of Dorset's odder couples. She was a tiny, high-strung Chihuahua of a woman in her thirties with frizzy black hair and slightly protruding dark eyes. Nice little figure, although she hid it underneath a baggy fleece top and loose-fitting jeans. Lem was a gruff bear who reveled in looking menacing. It was how he got a measure of respect from the blue bloods. The man was not only mammoth but he shaved his head and wore a ZZ Top beard halfway down his chest. He also carried a large knife in a sheath on his belt, just in case he needed a blade at an eggnog party. Lem owned Champlain Landscaping. During the warm months he and his crew of mow boys tended the lawns in Dorset. This time of year they plowed driveways and delivered firewood. Between Lem's business and the money Tina made cleaning houses, they made out pretty well for a couple of teen sweethearts who'd barely finished high school. Tina was already pregnant with their daughter, Kylie, by then. Kylie was eighteen now and when you saw her and Tina around town together you'd swear they were sisters. Kylie was tiny like she was.

"How's Kylie doing?" Des asked them.

"Don't get me started," Lem growled.

"She's fine," Tina said, shooting a look at him—and then at Mitch, who had inched his way over by her side. "No more weenies for you."

"Does that mean I can have a deviled egg?"

"One," she allowed.

"I love you, Tina," Mitch said, popping it into his mouth.

"Kylie's *not* fine," Lem muttered at her.

"We want her to go to nursing school," Tina said with a weary sigh. "All she wants to do is party and shop."

"That girl can't be trusted with a credit card," Lem said. "I had to take hers away and tear 'em up."

Tina's cell phone vibrated in the pocket of her fleece top. "Hold these for a sec, will you, Lemmy?"

He took the platters from her so she could read the text message on her phone's screen. "You're as bad as Kylie," he complained as she thumbed out a response. "On that damned thing every second."

"It's my *mom,* will ya? She moved in with her cousin in Philly last month," Tina explained, her eyes never leaving the screen. "And now she texts me a hundred times a day. There, all done, okay?" She tucked the phone back in her pocket and took the platters back from him. "What were we talking about?"

"Kylie." Des couldn't help notice the chippy vibe Tina and Lem gave off. "Is she seeing anyone special these days?"

"She's been spending a little time with Pat Faulstich," Lem replied.

"Well, *that* won't last," Tina assured him. "I *don't* want her mixed up with one of your plow monkeys."

"Pat's a good kid. He works hard."

"He's a no-good cheesehead."

17

"Hey, I have a great idea," Hank Merrill put in as he snatched a cocktail weenie from Tina's platter. "Why don't we fix her up with Casey?"

Lem let out a huge laugh. "Brilliant idea."

"Isn't it? What do you think, hon?" Hank asked Paulette as she joined them. "Kylie Champlain and your bouncing baby boy?"

Dorset's postmaster considered her response carefully before she said, "I think that you'd better slow down on that eggnog. And don't be nasty." Paulette was Hank's boss, if anyone cared to get technical. She'd gone to work as a carrier for Rut Peck back when she was in her twenties. She was in her early fifties now. A tall, taut, good-looking woman with a strong jaw and long, beautiful black hair streaked with silver. Also a tight-lipped, controlled woman who seemed to be under a great deal of strain. Worry lines furrowed her brow. Casey was her twenty-eight-year-old son from a marriage that had ended in divorce long ago. Paulette had wangled him a part-time job as a weekend carrier. He lived in the basement of the house she shared with Hank.

"I'm not being nasty," insisted Hank, who was evidently well into the high-octane eggnog. "Just saying Casey and Kylie would make a nice couple. Am I right or am I right?" he asked Lem.

"Totally right," Lem assured him with a big grin.

Lem liked Hank. Everyone liked Hank. He was a goofy, amiable and extremely active fellow around Dorset. In addition to his duties on the fire department, he coached the girls' high school basketball team and played tuba in the Dorset town band. Most Saturdays, he could be found working the second chair for John the Barber. Hank was lanky and splay footed with thinning sandy-colored hair and an extremely large, busy Adam's apple. He had the wheezy laugh of a longtime smoker. He also had a habit of sucking on his teeth, which were crooked and rather horsy.

"Casey *ought* to find himself a nice girl," Hank went on, pausing to take another gulp of his eggnog. "Not to mention a full-time job and his own place to live. He spends all day in our basement stuffing his face and watching TV. And all night at the Rustic drinking beer and watching TV. That kid must spend eighteen hours a day in front of the TV."

"Sounds good to me," Mitch said. "I'd take that deal."

"So would I," Hank agreed. "I'd like to know how he got so lucky."

"Casey has issues," Paulette said to him in a distinctly cool voice.

"He's not the only one," Bella interjected, wagging a stubby finger at Hank. "I have an issue with *you*. I have gotten no mail for the past two days, mister. Not so much as a single Chanukah card. And I still haven't received my three-month supply of Lipitor. My online pharmacy mailed it to me from Dayton, Ohio, ten days ago."

"It's the snow, Mrs. Tillis," Paulette explained. "Our out-of-state-mail isn't coming in at Bradley Airport because the planes can't land. And our trucks can't make it here from Norwich because the governor keeps closing the highways."

"That part I understand." Bella turned her piercing gaze back at Hank. "But how come you didn't say one word about the marble cake I left in my box for you? I baked it for you special."

Hank's mouth opened but no sound came out. He looked totally thrown.

Paulette stepped into the awkward silence. "Lem, all of this snow must be good for *your* business."

"You'd think so," he acknowledged, scratching at his beard with a thumbnail the size of a clamshell. It wasn't a very clean-looking thumbnail. It wasn't a very clean-looking beard either. "Only, I've been working harder than I ever have, plowing day and night, and I'm practically going broke. They keep jacking up the price of road salt for one thing. And, well, this is Dorset. People don't pay their bills." He glanced over in the direction of First Select-man Paffin. "Especially the rich ones. Keep telling me they left my money out in their mailbox. Except, guess what? The money's not there."

"How do you explain that?" Des asked.

He shrugged his big shoulders. "Easy. They got no problem lying to people like me."

"Get out, my next door neighbors decided to show," Mitch ex-claimed as Bryce Peck and Josie Cantro started across the parlor toward them.

Bryce Peck was the black sheep of Dorset's blue-blooded founding family. An aging wild child who'd spent his entire adult life running away from his life of privilege only to return home this past August as a gaunt, weathered burnout case. Bryce's ex-tremely tight-assed older brother, Preston, was allowing him to winter over in the family's prized eight-bedroom summer house out on Big Sister in exchange for Bryce serving as the island's caretaker. Des imagined that Bryce had been quite dashing in his youth. He was tall and broad shouldered, with deep-set dark eyes and high, hard cheekbones. But now, at age forty-six, he was a haunted shell of a man, his face ravaged by decades of hard living. Word was he'd been a heavy drinker. Heavy into any drugs, legal and illegal, that made you numb. Those deep-set eyes of his had a frightened look in them. And his work-roughened hands never stopped trembling. Mitch got along well with him. Mitch was gifted that way. But Bryce stayed away from most people. He was a moody, withdrawn man who was uneasy in social settings.

Especially now that he was clean and sober thanks to Josie

Cantro, a blonde who was fifteen years younger than Bryce. Josie didn't come from money. Didn't come from Dorset. She was from somewhere up in Maine. But she'd built herself a thriving little business as Dorset's resident life coach. Josie was one of those relentlessly upbeat women who helped other people do things like lose weight. She'd helped Bryce wean himself off of booze and pills. And in the process they'd fallen in love. She'd moved in with him just before Thanksgiving. Josie was always perky, always smiling that sunny smile of hers. She practically glowed. Not exactly a beauty. Her face was too round. And she had a turned-up little pug nose. But she was definitely a honey, with big blue eyes, a long mane of creamy blond hair and a slammin' bod. A health food junkie and fitness freak who'd taken to dragging neighbor Mitch out for morning beach runs in the snow. Also to rummaging through his kitchen for evil junk food. Josie's heart was in the right place. Des had no doubt it was because of her that Bryce had shown up here to pay his respects to his cousin Rut. She also had no doubt that Josie had done many people around Dorset a lot of good. And yet, Des couldn't shake the feeling that something about the woman was wrong. It was not, repeat not, a jealousy thing. Des didn't worry about Mitch. But her cop instincts kept telling her that nobody was as unfailingly smiley faced as Josie Cantro was—not unless they were fronting.

"Hey, naybs, are you up for a snow run tomorrow morning?" Josie asked Mitch brightly when she and Bryce reached them.

"Absolutely, naybs," Mitch answered just as brightly.

Or maybe I'm just being bitchy because I hate the stupid nickname that he and his vanilla blonde neighbor have for each other.

Bryce, meanwhile, stood there looking as if he wanted to flee through the nearest exit. When Mitch put a hand on his shoulder the poor man practically jumped out of his skin.

"Easy there, pardner," Mitch said. "You're among friends."

Bryce nodded his head, shuddering. "For a second I-I just couldn't . . ."

"Couldn't what, Bryce?"

"Remember what I was doing here."

Josie turned her attention to Hank. "Dude, how are *you* doing?"

"Doing great." Hank patted his shirt pocket. "Got my nicotine gum right here if I need it. So far I haven't."

"*And* he hasn't had a cigarette in two months," Paulette put in proudly. "All thanks to you, Josie."

"It wasn't me. It was all Hank. Hank's the man." Now Josie's blue-eyed gaze fell on Des. "I am so totally hating you right this second."

"And this would be because? . . ."

She was staring longingly at Des's skinny jeans. "I exercise two hours a day. I subsist on wild greens and tree bark. And when I tried on a pair of those I looked like I ought to be playing left tackle for the New England Patriots."

"I find that hard to believe."

"Believe, Trooper Des. These thighs are seriously chunky. And we won't even discuss my butt."

Old Rut waddled his way over toward them, his face aglow. "Thanks again, young lady," he said to Tina. "This is a wonderful evening."

"My pleasure, Mr. Peck."

"Everybody enjoying that eggnog?"

"You bet," Lem said.

Rut raised an eyebrow at Mitch. "There's, um, something I want to show you down in the cellar, young fella."

"Are we talking about what I think we're talking about?"

Rut nodded. "I saved one last case for a special occasion. And this here is it." Clearly, they were talking about a case of the old postmaster's home-brewed stout. "Would you mind lugging it upstairs for me?"

"You are on," Mitch assured him.

"Fine and dandy. I'll meet you down there in half a tick. Just have to stop off and take a pee. Or try. I may be a while, if you catch my drift."

Nonetheless, Mitch headed off toward the kitchen with him.

Des watched them go, then turned to discover Josie was smiling at her. "You and Mitch are so fortunate that you found each other," she said.

"Yes, we are," Des said politely, all the while thinking: *I really don't like Josie Cantro.*

Chapter 2

I really like Josie Cantro, Mitch reflected as he made his way down the steep stairs into Rut Peck's dimly lit cellar. True, his new neighbor could get a bit overzealous when it came to dietary matters. She'd uncovered his secret caches of Cocoa Puffs three times so far and hurled them into the trash. But in the world of positive energy Josie was what's known as a carrier. Ever since Mitch had lost his beloved wife, Maisie, to ovarian cancer he'd had very little use for the company of his fellow New York critics, a blasé breed who were unremittingly sarcastic, sour and smug. Mitch vastly preferred people like Josie, enthusiastic people who embraced the joy of being alive.

And she'd sure worked miracles with Bryce. The man who'd shown up next door to Mitch at summer's end had been a lost soul who had nowhere else to go. Mitch had been glad when Bryce's older brother, Preston, an uber-rich Chicago commodities trader, permitted him to stay on as Big Sister's winter caretaker. Winters were rugged out on Big Sister, the forty acres of Yankee paradise that Mitch was lucky enough to call home. There were five precious old Peck family houses on the island, not counting Mitch's two hundred-year-old post-and-beam caretaker's cottage and the decommissioned lighthouse that was the second tallest in New England. Last winter there'd been a ton of storm damage to the rickety wooden causeway that connected the private island to the Peck's Point Nature Preserve. Also to the Peck family houses. But until Josie came along, Bryce had to qualify as New England's most hands-off caretaker. All he did was drink beer, pop Vicodin and watch the Cartoon Network. Did no chores. Rarely left the island. Spoke to no one. It was the Peck family's attorney, Glynis Fairchild-Forniaux, who'd gently urged him to contact Josie. Unexpectedly, the two of them had fallen in love. Once she moved in, Bryce was transformed into a dutiful caretaker from dawn until dusk. He took a chainsaw to the trees that had come down when Tropical Storm Gail brushed past them in October. Replaced several rotting planks and railings in the causeway. And when the blizzards started coming, one after another, he kept the causeway clear with the Pecks' mammoth John Deere snow thrower. Mitch liked having Bryce and Josie around. They'd invited him over a few times for her three-alarm Thai vegan dinners. Josie would chatter away gaily. Sometimes Bryce would even stir from his remote silence and join the conversation. She was working wonders with the guy.

Rut Peck's cellar reeked of damp concrete, mold and something else that smelled vaguely like decaying potatoes. There wasn't much headroom down there. Mitch's curly hair very nearly brushed the floor joists over his head. Cardboard boxes, suitcases and old steamer trunks were piled everywhere. There was a workbench against one wall, built-in cupboards against another. The only light came from one naked bulb in the stairwell.

Mitch heard footsteps on the stairs behind him almost as soon as he got down there. "That didn't take you long at all," he said. Only it wasn't the old postmaster. "Oh, hey, I thought you were Rut."

"Nope, still me," Bryce Peck said, dragging deeply on a cigarette. "For now, anyhow. Just an awkward stage." Bryce had a strange, elliptical way of talking. He often seemed to be not all there—not all there as in part of him was somewhere else that was far away and incredibly scary. "If Josie catches me smoking she'll skin me alive. But I'm desperate, man. Cigarettes are the only vice I have left." His eyes flicked warily into the cellar's darkened corners. "Damn, I haven't been down in a basement this small since I left Bozeman."

"What were you doing there?" Mitch asked. Bryce had never mentioned Bozeman before.

"Working construction," he replied. "Until I fell off a roof. Broke my collarbone. Learned a valuable lesson though."

"What was that, Bryce?"

"Stay off of roofs."

Mitch knew that Bryce had cracked up a motorcycle in his youth and that it still caused him a lot of back pain. Hence the Vicodin. He hadn't known about the roofing accident. Bryce never talked about his past—until he suddenly chose to.

Upstairs, the partygoers erupted into raucous laughter.

Bryce shot a worried glance at the stairway. "I hate parties. Hate having to *pretend*. Especially clean and sober. It ain't easy, man." He stubbed out his cigarette and immediately lit another one. "I have to remember to breathe. That's what Josie's always telling me."

"I know," said Mitch, who'd suffered from panic attacks after Maisie died. The attacks didn't go away until he rented his cottage on Big Sister and met Des. "Parties have always given me the jim-jams."

"Other people seem to enjoy them."

"Don't kid yourself. They're just here for Rut," Mitch said, hearing footsteps on the cellar stairs again.

This time it was Rut, puffing and wheezing as he came slowly down. "Have you taken up smoking cigareets, Mitch?"

"That would be me, sir," Bryce said.

The old man smiled at him genially. "How are you, young fella?"

"Doing okay, sir."

"Sure you are. We're all doing okay. And you don't have to 'sir' me. Your dad was my second cousin. And a Peck is a Peck. Good to have you back in town, son. You belong here."

Bryce looked at him curiously. "Do I?"

"Yes, you do. My young friend and I are about to tear into the last of my home-brewed stout. Can I interest you in a bottle?"

"None for me, thanks. I'd better head back up. Josie worries about me."

"Treat her right, son. That one's a keeper."

Bryce smiled faintly. "Yes, she is." He stubbed his cigarette out under his heel, carefully picked up both butts and carried them upstairs with him.

Rut watched him go, shaking his head sadly. "That boy could have done anything he wanted to—if he'd just learned how to like himself a little bit. But he never figured out how."

"Any idea why?"

Rut peered at him through his thick glasses. "You don't know the story?"

"I know he has a rich older brother."

"Preston's his half-brother, actually."

"Beyond that he doesn't talk much."

"Me, I like to talk. Makes me awful thirsty though. You'll find what we're looking for in that jelly cupboard over there."

Mitch opened the cupboard and pulled out a heavy, old-fashioned wooden case that held twenty-four brown bottles of Rut's prized stout. He set it down gently on the workbench.

Rut opened two bottles and handed Mitch one. Then he settled himself down on a steamer trunk with his and took a long gulp.

"Ahh, that's the good stuff. Just the right temperature, too. If it's too cold you can't taste it." He took another gulp before he said, "Bryce never had a chance. Wasn't his fault. That's why I feel so sorry for him. His father, old Lucas, must have been close to sixty when Bryce was born. Lucas was an investment banker in the city. He and his wife, Libby, had themselves a big apartment on Park Avenue. Their boy Preston was in his senior year at Cornell when Lucas fell head over you-know-what for a twenty-three-year-old lingerie model. He divorced Libby, married the girl and had Bryce with her. Less than a year after Bryce was born she took off with some tennis player. Abandoned Lucas and her baby."

Mitch leaned against the workbench and drank his stout, which was even tastier than he remembered. "What happened to her after that?"

"She died in a car crash down in Mexico a few months later. Left Lucas with a baby boy he really didn't want. Libby sure didn't want anything to do with Bryce. Neither did Preston, who considered him a bastard child. So the boy ended up being raised in the house out on Big Sister by an elderly governess. He went to school here in town. Made friends here. Dorset was his home. He was a nice boy, too. Not a mean bone in his body. He was just unloved, I guess you'd say. Lucas died when Bryce was twelve or so. Libby was dead by then herself. Bryce was pretty much on his own after that. Lucas did leave him a small trust fund but it was Preston who controlled the purse strings. He still does. And Preston is a coldhearted SOB. First thing he did after he took over his father's financial affairs was kick Bryce out of the only home he knew. Shipped him off to a military academy. The boy came home to Dorset every summer. But Preston, who had a wife and family of his own by now, didn't want him with them on Big Sister. Bryce had to bunk with childhood friends. Until one day he took off and never came back. Boy's been roaming the world ever since, working odd jobs, living hard. This is his home. He belongs here. I hope he can find himself some happiness with that nice blonde." Rut drank down the last of his stout, smacking his lips contentedly. "Ready for another?"

"You talked me into it." Mitch opened two more bottles and handed one to Rut, who seemed to be in no hurry to go back upstairs to his own party.

"Mitch, there's . . . something I need to talk to you about," he said, clearing his throat. "This is on the quiet. Don't want anyone else to hear about it—except for one special person."

"Would that one special person be our resident trooper?"

"Correct. But she isn't hearing this through official channels. It's strictly the man in her life passing along a little something he heard about, okay?"

"Okay, Rut. What is it?"

The old postmaster took a deep breath, letting it out slowly. "We have us a grinch working the Historic District again. This happened once before when times were hard, back when Bush One was president."

"I'm going to need you to translate that for me, Rut."

"Somebody's been stealing the mail from the curbside boxes on Hank Merrill's route."

"So the snow's not to blame for why people like Bella Tillis haven't been getting their mail?"

"That's correct. It's a grinch. And Paulette's real upset about it. I've never seen her so upset."

"Does she know you're talking to me about it?"

"Well, sir, she does and she doesn't. I told her I might have a quiet way of tiptoeing the matter in through the back door. The key word is 'quiet.'"

Mitch looked at him curiously. "Forgive me for being dense, but why does this have to be such a deep, dark secret?"

"Because stealing the U.S. Mail is a serious federal crime, my young friend. Any sort of official inquiry would have to be conducted by the postal inspectors. That'd mean strangers who don't understand our local customs swooping in from God knows where and making a mess of things. Not to mention leaving a black mark on Paulette's record. That wouldn't be fair to her. I mean, hell, it's not as if the grinch is actually going after the U.S. Mail."

"What *is* he going after?"

Rut lowered his voice to a whisper. "Hank's Christmas tips."

"Oh, I see . . ."

The tipping of mail carriers at Christmas time violated the rules of the U.S. Postal Service. Members of the public weren't supposed to put money or gifts out for carriers. And carriers weren't supposed to accept them. But it was a time-honored tradition in Dorset to leave a little something out for a popular carrier like Hank. An envelope with twenty dollars in it. A plate of home-baked Christmas cookies. Or a marble cake like the one Bella had told Hank she'd made him. Pretty much everyone in the Historic District left something out for Hank. The cash he donated to the Food Pantry. The cookies got passed around at the Post Office. And the higher-ups at the U.S. Postal Service were none the wiser.

"And Hank's tips aren't all that this grinch is after," Rut confided. "Quite a few of Lem Champlain's customers transact business with Lem by way of their mailboxes. I don't have to tell you Lem's been a busy man this month. I also don't have to tell you that those mailboxes aren't supposed to be used for anything except officially stamped and posted U.S. Mail."

Mitch sipped his stout, nodding. "How much money is Lem out?"

"Tina told me he's short nearly two grand that his customers swear they put out for him. Mitch, I'd sure hate to see Paulette get in any kind of trouble with the Postal Service over this. I'm the one who hired her, you know—thirty years ago this past November. I'm real fond of that young lady." He shifted his weight around on the trunk uncomfortably. "More than fond. I've been madly in love with that gorgeous, leggy creature from the first moment I set eyes on her."

"Are we talking about Paulette *Zander?*"

"We are. All you see upstairs right now is a tired middle-aged lady. You should have seen her back in the day. My God, what a willowy thing of beauty she was."

"Did you two ever? . . ."

"No, sir. I was a married man. Also old enough to be her father. She's never once thought about me that way. But I used to dream about her and me together. Still do when I'm lying in bed all by myself at night. That's what you do when you get to be my age. You lie in your bed at night thinking about the women who you wish you'd slept with but never did. It's pretty much all you think about. Just you wait and see." He let out a sigh of regret. "That ex-husband of hers, Clint, didn't know what a treasure she was. Took off for Florida back when Casey was a young'un and left her to raise him on her own. She was single for a long, long time before she took up with Hank."

"Hank seems like a decent guy."

"People seem to think so," Rut responded with a distinct lack of enthusiasm. "Tina's been cleaning for me for a lot of years. She keeps Lem's books, too. And she tells me things."

"What kind of things, Rut?"

"Lem hasn't been able to pay his men this month. It seems he's been blowing a whole lot of money in Mystic."

"What's in Mystic?"

"Not what—*who*. Debbie Leto, his old high school flame. Lem dated Debbie before he got Tina pregnant with Kylie. A lot of folks believe Lem never got over Debbie, and Debbie's rich dentist husband just dumped her for his young hygienist. Tina thinks Lem's wining and dining her. They aren't exactly happy together anymore, truth be told. Tina's got herself someone, too."

"Anyone we know?"

"He's not local or I would have heard. But she's got someone. I know that girl. She's got a new spring in her step."

Mitch sorted his way through the choice morsels of gossip that Rut had fed him, moving them around this way and that way. "Rut, are you suggesting that Lem Champlain is our grinch?"

Rut lowered his gaze. "Lem would give you the shirt off of his back if you needed it. But he's also a horse thief, same as his father was. Let's say he wanted to hide a nice chunk of change from Tina and spend it on Debbie. He *could* claim that a grinch has been stealing it from those mailboxes right along with Hank's tips and no one would be the wiser."

"Is Lem that crafty?"

"Lem's twice that crafty. And he's crazy in love with Debbie. Or so Tina says." Rut drank down the last of his beer, sighing. "A man in love is liable to do some mighty stupid things."

Mitch studied the old man carefully. He kept sensing that there was more to this that Rut wasn't telling him. Rut seemed unsettled. And he couldn't quite look him in the eye. "Rut, what's really going on here?"

The old postmaster stayed silent for a long moment, his eyes fastened on the concrete floor. "Mitch, that's what I'd like your lady friend to find out."

———

"Okay, wait, I'm missing something huge here."

"Give me a few more minutes and I'll be ready for you again, I promise."

Des swatted at him playfully as they cuddled in his bed beneath the down comforter and Clemmie and Quirt, listening to the surf crash against the rocks. It wasn't unusual for Clemmie, Mitch's ottoman-shaped house cat, to snuggle with them in the sleeping loft. But it was rare for Quirt, his lean, mean, outdoor hunter, who'd only taken to joining them after the island's snow cover became knee-high.

"I don't get it. What does Rut want me to do?"

Mitch nuzzled her neck, inhaling her intoxicating scent, which was one part cinnamon, two parts her. "Have a conversation with Paulette, I guess."

"But if we have a grinch . . ."

"We definitely have a grinch. No if about it."

"Why hasn't *she* said something to me?"

"Because then it would qualify as the postmaster of Dorset officially reaching out to the Connecticut State Police. Rut doesn't want her to get in trouble with the postal inspectors over our quaint, small-town ways. He has a genuine soft spot for Paulette, it turns out. And I don't mean the sweet, fatherly kind."

"Really?" Her almond-shaped pale green eyes shined at him in the candlelight. "At his age?"

"There's no expiration date on a man's erotic yearnings. Or so I've been informed. It'll be a few decades before I can confirm that."

Des laid her head on his chest, wrapping her arms around him. "I just realized something truly heinous. I have to get dressed and go home."

"No, you don't."

"Yeah, I do. I'll be on fender-bender detail once the snow gets here."

The newest blizzard was supposed to arrive a couple of hours before dawn. At least eighteen inches of the white stuff were expected to fall before a warm front moved in by late afternoon and the snow turned to sleet, frozen rain and then just plain rain. Buckets of it.

"Besides, if I don't leave now I might get stranded out here."

"Sounds good to me. There's plenty of food, wine and firewood. We can finish decorating my Chanukah bush. Or Christmas tree, as you prefer to call it."

It was a six-foot balsam fir that he'd felled with an axe in the island's dense forest and lugged home through the snow just like an old-time Yankee. He'd adorned it with seashells, pinecones and other found objects, including the teeny-tiny yellow string bikini that Des had worn last summer. Although for some mysterious reason it kept vanishing from the tree and showing up back in the wardrobe cupboard.

"Or we could just hide here under the covers. I still have that magic feather in the nightstand."

"Baby, I have to go. The snow is going to start any minute."

Mitch ran his hands up and down her impossibly smooth, sleek body, caressing her gently. "Are you sure there's no way I can convince you to stay just a little while longer?"

She let out a soft whimper and then they didn't talk about much of anything for quite a while longer.

Fat snowflakes were starting to patter against the skylight over the bed when she left at 4:00 A.M. Mitch dozed off after that, but when dawn arrived Quirt woke him back up, anxious to take care of some personal business. Mitch went down the narrow stairs and let him out. The snow was coming down hard now.

Within seconds Quirt was scratching at the door, wanting back in. Mitch obliged him, then put the coffee on and built a fire in the stone fireplace. His post-and-beam cottage was basically one big room with bay windows facing the water in three different directions. There was a kitchen and bath, the sleeping loft and that was it. The moth-eaten overstuffed chairs and non-matching loveseat had been taking up space in one of his neighbor's barns. The coffee table was an ancient rowboat with an old storm window over it. Mitch's desk was a mahogany door that he'd found at the dump and set atop two sawhorses. His sky blue Fender Stratocaster and monster stack of amps filled one corner of the room, waiting there for whenever he felt like cutting loose. Books and DVDs were piled here, there, everywhere.

While the coffee brewed he did some thermal layering for his beach run. First an undershirt and long johns of Capilene. Then polar fleece sweat pants, a cotton turtleneck and his Columbia University hoodie. On his feet he wore heavy merino wool socks and his New Balance Gore-Tex trail runners. Properly swaddled he poured himself some coffee, fired up his computer and got to work. Mitch had been the lead film critic for the most distinguished daily newspaper in New York City until it was bought out by a media empire that tried to morph him into a cable news quote slut. Now he wrote quirky essays for an e-zine that had been launched by his old editor. This morning he was saluting some of the greatest unheralded movie scores of all time. In today's connected online world that meant showing his readers what he was talking about, not just telling them. As Mitch sipped his coffee he poked around until he found a YouTube video link of the Los Angeles Philharmonic performing the incredible chase music that Bernard Herrmann had composed for *On Dangerous Ground,* Nicholas Ray's noir classic. And another of David Amram at the

Montreal Jazz Festival playing his profoundly heartbreaking score to Elia Kazan's *Splendor in the Grass*. Mitch had just created links to three of Kris Kristofferson's original songs from *Cisco Pike*, the 1972 cult classic, when he heard a pounding on his front door.

"Come on in, naybs!"

"It's go time, naybs," Josie exclaimed as she came bounding through the door, her Bates College hoodie dusted with snow. She wore a stocking cap under the hood to protect her ears and mittens on her hands. For leggings she had on water-resistant rain pants.

"Be with you in one sec. And don't bother looking because you won't find anything."

"I'll be the judge of that," she said, heading straight for his kitchen. Mitch could hear her opening and closing cupboards and drawers. "Clearly, you've become more devious. . . ." To his horror, the cursed cereal killer was now rummaging around in his refrigerator, where it took her less than thirty seconds to find his cache of Cocoa Puffs buried in the vegetable bin, underneath the carrots and potatoes. She returned to the living room, shaking her head with disapproval. "You'll have to do better than that, fatty."

"Damn, Josie, you are killing me."

"No, *you* are killing yourself. Do you have any idea what's in these?"

"Really tasty stuff."

"Really tasty chemicals and artificial *everything*. You're a smart man, Mitch. I can't bear the idea of you eating a big bowl of stupid for breakfast."

"I'm going to regret asking this but what did *you* have?"

"A banana and raw kale smoothie."

"I may vomit."

"It was delicious and full of nutrients."

"Just exactly what color is a concoction like that? No, don't tell me—I *will* vomit."

She returned to the kitchen and dumped his Cocoa Puffs into the trash. "Promise me you won't buy this crap anymore."

"Oh, all right. I promise you."

"Do you mean that?"

"No."

"Naybs, you are hopeless. I don't even know why I try."

He fetched his gloves and stocking cap, grinning at her. "I don't either."

It was a fluffy, pure-white snow and there was almost no wind. Just a dreamy, wonderful silence. Mitch loved how quiet the world got when it snowed this way. He and Josie tromped their way down the narrow pathway in the thigh-high drifts that their own footsteps had made on previous mornings. Mitch still could not believe how much snow there was. It was as if somebody had buried the whole island beneath three feet of shaving cream. There was no trace of recognizable landscape anywhere. The shuttered summer houses looked like igloos.

The tide was going out, exposing a smooth, firm strip of beach. They ran side by side, their pace slow but steady, snowflakes smacking them in the face. They'd taken to running an hour's worth of laps around the island. Mitch had no idea how many miles that was. Didn't really care. It was how much time you put in that mattered, not how far you went. Josie ran very erect and was never out of breath. She was five-feet-seven, tops. Mitch's legs were definitely longer. Yet he always sensed that Dorset's life coach was dialing down for his benefit. If she wanted to she could take off on him like the Road Runner.

"How did Bryce do at the party?" she asked as they jogged past a trio of gulls searching for their breakfast at the water's edge.

"He seemed okay," Mitch puffed. "Why are you asking?"

"Because he's not okay. He's not even within shouting distance of okay. He really, really didn't want to go. And he would only stay for a half hour. We came home and watched one of your Budd Boetticher westerns with Randolph Scott. Bryce loves those movies. So do I. There's something so intensely real about them. And Randolph Scott is just so calm and sure. Bryce *isn't* calm or sure. He's still trying to figure out how to live with himself when he's sober. That's not easy, Mitch. He's been self-medicating since he was thirteen—alcohol, pot, coke, ludes. Hell, when he first came to me he was *still* getting Sheened every night. And wasn't taking care of himself at all. Would you believe he hadn't had his teeth cleaned for twelve whole years?"

"And I'm guessing he didn't floss daily."

"He didn't want to be that guy anymore. And we've made a lot of progress. He's learning how to hold himself responsible for the choices he makes. We've broken his pattern of dependency on Vicodin and Xanax. We practice yoga twice a day for his back pain, perform breathing exercises for his anxiety. His nutrition is much, much better. And it's good for him to have work to do out here. It keeps his mind occupied and his hands busy." She wrinkled her pink snub of a nose. "Gosh knows he doesn't use them for anything else."

"What's that supposed to mean?"

"Nothing. We just had a bit of a tiff this morning, that's all." She let out a laugh as they ran past the old lighthouse. "This situation is rich with irony."

"What situation?"

"I spend all day long trying to help people with their problems, and I have no one to talk to about my own."

"Sure you do. You have me. That's what running buddies are for."

"Our love life has . . ." Josie glanced over at him, her mouth tightening. "It's become nonexistent. He has no interest in me at all anymore."

"Have you talked to him about it?"

"I just tried. That's what our tiff was about. He said, and I quote, 'You have no idea what it's like to be me.' I said, 'Hey, mister, let's you and me climb out of that pity pit, preferably while we're both naked.' And he said, 'This is the real me. Get used to it or get lost.' He got really withdrawn and quiet after that. And then I left to run with you. I honestly don't know what's happened, Mitch. Things were so great between us that way. Now we lie in bed night after night and he never so much as touches me."

"That's pretty hard to imagine."

She arched an eyebrow at him. "Meaning? . . ."

"You're a good-looking woman, naybs."

"I appreciate the compliment, but I haven't felt like one lately. I watched you and Des standing there together last night, glowing with so much love for each other, and it made me ache inside. I wish Bryce and I had that. I-I thought we did. But he's pulling away from me and I don't know how to hold on to him. Bryce is someone who has never experienced any kind of love. He's never belonged to a family. Never belonged anywhere. And he's really a very sensitive man. He told me once that he used to be angry at the world. He isn't angry anymore. But he still doesn't trust anyone. And he for damned sure won't let anyone in. He's a project. I knew that going in. He has his good days and his bad days. Today's a bad day. He was seeing a shrink up in Essex before I took him on as a client. He decided to stop seeing him a few weeks ago. Maybe that wasn't such a good idea. Maybe he needs to talk out his underlying problems some more. I'm going to suggest that real gently when I get back." She flashed a faint smile at Mitch. "Sorry to dump all of this on you."

"Don't be sorry. I told you—that's what running buddies are for."

The snow was falling even harder by the time Mitch parted company with Josie and trudged back to his cottage, exhausted but invigorated. He brushed his snow-caked hoodie off on the front porch before he went inside and peeled off his thermal layers one by one one en route to a hot shower, which felt pretty damned good. He lingered in there for a few minutes, letting the hot water beat down on him. By now his stomach was growling. He was thinking about those Cocoa Puffs that Josie had tossed in the trash. Thinking that maybe he could fish them out, wash them one puff at a time and dry them in the toaster oven. But then it occurred to him that doing this would signify that he was a truly diseased person. No, those Cocoa Puffs were history, he decided as he toweled himself dry. He'd have to settle for the same dee-licious kibble that he fed the cats, repackaged under its human brand name—Grape-Nuts.

He was getting dressed when someone pounded on his front door. Josie came bursting in, still wearing her snow-caked running clothes. Her blue eyes were bulging and she was speechless.

"What is it, naybs? What's wrong?"

"Bryce is . . . he's lying in bed with a bunch of empty pill bottles and a bottle of Cuervo," she gulped. "He's gone, Mitch."

"Gone? What do you mean he's gone?"

"He OD'd. He left a suicide note and everything. Bryce is dead."

CHAPTER 3

AT LEAST FOUR INCHES of fresh snow had fallen since Des drove home from Mitch's place to put in some time on her portrait of Titus Smart, age nine, whose aunt Marcella, age sixteen, had smashed him in the face with a crowbar approximately twenty-seven times. When Des had asked the blood-spattered Marcella why she'd done it she calmly replied, "I didn't care for the way he was looking at me." And so Des not-so-calmly drew and drew. Sleep was not an option, she reflected as she drove her way back out to Big Sister, the Crown Vic's wipers shoving the flakes aside. It was not quite 8:00 A.M. But, happily, the town plowman had made an early pass through the Peck Point Nature Preserve. She used her key card to raise the barricade and inched her way out onto the narrow wooden causeway, following the Jewett girls' tire tracks through the deepening snow with great care. It was easy to fishtail on the causeway and sideswipe the railing. Easy to go *through* the railing and right down into the angry surf below.

Mitch's bulbous 1956 kidney-colored Studebaker pickup was sitting in his driveway under the fresh blanket of snow. Des drove on past it to Preston Peck's mammoth, natural-shingled beach house and pulled up next to the Jewett girls' volunteer ambulance van, which they'd parked outside of the house's attached four-car garage. Both double-wide garage doors were up. Bryce's Jeep Wrangler and Josie's Subaru Forester were parked inside along with a rider mower and a snow thrower. There was a cluttered handyman's workbench. A chainsaw, weed whacker and other assorted power-driven yard gear hung from hooks on the walls. Lawn furniture and window screens had been stored in the rafters along with the net from the island's tennis court.

Des squared her big Smokey hat on her head and got out. Headed through the garage past two stacks of firewood and into the house's mudroom, stamping the snow from her black lace-up boots. The kitchen was spotless and smelled of fresh brewed coffee. It was eerily quiet. Her footsteps resounded like a kettle drum as she strode down the hall into the den, where it didn't look so much like Christmas in Connecticut as it did Christmas in Miami Beach. The sofa where Josie Cantro sat slumped next to Mitch, huge-eyed with grief, was white wicker with pale blue cushions. Same as the armchairs. The coffee table was white wicker, too. There were no rugs. Just a bare wooden floor that had been painted blue ages ago and become gently worn by thousands of sandy footprints. The summery décor clashed sharply with the snow that was falling outside of the windows that looked out over the sound. Also with the spindly little Christmas tree that stood there in the corner. There was a fireplace but no fire was going. There was a flat screen TV. There was a bookcase that was stocked with old-time rainy day diversions like jigsaw puzzles and Monopoly.

Mitch wore a pair of jeans and a heavy turtleneck sweater. Josie was still dressed in snow-dampened running clothes. Mitch was talking to her in a soft, comforting voice. She barely seemed to hear him.

He glanced up at Des and said, "I made coffee. Want some?"

She shook her head. "Where is he?"

"Through there." He gestured toward a doorway next to the bookcase.

It led to a bedroom that was right off of the den. A bedroom that was so tiny that Des guessed it was a converted sunporch. There was barely enough room for a chest of drawers, a pair of nightstands and the double bed where the late Bryce Peck lay propped up against a couple of pillows, his head flopped over to one side like a Raggedy Andy doll. His eyes were closed, his complexion already faintly bluish. The Jewett girls were attending to him in their usual quiet, efficient manner. Bryce's stringy hair was uncombed, his gaunt, weathered face unshaven. He wore a ratty old tie-dyed T-shirt over a long-sleeved thermal undershirt. His hands lay open on the bed, palms up. Next to his right hand there were three empty prescription pill bottles. Next to his left lay an empty fifth of Jose Cuervo Gold tequila.

A hand-scrawled note on a yellow Post-it was affixed to Bryce's chest. Des read it, frowning, before she said, "Good morning, girls."

"Oh, it's a lovely one," Marge responded.

"What did he take?"

"Quite some cocktail," Mary said. "We're looking at twenty-four Xanax, thirty Vicodin and another thirty Ambien sleep aids."

"Were they his pills?"

Mary nodded. "Prescribed by Ed Swibold, that country club shrink up in Essex. The prescriptions were filled in November."

"Mind you, we have no way of knowing if all three pill bottles were full," Marge pointed out. "But Josie swears that they were. Also that the fifth of Cuervo had never been opened. She told us Bryce was alive when she left to go running with Mitch. She was gone for an hour and change. By the time she got back here, he was dead."

"Say those pill bottles *were* full. Would they be enough to kill him within the time frame we're talking about?"

"Him and a good-sized herd of elephants," Marge affirmed.

Des glanced around the room. No furniture was overturned,

no lamps or windows broken. She moved in more closely and examined Bryce's skull, throat and hands. Saw no head wounds. No bruising around his throat. No fresh scratches on his hands. No skin, blood or other foreign matter under his nails. There was no reason to think that Bryce's death was anything other than what it appeared to be—a straight suicide by a man who had a long history of emotional problems and drug dependency. As resident trooper her job now was to report her preliminary observations to the Troop F barracks in Westbrook and obtain contact information for the victim's next of kin. A detective would take over from there. And a death investigator from the Medical Examiner's office in Farmington would slog his way down to photograph the body and take Josie's statement. After that, Bryce's body would be delivered by hearse to Farmington for an autopsy. The M.E.'s people no longer transported bodies in their own fleet of vans. The job had been outsourced to undertakers.

Des studied that hand-scrawled Post-it on Bryce's chest again, which read: *Just an awkward stage.* "What do you suppose that means?" she wondered aloud.

"Bryce used to say that to me whenever he went off into one of his dark places," Josie answered softly, standing there in the doorway with Mitch. "He'd shrug his shoulders and say 'It's just an awkward stage.' I ought to have those words carved on his headstone except . . ."

"Except what, Josie?"

"He told me he wanted to be cremated."

"So his death was something that you two had talked about?"

"He talked about it all of the time. I kept telling the gnarly doofus that I intended to keep him around for a good thirty years. But he . . . he didn't expect to be around for long."

Des nodded, glancing around at the cramped little room.

"We've been sleeping down here to save on the fuel bill," Josie explained. "It costs a fortune to heat this big old place. We don't go upstairs at all."

"About those pill bottles," Des said. "You're sure they were full?"

"Positive. I count them every morning to make sure. He wasn't taking any of that stuff anymore. Their presence in our medicine chest was entirely totemic."

"Entirely what?"

"They were symbolic. They represented what he didn't need anymore."

"Was that your idea or Bryce's?"

"It was something we both agreed to."

The tiny room fell silent as all of them stood there trying not to look at her dead boyfriend.

"Josie, why don't we continue this conversation in the kitchen?"

Mitch joined them, topping off Josie's coffee mug and his own before he sat with them at the round oak table.

"I don't happen to believe in pills," Josie stated firmly. "I don't think they make you healthy—just drug dependent. I'm strictly about self-healing that utilizes energy-based modalities and mind-body practices."

"Forgive me, but I don't understand what you just said."

"I'm saying that we concentrated on harnessing the vast power of Bryce's mind to return his body to its natural state of being. We detoxified his system of artificial chemicals. We reduced his stress levels. We placed him on a . . ." She trailed off, staring at Des accusingly. "You think I'm full of crap, don't you?"

"That's not true at all, Josie," Des said.

"Yes, it is. I can see it in your eyes. I happen to be a fully accredited life coach, you know. People *value* what I do. You would, too, if you needed me. You don't. You're someone who has tremendous personal discipline. You exercise, eat right, don't smoke or do drugs. You've got it together."

Des glanced down at the graphite stick residue that was always there underneath the middle fingernail of her right hand. *Yeah, I've got it together. I just see dead people is all.*

"But most people aren't like you, Des. They're weak. And an amazing number of them don't like themselves very much. I have one client who pays me seventy-five dollars an hour just to go grocery shopping with her twice a week. She says she'd be lost without me. This is an affluent, well-educated career woman. You wouldn't think she'd need me, but she does. Most of my clients do."

"Bryce was more than a client to you."

"Much more," Josie acknowledged, lowering her blue eyes. "That . . . never happened before. I've never fallen in love with a client. I can't explain it."

"You don't have to."

The Jewett girls were done in the bedroom. They said their good-byes and headed back out by way of the mudroom. Des heard their van start up and pull away.

Josie gazed out the kitchen window at the snow, which was now coming down so hard that you could barely see across the beach to the water. "I could never, ever convince him that he deserved to be loved. And he was *so* depressed this morning that I decided he ought to see Dr. Swibold again. Mitch and I were talking about it while we were running."

"It's true, we were," he confirmed.

"Josie, is there any chance Bryce was self-medicating without your knowledge? Scoring drugs on his own?"

"I don't believe so. He hardly ever left the island. Didn't hang out with anyone. Plus he was flat broke. The monthly check from his trust fund barely covered a week's worth of groceries."

"If that's the case then how did he pay you? When he was see-ing you professionally, I mean. You say you charge seventy-five dollars an hour. Where was the money coming from?"

"Why is that important?" Josie asked, sipping her coffee.

"It may not be. I'm just wondering."

"Preston paid for it. Also for Bryce's sessions with Dr. Swibold. Preston and Bryce had a-a strained relationship. When Bryce showed up last summer it hit Preston really hard. He told me he felt awful about the way he'd treated Bryce. Preston is in his sixties now, and he's had two heart attacks. I got the impression that he didn't want Bryce sitting on his conscience."

"So you've been in personal contact with Preston?"

"By phone and e-mail. And he sent me checks from Chicago when I was coaching Bryce."

"I'll need a phone number for him."

Josie fetched her Blackberry from the counter and gave Des Preston's home and office numbers. "Bryce was a real hard case at first," she recalled sadly. "He hated the idea of seeing someone like me. Many of my male clients do. Men flat-out hate to ask for help."

Des was already well aware of this. It explained why most of the suicides she'd caught in her career were men—going all of the way back to her rookie year, second week on the job, when one of them decided to throw his gray flannel self in front of the 7:32 Metro-North train out of Stamford. Women create support groups for each other. They share their feelings with their friends. Talk. Confide. Depend on each other. Men are taught to be self-reliant. When things go bad they don't reach out, just retreat into gloomy, lonely isolation. The holiday season, with its feel-goody emphasis on family and loved ones, can be particularly hard for them.

"I can't imagine what I'll do now," Josie said, staring down into her coffee mug. "Bryce was such a big part of my life."

"I'm sure Preston won't mind if you stay here for a while," Mitch said. "Under the circumstances, I mean."

Josie looked at him narrowly "It's not up to Preston to mind or not mind. This house doesn't belong to him."

Mitch glanced at Des curiously before he turned back to Josie. "What do you mean?"

"I mean that Bryce wasn't the caretaker of this place," she replied. "He owned it. Lucas left it to him. Ask the family lawyer if you don't believe me. Ask Glynis. She'll tell you. Preston held the purse strings to Bryce's trust fund, but Bryce has owned this house since the day he turned twenty-one. Preston wasn't 'allowing' Bryce to stay here. It was Bryce who was 'allowing' Preston and his family to spend their summers here. Bryce knew how much it meant to Preston's kids to return to Big Sister every summer. They have happy memories of this place. Bryce had happy childhood memories himself. This had been his home until Preston kicked him the hell out. But it's not Preston's house. It was Bryce's and he—he . . ." Josie broke off, breathing deeply in and out. "I hardly ever drink coffee. It's making me all buzzy and I'm rattling on."

"You're not," Des assured her.

"Bryce really loved this island," she said, her eyes growing shiny. "He'd gotten so tired of being rootless. Wanted to settle down here and stay put. Maybe even start a family of his own. Everyone in town thought he was the caretaker. He went ahead and let them think it. That was Bryce's way. He liked for people to think he was a cheese head, but he wasn't. Did you know he had a Master's degree in literature from the University of Montana? He was incredibly well-read and insightful."

"He told me he worked construction in Bozeman," Mitch said.

"To put himself through school," Josie said, nodding. "Des, what happens now?"

"There's a process. Another officer will come and ask you more questions. So will someone from the Medical Examiner's office."

"What's the point? It's obvious what happened." She puffed out her cheeks. "Sorry, there's a 'process.' I get it. Will I need to be here all day? Because I have clients to see."

"I'm sure they'll understand if you have to reschedule."

"No, they *won't* understand," Josie said emphatically. "They rely on me."

"Then do what you got to do," Des responded. People coped with grief in their own ways. If Josie needed to be there for her clients then so be it.

She was gazing out the window again at the snow. "He really did want to be cremated. But I guess I won't have any say in that, will I?"

"That's a family matter," Des said. "All I can tell you is that those arrangements will be on hold until the Medical Examiner completes the autopsy."

Josie's eyes widened. "They have to do an autopsy?"

"I'm afraid so. This type of situation is what we call an untimely death. Autopsy's pretty much automatic. Bryce's blood will have to be tested. It may be several days before they have the preliminary toxicology findings, though it usually goes faster if they have a specific idea of what to look for."

Josie cocked her head at Des curiously. "Why do I get the feeling that you've been through this 'process' before?"

"Only because I have."

Too damned many times.

Des made a slow circuit through the Dorset Street Historic District. By now the fresh snow had to be six inches deep. The schools were closed for the day. So was Town Hall. When she reached

Big Branch Road, Des made a left turn—her hands loose on the steering wheel, foot gentle on the gas pedal—and eased on through the business district, which was adorned up the wazoo with Christmas decorations and lights. The A&P was open, though there were very few cars in the lot. The antique shops, clothing stores and art galleries were open as well. 'Twas the week before Christmas and the economy sucked. No way the shop-keepers were staying home. Lem Champlain's plow monkeys were out keeping the parking lots clear. Or trying.

McGee's Diner on the Shore Road was a shabby, much-beloved local landmark. During the summer it teemed with sunburned, boisterous beachgoers who stopped there to munch on lobster rolls and gaze out the windows at Dick McGee's million-dollar view of the Big Sister lighthouse. On a snowy December morning Des figured it would be a nice, quiet place to meet Paulette Zander for a cup of coffee.

A red Champlain Landscaping plow pickup was the only vehicle parked out front when Des got there. Pat Faulstich, the young Swamp Yankee who'd been spending time with Kylie Champlain, sat hunched over a mug of coffee at the counter, a wool stocking cap pulled low over his head. He glanced up at Des when she came in, then looked back down at his coffee, shifting his shoulders uncomfortably. Pat had a reddish see-through beard and a thick neck. He was thick through the chest and shoulders, too. Wore a heavy wool shirt, jeans and work boots. A pea coat hung from a peg on the wall next to him. No one else was in the place—unless you count Nat King Cole, who was singing Christmas carols on the radio in the kitchen.

Dick's waitress, Sandy, came out of there with a paper bag and a Thermos bottle and set them in front of Pat. "Here you be, young sir, four ham-and-cheese sandwiches. And I topped off your coffee—black with lots of sugar."

Pat thanked her and put his pea coat back on. Then he grabbed the bag and Thermos and clomped out of there, his gaze avoiding Des's as she sat down in a booth. When he got outside he stopped to light a cigarette, watching Des through the front window. Des watched him back. She made him nervous. She made all of the local boys nervous. He got into his truck, his jaw stuck out defiantly, then started it up and pulled away just as Paulette arrived in her Nissan Pathfinder.

Dorset's postmaster came in out of the snow wearing one of those full-length quilted down coats that don't look good on anyone. Not unless an overcooked bratwurst is your idea of looking good. Paulette wore her long silver-streaked hair in a ponytail today, but she still had the same tense, preoccupied look on her face that she'd had last night at Rut's party. She took off her coat and slid into the booth across from Des, sitting in tight silence while Sandy poured their coffee.

"What's going on?" Des asked her after Sandy returned to the kitchen.

"Same old sloppy mess," Paulette answered nervously, pouring cream into her coffee. "We'll be out there delivering what we have, but these snow days really do a number on my carriers. Those decrepit old Grumman LLVs of ours are just no good in the snow. Do you know what LLV stands for? *Long Life Vehicle*. To which I say *LOL*. Half of ours are falling to pieces." She removed a paper napkin from the dispenser and tore off a piece, rolling it between her thumb and forefinger until it was a teeny, tiny ball. She set the ball next to her spoon, then tore off another piece of napkin and began rolling that.

Des watched her doing this for a moment before she said, "Shall we talk about what we need to talk about?"

Paulette bit down on her lower lip, fastening it between her teeth. "What did Rut tell you?"

"Not a thing. It was Mitch who he reached out to. He told him that a grinch has been stealing Hank's Christmas tips and Lem's plow money. Lem claims he's missing a couple of thou." Although that particular aspect was a bit iffy. Rut also told Mitch that Lem was tomcatting with an old sweetheart and might be hiding the money from Tina to pay for his fun. "Rut's hoping we can keep it in the Dorset family because the postal inspectors won't exactly be down with our quaint, small-town ways."

Paulette sat there in stiff silence, rolling another piece of napkin into a teeny, tiny ball and setting it next to her spoon. There were already four tight little balls there.

Des shoved her heavy horn-rimmed glasses up her nose. "There's more happening than Rut let on, isn't there?"

Paulette responded with a brief nod of her head. "Last Monday a dog walker found a huge batch of Hank's mail in a ditch on Johnny Cake Hill Road. Practically every envelope Hank delivered in the Historic District that morning had been slashed open. Some contents were missing. Others were simply discarded."

"Did they take the credit card statements, bank statements and such?"

Paulette shook her head. "They weren't interested in those. Or in the paid bills that folks had put out for Hank to take. We found dozens of personal checks to mortgage companies, Connecticut Light and Power, you name it."

"Then it doesn't sound like we're dealing with identity thieves. What *did* they take?"

"Anything and everything of value. People mail all sorts of

gifts to their friends and relatives this time of year. They send Christmas cards with cash or prepaid retail gift cards tucked inside. And a million small packages that'll fit inside of any mailbox—DVDs, CDs, iPods, Kindles. It's kind of ironic, really."

"What is, Paulette?"

"This is the age of high-tech security. We have elaborate systems to protect our homes and our cars. Yet our mailboxes still sit there by the curb, unlocked and unprotected, twenty-four hours a day. Some folks in town prefer to keep a P.O. box for that reason, but not as many as you'd think."

"Are things disappearing from other routes besides Hank's?"

"Just Hank's, near as I can tell."

"And how long has this been going on?"

"About two weeks. Hank's furious. He's taking it personally."

"Should he be?"

Paulette's eyes crinkled at her. "What do you mean?"

"I mean is someone purposely singling him out?"

"I can't imagine why they would. Hank's my most popular carrier. I have no idea why his route is being hit—beyond the simple, obvious reason."

"Paulette, nothing about this is simple or obvious to me."

"Hank's route is the Historic District, which has the highest concentration of wealthy people packed into the fewest number of miles."

"As opposed to a rural route, you mean."

"Exactly."

"Has anyone reported suspicious behavior of any kind? A stranger rummaging through mailboxes, anything like that?"

"Nothing like that, Des."

One of the town's big orange plow trucks rumbled by on Shore Road, its plow blade shaking the foundation of the old wood-framed diner. On the radio, Nat King Cole was singing about chestnuts roasting on an open fire.

"The mail was discarded on Johnny Cake," Des mused aloud. "That tells me it's someone local. Out-of-town pros would have taken it with them."

"I wouldn't be surprised if it's a couple of teenaged kids."

Des gazed out the window at the marsh. The snow was coming down so hard she couldn't make out the lighthouse in the distance. "How, Paulette? How do a couple of young cheese heads cruise through the Historic District on multiple occasions, raid peoples mailboxes in broad daylight—it *must* be broad daylight because the boxes are full—and not one person has noticed them? A lot of folks are home during the day right now. The schoolkids are getting one snow day after another. The college kids are back for Christmas break. Plus we've got our share of retirees living in the Historic District. The arrival of the mail is the highlight of their morning. I find it hard to believe that anyone could hit those boxes repeatedly without being spotted."

Paulette made another napkin ball with her thumb and fore-finger and placed it next to her spoon. That made eight, nine, ten of them. "Quite a few of the houses are set back pretty far from the road."

"And quite a few of them aren't. Plus the Historic District is *busy*. People go in and out of Town Hall all day long. I'm thinking our grinch must be someone who has a legitimate reason to be accessing the boxes. Like, say, one of Lem's plow boys."

Paulette's eyes narrowed. "Or one of my other carriers?"

"Well, yeah."

"Des, I can't vouch for Lem's people but I can vouch for all ten of my full-time carriers and my five part-time subs. They're honest, hardworking people. Every single one of them has passed the postal exam and undergone a thorough background check—including my son, Casey. There's no nepotism in the U.S. Postal Service."

"Casey's a part-timer?"

Paulette nodded. "I'm hoping he'll be able to go full-time within the next two years—*if* they're hiring. All we hear about these days are cutbacks and givebacks. But it's still a good career. And Casey's a good kid. Well, he's not a kid anymore. He's twenty-eight. But he's one of those young men who . . ." Paulette searched for the words. "Some of them need extra time to find their way."

"From the way Hank was talking last night, it sounded like he and Casey don't exactly get along."

"That was just the eggnog talking. They're fine. He'd like to see Casey living in his own place, that's all. So would I. Nothing would make me happier than Casey settling down with a nice girl instead of hanging around at the Rustic with that drugged-out skank Gigi Garanski."

The Rustic Inn was Dorset's designated skeejie boy bar. Most of the brawls that Des had to break up during the course of a month took place there. "So Casey's into Gigi?"

Paulette nodded glumly. "And Gigi's not even his girl. She goes with Tommy Stratton."

Whenever there was a brawl at the Rustic, Tommy Stratton was usually in the middle of it. Most people in Dorset knew him as Tommy the Pinhead. He was unsavory, unbright and scary. Hired muscle who was connected with the Costagno crime family. The Costagnos had an iron hold on whatever bad went on in Connecticut, Rhode Island and Western Massachusetts.

Sandy came over and refilled their cups.

Paulette dumped more cream in hers. "Can you help me, Des?"

"I'm still waiting for you to tell me the rest."

"I don't know what you mean."

Des glared at her. "Yes, you do."

Paulette cocked her head at her curiously. "No, I don't. And I don't understand why you're being so confrontational."

"Because you're disrespecting me and I don't like it. Are you going to say the words or do I have to say them?"

Paulette sat there in tight silence, reddening.

"Fine, I'll say them. I used to live with a seventy-eight-year-old woman who happens to be one of those people whose mail has gone missing."

Paulette grimaced. "Mrs. Tillis, I know. She gave me an earful last night."

"That wasn't an earful. If you want an earful just get her started on Rush Limbaugh. Bella's in good health for a woman her age. But she takes quite a few prescription meds—Lipitor for her cholestorol, Celebrex for her arthritis pain, Synthroid for her thyroid, Boniva for her osteoporosis and two or three others that I can't think of right now. She gets them by mail from her online pharmacy. People of all ages get their meds that way. A lot of those people have high annual deductibles on their health plans. When December rolls around they try to stock up because they've finally met their deductible and, lo and behold, their insurer actually has to foot the bill. This happens to be December, Paulette. Those mailboxes on Hank's route are *bursting* with little bubble-wrapped pouches full of meds. It's a violation of the Controlled Substances Act for online pharmacies to send anabolic steroids or Oxycontin through the U.S. Mail. But they can send just about anything else. Meds that wake you up. Meds that knock you out. Meds that make you feel happy all over. The high school kids here in Dorset love to party with that stuff. Every time I bust up a late-night beer bash I find heaps of Vicodin, Percocet, Valium, Xanax, Prozac, you name it. And, cue the drum roll, it's all just sitting out there in those mailboxes waiting for someone to snatch it and sell it. We are *not* talking about someone taking Hank's Christmas cookies or a DVD stocking-stuffer of *Cars 2*. We are talking about the illegal trafficking of prescription drugs. Now, were you *ever* going to mention that to me or were you just hoping that I'm totally stupid?"

Paulette breathed in and out for a long moment, her right eye twitching slightly. Then she reached for her coffee mug and took a sip, the mug trembling in her hand. "I'm not real proud of myself right now. I'm supposed to be in charge. I *am* in charge. I do a damned good job, too. My people work hard and smart and safe. They respect me. And, at the first sign of trouble, what do I do? Go running to good old Rut. I guess I feel like I'm in over my head," she confessed. "And I'm a little ashamed of myself. A lot ashamed. I apologize."

"Apology accepted."

She gazed at Des searchingly. "Can you help me?"

"I'm sympathetic to your situation. The postal inspectors won't understand our local customs. You don't want Hank to get in trouble. I get that. But this may be a serious matter. I don't have a lot of leeway here."

Des's cell phone vibrated on her belt. The 911 dispatcher was calling to report that the owner of the Village Bootery had just apprehended a shoplifter trying to slip out of the door with a four-hundred-dollar pair of Ugg boots.

The shoplifter was eighteen-year-old Kylie Champlain.

Des stood up and reached for her Gore-Tex storm parka. "Paulette, I'll be in touch, okay?" Then she hurried outside, jumped into her cruiser and took off.

It was beginning to look a lot like Christmas.

CHAPTER 4

ORDINARILY, THE HISTORIC DISTRICT was one of the most splendid sights on earth when snow was coming down. And there had to be a blanket of eight inches of it by now, Mitch figured as he drove past the fork to Johnny Cake Hill Road. Dozens of neighborhood kids were sledding down the steep hill that was, in warmer months, the third fairway of the country club. He took it slow and easy when he rounded the bend by the steepled white Congregational Church. He had snow tires on his old Studey pickup, not to mention two sixty-pound sand bags positioned over each rear wheel. But it still didn't handle well in heavy snow like this, which clung to the majestic old maples and the beautiful colonial mansions that were all decorated for the holidays.

Ordinarily, it warmed Mitch's insides to make this drive on such a morning. The frantic modern world was forced to surrender to a kinder, gentler pace from out of another era. It was all so peacefully unreal that he half-expected to hear a director, most likely Frank Capra, holler, "And . . . *action!*" But Dorset Street was no movie set. And this was no movie. And today Mitch's insides weren't feeling warm at all. Because Bryce Peck's very real life had abruptly ended this morning. What Mitch felt inside was a hollow emptiness. The quiet that enveloped him as he drove along wasn't serene. It was ominous. Because Mitch had been there himself. Wrestled with his own demons after Maisie died. For months he'd seen no point in going on. Only his own pain. He couldn't imagine that the pain would ever end. Didn't believe it ever would. He remembered quite clearly the words he'd said to himself that first rainy night he'd arrived in this little gem of a town on a Weekend Getaway assignment for the newspaper's travel section. He'd checked into his room at the Frederick House Inn. Taken a bath in the claw-footed tub. Then burrowed into his canopied bed and, lying there grief-stricken and alone, had thought: *I am so glad I do not own a gun for my personal protection. Because if I had one I would shoot myself.*

Bryce had been clean and sober. A terrific woman loved him and believed in him. He was home again. Hell, he even owned that beautiful home, according to Josie, who had both a professional and personal stake in him. And now he had nothing and no one. Bryce had had every reason to stare down his demons and keep on going. And yet he'd chosen death. Why? *"Just an awkward stage,"* he'd scrawled on that stupid Post-it. As if that explained a goddamned thing.

It would be a white Christmas this year. No doubt about that. But it would not be a merry one.

When Mitch reached Maple Lane he pulled up outside of Rut's little farmhouse and got out, surrounded by the snowy silence as he tromped his way to the front door. Last night's party hadn't been the old postmaster's only Christmas gift. Madge and Mary had also granted his deepest wish, which was to spend a night in his own bed instead of returning to Essex Meadows. Thanks to the blizzard, he wasn't going anywhere now. The sisters were looking in on him regularly to make sure he was okay.

Rut answered the door wearing a navy blue wool bathrobe over a flannel shirt, baggy slacks and carpet slippers. "Good morning, young fella," he said, turning up both of his hearing aids. "I can see from your long face that you've come to bring me some sad news. I'll spare you the discomfort. I already heard about him from the Jewett girls. So let's you and me crack open a couple of bottles of stout and drink to the poor son of a bitch. Somebody ought to."

"All right, Rut," Mitch said, unzipping his coat.

"Nice to be back in my own place, let me tell you," Rut chattered as he led him into the parlor, where a fire was going in the potbelly stove. "Not that I've had more than two minutes to myself. Mary insisted on tucking me into bed last night at ten o'clock sharp. Made sure I took my pills. And when I opened my eyes at six this morning Madge was already here to feed me my breakfast and more pills. And then Tina showed up to clean up from last night. She just left. I'll let you in on a little secret—the timing of this here snowstorm suits me just fine. I'd much rather be here than at some halfway house for the soon-to-be departed. But the doctors won't allow me to be on my own anymore. It seems I get to thinking on things and forget where I am."

"That happens to me with great regularity."

"At your age it's okay. But when you get to be my age people take a mighty dim view of it—especially when you're behind the wheel of a moving automobile at the time." Rut tottered into the kitchen and returned a moment later carrying two glasses of foamy stout on a serving tray along with a plate of leftover deviled eggs and ham sandwiches. He set the tray on the coffee table. They raised their glasses in the air. "Here's to Bryce, who never had a happy day in his life," the old fellow declared. "I hope he's found himself some peace."

They drank. Then Rut eased himself slowly down into his favorite overstuffed chair, his slippered feet up on the ottoman.

Mitch sat in a chair across the coffee table from him, helping himself to a deviled egg. "Is it true that he owned the house on Big Sister?"

"He did indeed," Rut confirmed. "Lucas left it to him, which riled Preston to no end, let me tell you."

"Why didn't Bryce want anyone to know about it?"

Rut shrugged his soft shoulders. "That was Bryce. He had a renegade streak a mile wide. A tough one to get to know, too. Talked to hardly a soul here in town except for Glynis."

"The family's lawyer?"

Rut nodded his head. "I hear he paid a call on her last week."

"How did you hear that?"

"Her secretary happens to be a cousin of mine."

"Rut, is there anyone in Dorset who *isn't* a cousin of yours?"

"Bryce and Glynis were childhood friends, you know. Back before Lucas died and Preston gave Bryce the boot."

"Was Bryce visiting her as his friend or his lawyer?"

"That sort of information my cousin can't share with me. She'd lose her job." Rut sipped his stout. "The house will pass to Preston now. He'll be mighty pleased about that."

"You're not the first person who's said that to me today."

Rut peered at Mitch over the rim of his glass. "Josie's a fine looking girl. High-spirited, too. She'll find herself another fellow pretty fast. Or one will find her."

"I suppose so."

Rut continued to peer at him. "Anything you want to get off your chest?"

"Such as? . . ."

"I had my eye on Josie last night. Something about the way she kept watching one of the other fellas at the party gave me the impression she wasn't entirely content with Bryce. We're both men here, so there's no point in tiptoeing around—it was you who she was looking at. And it's been you sharing that island with them these past months. Bryce was quite a bit older than Josie. Also plenty frayed around the edges. Everybody knows that you and Josie are friends. Wouldn't surprise me one bit if you were a little something more than that. Can't say I'd blame you—a healthy young cocksman such as yourself."

"Rut, I'm the Jewish film critic from New York, remember? I think you're confusing me with someone else."

"It isn't someone else who keeps Dorset's resident trooper glowing. That there is one contented woman, let me tell you. Always a smile on her face. Any man who can satisfy a gorgeous handful like Miss Desiree Mitry, well, the fellows at the firehouse have nothing but admiration for you, Mitch. Fact is, you're something of a hero to them."

"This is an actual topic of conversation at the firehouse?"

"Heck yeah. What do you think they talk about—fire safety procedures? And that's just the fellas. Imagine what the gals over at the Town and Country beauty salon are saying."

"I'd rather not, if you don't mind," Mitch said unhappily. This was the downside to living in a small town. Everyone thought they owned a front-row seat to your private life. "Rut, there's nothing going on between Josie and me. Des is the only woman in my life."

"Glad to hear it. I felt the same way myself about my Enid, God rest her soul."

"You told me last night that you lusted after Paulette Zander for years."

"Still do, truth be told," Rut conceded. "But thinking about it and *doing* it are two entirely different things. I always figured a man's free to dream about any woman he chooses just so long as he doesn't cross the Mendoza Line."

"I think you mean the Maginot Line."

The old fellow frowned at him. "I do?"

"The Mendoza Line refers to Mario Mendoza, the famously

light-hitting major league shortstop of the seventies. He was so deficient with a bat in his hands that cracking .200 came to be known as the Mendoza Line."

"I think you're wrong about that one, young fella."

"I could be," said Mitch, who'd learned never to argue with anyone who was over the age of eighty. There was no point. He reached for a ham sandwich and took a bite, chewing on it thoughtfully. "What do the guys at the firehouse say about Hank Merrill?"

"Hank's an affable fella. Everybody likes Hank."

"Everybody except for you, you mean."

"Don't think I follow you."

"I got the distinct impression last night that you don't care for him."

"Naw, Hank's okay," the old postmaster said grudgingly. "You just need to understand the background of the situation. Paulette fell to pieces when that husband of hers, Clint, ran off. Just sat there in her house day and night drinking cheap white wine and chain-smoking cigarettes. Stopped showing up for work. Any other postmaster would have canned her. But I covered for her. And she got through it eventually. Sobered up, quit smoking. Only, it was like a part of her died inside. She was never the same person again. When I first met Paulette she was a lighthearted gal, quick to laugh, with a smile that'd make you melt. Want to know something? I can't remember the last time I saw Paulette smile." He shook his tufty white head. "When she took up with Hank it had been a lot of years since she'd had a man friend. And, well, Hank was still a married man at the time. Cheating on his wife Mary Ann, to put it plain and simple. He and Paulette used to sneak off to the Yankee Doodle for hot-sheet matinees. I didn't approve. Figured he was using that beautiful, lonely woman strictly for the sex. Turned out I was wrong about that. Hank did leave Mary Ann for her."

"But you still don't approve."

Rut shifted uneasily in the chair. "I don't think he's good enough for her. It's nothing personal. I'd feel that way about any man who came into her life."

"So that's all there is to it?"

Rut studied him suspiciously. "What are you getting at?"

Mitch drank down the last of his stout. "Does Hank have money troubles?"

"You know anyone these days who doesn't? But now that you mention it, he *is* trying to dig himself out of a deep hole. Believe me, a fella doesn't work second chair for John the Barber every Saturday unless he's seriously short of cash." Rut gazed at Mitch's empty glass. "You ready for another?"

"Sure thing."

The old man bustled out to the kitchen with their empty glasses, refilled them and returned. "It didn't take long for Mary Ann to find out that Hank was cheating on her with Paulette," he recalled, settling back down in his chair. "She was mad as hell—especially when he asked her for a divorce. Paulette felt terrible about breaking up Hank's marriage. But I've always figured you can't bust up a marriage unless it's already broken. Mary Ann's lawyer saw to it that their assets were divided in a way that was highly favorable to her, on top of which he has to pay her monthly alimony."

"Is she still living in Dorset?"

"She moved to Farmington. Works at a day care center up there for a whopping nine bucks an hour. Mary Ann is one bitter woman. Or so I hear. Anyhow, about a year after the divorce was finalized, Hank's mother passed away in Rochester, New York. That's where he's from originally. She was by no means wealthy, but she did own her own home free and clear. Hank sold it and cleared enough to make a down payment on a fixer-upper cottage up by Uncas Lake. Hank's good with his hands. He renovated the place himself, sold it for a tidy profit and bought himself another fixer-upper. Mary Ann eventually heard about this from one of her girlfriends in town and, well, it turns out that either Hank's lawyer didn't explain the terms of the divorce settlement to him or Hank didn't listen. Because Mary Ann was entitled not only to her share of their assets at the time they split up but also to any assets he might come into *in the future*—namely his mother's house in Rochester *and* the net proceeds from the fixer-upper he sold. Hank hired himself a new lawyer and tried to contest it but he lost. Now he owes Mary Ann close to seventy grand. Hasn't got a nickel of it. The money's all tied up in the other fixer-upper. The only way he can pay her is to sell it, except nobody's buying a damned thing these days. This house right here has been on the market for nearly a year and I haven't had one single offer. Until Hank is able to sell his cottage and lay a lump sum on Mary Ann, he has to scramble to make a structured monthly payment that the lawyers drew up. This is on top of the alimony he's already paying her. Hank's in deep. And he can't very well ask Paulette for help. That wouldn't be right." He looked at Mitch shrewdly. "Why are you asking me about Hank's money troubles?"

"Just curious," said Mitch, who was much more than curious. He was keenly interested. Because a grinch was stealing from the mailboxes on Hank's route. Because Hank owed his ex-wife a fortune. And because if there was one thing he'd learned from Des it was that the solution to a case is often the obvious one that's staring you right smack-dab in the face.

Meaning that the grinch was none other than Hank himself.

CHAPTER 5

DES WAS JUST PULLING into the shopping plaza directly across from the A&P when little Kylie Champlain came sprinting out the door of the Village Bootery with a pair of Ugg boots clutched under one arm and a look of total panic on her young face. Kylie jumped into a silver Honda Civic with the boots, started up the engine and took off. Or tried to—her wheels just kept spinning. The blizzard had dumped ten inches of the white stuff on the pavement by now and her daddy's plowboys hadn't hit the parking lot for a while. Then Des saw Joanie Tooker, who owned Village Bootery, come staggering out the door, clutching her elbow in pain. Des found out later that as soon as Kylie spotted Des's cruiser she'd shoved Joanie, age sixty-one, roughly to the floor and escaped out the door. Joanie, who'd known Kylie for the girl's entire life, suffered a dislocated elbow.

Des climbed out of her cruiser and motioned Kylie to get out of her Honda. "Come on, Kylie, let's talk this out!"

Kylie floored it, the Honda's wheels spinning and spinning. She was absolutely determined to rabbit on Des.

"Kylie, stop this, will you?"

No use. Kylie's wheels caught hold and she went skidding out of the lot onto Big Branch heading way too fast in the direction of Old Boston Post Road. Des considered letting her go. Simply putting out a BOLO alert. She had Kylie's license plate number. Knew where the girl lived. But she was concerned. Kylie was so panicky that she might crash into somebody. And so, reluctantly, Des took off after her, hoping that the reality of seeing flashing lights in her rearview mirror would jolt some sense into the little fool.

It was the most pathetic high-speed chase Des had ever been involved in. Not that it qualified as a high-speed chase, since neither of them could do more than twenty in the dense snow. And Des wasn't even trying to gain ground. She didn't want to make Kylie drive faster in these blizzard conditions. Just wanted her to know that it was pointless to keep going and that she ought to do the sane, adult thing and pull over.

Good luck with that.

At the intersection with Old Boston Post Road Kylie ran the red light, which ranked as the least of her worries right now, and attempted a sharp left turn. Instead, she made a full 360-degree doughnut in the deep snow before she came to a complete stop right in the middle of the intersection. Thankfully, there were no other cars around. Des came to a halt twenty feet away and gestured for Kylie to get out of the Honda.

And good luck with that.

Kylie floored it again and went slip-sliding her way north on Old Boston Post Road in the direction of Uncas Lake. Again, Des thought about leaving her be. But the girl presented a clear danger to herself and others. Des couldn't just let her go.

The Post Road had been plowed within the past few minutes. Or at least a single lane had. Kylie powered her Honda all of the way up to thirty as she headed north in the center of the plowed lane. Des continued to give her plenty of room, praying that they didn't encounter any oncoming traffic. As she went past the turnoff for Frederick Lane Kylie caught up with the town's big orange plow truck and began to overtake it. Reality alert: Only a total nutso tries to pass a snowplow in the middle of a blizzard. Kylie

Champlain had gone total nutso. Actually veered around the plow truck and started to pass it. Until, that is, she practically drove head-on into the oncoming Dodge Ram that was inching its way down the Post Road. The Dodge Ram had to slam into a snowbank to avoid her as Kylie hit her brakes and spun out in the middle of the road. The plow truck driver had no chance to stop. Roared right on past her—missing her Honda by no more than six inches. Des brought her cruiser to a stop as Kylie sat there behind the wheel, eyes bulging with fright. The Dodge Ram's driver climbed out, waving his arms and cursing.

Des got out of her cruiser. "Please stop this, Kylie! Someone's going to get hurt!"

The girl was busy reaching for something now. Rolling down her window and throwing something out of the window into the road—the Ugg boots that she'd stolen.

"That's a good start, Kylie! Now why don't *you* get out of the car, too?"

But the little fool floored it again. Skidded around Des and started her way back down Old Boston Post Road in the direction they'd just come from. Des made sure that the Ram's driver was unhurt and had a working cell phone. Then she tossed the damned Ugg boots in her cruiser and took off after Kylie.

Now she had her siren on. Now she was pissed.

Back down at the intersection with Big Branch, Kylie tried to make a right turn and spun out again—only this time she caromed hard off of a Lexus that was waiting at the stoplight. But Kylie didn't stop, wouldn't stop. Just revved her engine until her wheels caught hold and slid her way back toward the shopping district, picking up speed as she went along. She was going way too fast when she arrived at the intersection where Big Branch dead-ended at Route 156. Directly across from the stoplight sat an old wood-framed house that had been converted into commercial office suites.

Now the girl had a choice to make. If she turned right she'd be heading north alongside the Connecticut River toward Dorset's bucolic farm country. If she turned left she'd be on her way down to the beach.

Left. She decided to go left.

She never made it.

Her Honda went into an uncontrolled spin and barreled head-on into the ground-floor suite of the office building. The sound of the crash was like a bomb going off in the snowy quiet.

Des radioed for emergency backup, then jumped out and ran to the Honda, which had hit the wooden building so hard that it ripped through the exterior *and* interior walls. The car's front end was *inside* the front office.

Kylie's door had popped open and her air bag had deployed. "My ankle!" she howled in pain. "My ankle!"

"Just try to relax and breathe, Kylie. Help is on its way."

"I'm sorry, Trooper Des! I'm so sorry!"

"It's okay. You're going to be okay."

"No, I'm not! My mom's gonna *kill* me!"

"Just keep breathing in and out, okay? I'll be right back."

"Don't leave me!"

"I'm not. I'm right here, I promise."

Des rushed inside the building. The ground floor front office belonged to Josie Cantro. The life coach's office door was locked but the frame had been knocked off-kilter by the crash, as if an earthquake had struck. Des shoved the door open with her shoulder and found, well, what she found was Josie groping around on the floor next to the office sofa for her jeans. Josie was naked. So was Casey Zander, who'd been getting busy with Josie on the sofa before Kylie and her Honda had so rudely interrupted them. Josie's camisole and panties were on the floor next to her jeans— ripped to shreds. Her left eye was swollen half-shut. She looked as if she'd been punched. Looked plenty dazed, too. So did Casey, whose forehead was bleeding. Fallen ceiling tiles were everywhere. Apparently, one of them had hit Casey, who was someone Des could happily have gone her entire life without ever seeing naked. Paulette's son didn't seem to be constructed out of muscle, bone or sinew. Just jiggly, moon-white blubber. He reminded Des of one of those grubs she sometimes dug up in the garden and had to squash.

She stood there in stunned silence, listening to the old building creak and groan around her. Steam hissed from the Honda's blown radiator. The baseboard heating pipes had ruptured and water was streaming from them onto the floor. Sheetrock powder wafted down from up above. Off in the distance, she could hear the sirens of the emergency responders.

"I-I thought the roof had collapsed," Josie stammered finally. "From the weight of so much snow."

"It may just do that. You're not safe in here. Get your clothes on and get out of here."

Neither of them moved. Just stared at her, blown away.

"Listen to me, if you folks don't get your clothes on *now* the firemen are going to find you this way. Everyone in town will talk. Do you understand?"

Josie nodded her head, blinking.

"Good. Now hurry up and get out. I have to search the rest of the building." Des darted back out into the hall. Josie's downstairs neighbor, a seamstress who did alterations and tailoring, was closed due to the storm. So were the accountant and home computer consultant upstairs. Josie and Casey were the only ones in the building. They were dressed by the time Des made it back down. Josie was rummaging through her desk drawers.

"Josie, what do you think you're doing?"

"I have to collect my files," she explained, her swollen eye twitching.

"No way. Not until the building inspector says it's okay. Let's go!"

The Jewett girls and two of Dorset's fire trucks had already made it to the scene. The volunteer firemen were attempting to extract Kylie Champlain from behind the wheel of her car. But Kylie was so freaked out that she was fighting them. Madge had to subdue her with an injection before they could wrestle her out of the car and stabilize her ankle. It was a bad break. Des could see bone sticking out of skin.

The rest of the men were preparing to search the building. Des assured them it was unoccupied. She also ordered them to stay out of Josie's office—which, as of right now, she was regarding as a potential crime scene. Though she saw no need to tell them that.

A second EMT van arrived now from Old Saybrook and took charge of transporting Kylie to the nearest emergency hospital, which was Lawrence and Memorial in New London. Highway I-95 was closed right now to all but emergency vehicles. If the plows were keeping up they might get her there in a half hour. On a normal day it would take ten minutes.

Des watched the EMT van take off, knowing she would have to prepare a detailed incident report for her troop commander. And this whole stupid mess would have to be reviewed by Internal Affairs. With the benefit of twenty-twenty hindsight they would demand to know why she hadn't just put out a BOLO and let Kylie go. But Des stood by what she'd done.

In the back of their van, The Jewett sisters tended to Casey's head wound and Josie's eye. While they did that Des called Tina Champlain to notify her that her daughter had just been injured in a one-vehicle accident while fleeing the scene of a crime. Tina took the news surprisingly calmly. She even thanked Des for calling before she rang off.

By now Josie was standing there in the snow with a cold pack pressed to her swollen eye.

Des showed her a smile. "How are you feeling?"

"Fine," she answered shortly. "But I need my files."

"I know you do. But you can't go back inside until we know it's safe. Sit with me for a minute, okay?"

They got into the front seat of her Crown Vic. Des cranked up the heater.

"Not my best morning ever," Josie said with a rueful shake of her blond head. "First my boyfriend kills himself. Now my office is toast. Who *was* that behind the wheel of the car?"

"Kylie Champlain."

"Is she going to be okay?"

"I'd rather talk about you, Josie. Want to tell me what was going on in there?"

"It . . . wasn't what it looked like," she responded quietly.

"Does that mean you don't want to swear out a criminal complaint?"

Josie looked at her, mystified. "A criminal complaint for what?"

"When I walked in that door your left eye was swollen and your underwear was in shreds on the floor. Was Casey sexually assaulting you?"

Josie let out a laugh. "No! Casey's been a client of mine for the past two months. No sexual assault of any kind was taking place."

"So what was?"

"A role-playing exercise."

72

"Does this type of exercise usually result in you getting a black eye?"

"He didn't mean to do it. He just got carried away."

"By what?"

"Casey lacks confidence when it comes to women. I'm doing what I can to empower him."

"So the sex was consensual."

"It was an *exercise*."

"Josie, are you romantically involved with Casey?"

She heaved an exasperated sigh. "I just told you—he's a client."

"I'm old-school when it comes to this life-coaching thing, so please forgive me if I come off as a bit dense. Are you telling me that consensual sex—consensual *rough* sex—is some kind of a teaching tool?"

"That's exactly right," Josie affirmed. "Sometimes the healing process calls for an unconventional approach on my part. But I'm willing to go there for my clients."

"I see. Just out of curiosity, how many other men with confidence issues count on you to 'go there' for them?"

Josie lowered the cold pack from her swollen eye, glaring at her. "I can't believe you'd ask me that."

"You'd believe it if you saw what I just saw. How many, Josie?"

Josie gazed out of her window at the snow coming down. "Any information regarding my clients is strictly confidential."

"Girl, you're not a medical practitioner. You aren't shielded by doctor-patient confidentiality."

"Look, what you walked in on was something that you can't comprehend," she said, her cheeks mottling with anger. "And you-you immediately jumped to the wrong conclusion because that's how your mind works. You make judgments about people. You sit there in your uniform and you decide who's good and who's bad."

"This isn't about me, Josie."

"Yes, it is. You're trying to make me out to be some kind of a hooker!"

"I'm trying to understand you."

"Nothing bad was going on in there! I'm trying to *help* that poor slob, okay? He needs to feel better about himself if he's ever going to have a productive, rewarding life."

"Did Bryce know about these role-playing exercises of yours?"

"I never discussed my clients with him," she answered quietly.

"Bryce had been a client himself. Were exercises part of his treatment?"

"I have nothing more to say to you," Josie replied. "We're done."

"Okay. Please stay here. I'll be back in a minute."

Des got out of her cruiser and hopped into the back of the EMT van, where the Jewett girls were bandaging the wound on Casey's forehead.

"How are you feeling, Casey?"

"I'm fine," he grunted.

"It's just a superficial wound," Madge informed her. "His pupils are normal and responsive to light. He has no dizziness or nausea."

"I'm *fine*," he repeated, this time with a whiny, hostile edge to his voice.

Casey Zander happened to be a whiny, hostile guy. Also an immature one. He was twenty-eight going on fourteen, a petulant, overgrown fat boy with a jowly face, a weak chin and a sulky, almost girlish rosebud mouth. He dyed his hair a garish henna color and wore it in a peculiarly retro *Meet the Beatles* mop top, complete with bangs that he combed down almost to his close-set eyes. The dye job contrasted starkly with his dark brown sideburns. He was dressed in a he-guy plaid wool shirt and corduroy pants. The shirt didn't flatter him. Fat boys should never do plaid.

74

It also didn't go along with his transgendery do. Des really, really didn't know what was up with that hair.

"Would you like me to notify your next of kin for you?" Des asked him. "That would be your mom, right?"

Casey tensed visibly. "Why do you need to call her?"

"You've suffered a head wound. Maybe you shouldn't be driving home."

"I'm not a kid. . . ."

"Didn't say you were."

"And I *don't* want you calling my mom, bitch."

Des raised an eyebrow at Madge and Mary. "What did he just call me?"

"I believe he called you a bitch," Mary replied tartly.

"He is one fierce customer," Madge chimed in. "Better watch out."

"Would you ladies excuse us for a sec?" Des asked them.

The sisters left them alone in the back of the ambulance.

"Want to tell me what was going on in there, Casey?"

"What did Josie say?" he demanded, fingering his bandaged forehead.

"I'm more interested in what you have to say."

He shrugged, his girlish mouth tightening. "We were having our regular weekly session. She's been trying to help me with—with . . ."

"With what, Casey?"

"I *don't* want to talk about it!"

"Has anybody ever told you that whiny never scores cool points? Women don't like to be around whiners—unless you're paying them to be with you."

"Look, you just shut up," Casey shot back. "You don't know anything about Josie and me."

"So school me."

"It's none of your damned business."

"Actually, it *is* my business, Casey. Bryce Peck took his own life this morning, but Josie wouldn't stay home to mourn his loss. She told me she had a client who needed her. That client would seem to be you."

He blinked at her in shock. "I-I didn't know. She didn't say a word."

"Pretty good deal for you. The field's clear now."

"Field?" He shook his mop top at her. "What field?"

"We're all adults here. If you and Josie have been getting busy behind Bryce's back that's your business. And if you two like it rough, well, so be it. Not my thing at all, let me tell you. Any man used his fists on me he'd be picking his teeth up out of the carpet for a week. Josie's had a real bad morning. She's upset. She's vulnerable. I'm wondering if I should be worried about her. You know her a lot better than I do. What do you think?"

Casey considered his answer carefully. "I think she'll be fine. I'll take care of her. I-I love her."

"Have you told her that?"

"Not exactly, but she knows how I feel. I mean, she must know."

"And what about Gigi Garanski? I hear you date her."

He let out a derisive snort. "You don't 'date' Gigi."

"Just use her for sex, you mean?"

"I'm not the only one who does," he said defensively. "But it's Josie who I want to be with. Josie's . . . She's wonderful."

Des studied this man-boy curiously. He was definitely bizarre, but what flavor of bizarre? Harmless or the other kind? "Okay, Casey. Thanks for your insight. I appreciate it." She hopped out and found Madge and Mary jawing in the snow with a couple of firefighters. "Is he okay to drive home?"

"I don't see why not," Madge replied. "Assuming he can dig out his car."

"Casey's a real catch, isn't he?" Mary said. "It's a shame he doesn't find himself a nice girl."

Des looked over at Josie Cantro, who was still sitting in the front seat of the Crown Vic nursing her swollen eye. "The boy's way ahead of you, Mary. He thinks he has."

Dorset's Post Office was located in a squat, brick-faced building that was plunked down all by itself in the same shopping center that was home to the A&P and to the local branch of First Niagara Bank, which had formerly been the local branch of New Alliance Bank and before that New Haven Savings Bank. Des thought that aside from the flagpole out front, the Post Office bore a remarkable resemblance to a Friendly's family restaurant.

She parked her cruiser out front and strode inside, allowing herself a sigh. She'd already seen a week's worth of action and it wasn't even 11:00 A.M. Days like this required stamina. Not the physical kind, which she had in abundance. The emotional kind. If she wasn't careful she could lose her patience with people. The public didn't care for snappish behavior from its sworn personnel. Especially sworn personnel who happened to be women of color.

There was a mud rug on the floor just inside the door of the vestibule. Flyers were tacked to a bulletin board there for the upcoming Dorset High production of *Fiddler on the Roof*. Inside the lobby, which was painted pea-soup green, a tinny sound system was playing Christmas carols. Tinsel was draped here, there, everywhere. But thanks to the blizzard there wasn't the usual crush of holiday customers waiting in line to send off presents. No customers waiting in line, period. There wasn't even anyone behind the counter. Billie, the counter clerk, had left a hand-lettered sign there that read, "*I'm out back. Holler.*"

Des didn't have to holler. The postmaster's office had a window that overlooked the parking lot. Paulette came right out of her office to escort Des in. The village's mail carriers hadn't left on their routes yet. Des could hear them out in back, joking with each other while they finished their sorting.

"Casey just phoned me," Paulette stated stiffly as she led Des into her small, spare office. There was a desk. There was a safe that was almost as big as the desk. There were no personal flourishes of any kind. No photos or Christmas cards. No invitation to sit down, either. "He was extremely upset. It seems he's had quite an ordeal."

"He has indeed. He got a cut on his head but he's okay."

"Did I hear him right? Kylie slammed her car *into* Josie's office?"

"I'm afraid so."

"Tina and Lem have had nothing but trouble with that little airhead. She's so irresponsible." Paulette raised her chin at Des. "Casey told me you were extremely abrupt with him."

"I'm sorry if he felt that way, but it was an emergency situation. Kylie suffered a serious injury. The building was in danger of collapsing. I had no time for kid gloves."

Paulette studied Des, her eyes crinkling. "And you had a job to do. I understand. Casey can be a bit thin-skinned sometimes. Hank thinks I babied him too much. He has trouble sticking to things. Gives up too easily when someone says no to him. And then gets all down on himself. I'm hoping Josie can help him find some direction. She sure worked wonders with Hank. Hank was a heavy smoker for thirty years. He quit when his doctor warned him that he was in the early stages of emphysema. But then he had some personal setbacks and before we knew it he was reach-

78

ing for the nearest Marlboro. Josie helped him kick the habit again. Hank thinks she's a miracle worker. Mind you, we knew Casey would flat-out reject the idea. So we had to be a bit devious. Josie arranged to 'accidentally' bump into him at the flu clinic back in October. He's been seeing her ever since."

"And do you think she's helping him?"

"Damned if I know. He seems a bit more confident, but it hasn't translated into any concrete changes. He hasn't moved out of the basement. He hasn't taken charge of his life. We'll see. These things don't happen overnight." Paulette bit down hard on her lower lip, studying Des once more. "Did you come here to tell me about Casey?"

"Actually, I'd like to speak with Hank."

"Absolutely. I believe he's still here. Shall I? . . ."

"That's okay, I'll find him."

Hank and the others were at their workstations loading bundles of mail and parcels into big rolling carts. A ton of parcels. Big boxes, the kind that Christmas toys come in. Small boxes, the kind that books and DVDs come in. And a whole lot of those bubble-wrapped pouches that prescription meds come in. The carriers were a casually dressed group of four women and six men. The standard outfit appeared to be fleece tops, jeans and snow boots. Most of them appeared to be in their thirties and forties. Hank was the oldest of the group. They were an upbeat bunch. Chatting and laughing with each other. If there was tension in the room Des wasn't sensing it—until they caught sight of her approaching them. The uniform had that effect on people. Especially when something nasty was going down. Clearly, they all knew about the grinch because they got real quiet.

"Morning, Hank. Have you got a minute to talk?"

"Sure thing, Des," he said easily.

The others decided that now would be a really good time to start rolling their carts toward the loading dock.

"You seem to have a lot of parcels today," Des observed.

"That's pretty much all that we have. The seven A.M. truck made it here from Norwich with our parcels and our flats but then they had to—"

"I'm sorry, 'flats' are? . . ."

"That's what we call our catalogues and junk mail," he explained. "Usually, a second truck shows up at 8:30 with our machine-sorted letters, but the governor had closed the highway by then." Hank fished a package of Nicorette gum from the pocket of his fleece top and popped a piece in his mouth, going to work on it with his crooked yellow teeth. "That was sad news about Bryce Peck. How's Josie holding up?"

"It hasn't been one of her better mornings. I understand it was your idea to put her together with Casey."

He shot a wary glance in the direction of Paulette's office, lowering his voice. "Believe me, that kid needs help. He's in a deep hole."

"What kind of a hole?"

"Let's just say he is one messed-up puppy, okay? Does nothing all day but sit in the basement watching TV. I thought maybe Josie could light a fire under him. She's such a supportive person. Believed in me so much that I didn't want to let her down." He cleared his throat uneasily. "I take it that Paulette's spoken to you about what's been going on. I'm glad. It's about time."

"What can you tell me, Hank?"

"Not much, to be perfectly honest."

"You have no idea what's happening?"

"None. And it's putting me in a really uncomfortable position. Like last night at Rut's party—Mrs. Tillis went to the trouble of baking me a marble cake and she thinks I'm rude because I didn't thank her. I never *got* the darned cake."

"It's not just marble cake that's going missing from your route. Paulette told me about the batch of mail that was found on Johnny Cake Hill Road."

He nodded grimly. "That's serious business. Stealing Christmas tips is one thing, but Paulette can't tolerate—*we* can't tolerate—someone stealing the U.S. Mail. If you can figure out who's doing it I'll take my hat off to you."

"Would you mind schooling me a little?"

"Not at all. Ask me anything you'd like."

"How long does it usually take you to complete your route?"

"Three, four hours. Depends on the volume of mail and the weather."

"Do you keep to the same schedule every day?"

"Paulette's real good about letting us make our own schedules—just as long as the folks get their mail. I'm usually here sorting by eight o'clock so I can get onto the basketball court with my high school girls by 3:30. Some of the others start later and stay later. And whether we want to take a lunch break or not is up to us. I just pull over somewhere quiet and have a quick sandwich in my truck. A lot of the others take a full hour off. Three of the girls drive their trucks back here and power walk to the health club at The Works. They've got a weight-loss contest going on. Whoever takes off the most pounds by New Year's Day wins a weekend in New York City."

"Hank, do you ever leave your truck unattended?"

"Well, yeah. Every time I have an accountable to deliver—that's your certified mail and express mail. If it has to be signed for and scanned then I have to get out and knock on the front door. Same thing's true when I have a parcel that's too big for the box. Like a lot of folks get those forty-pound cartons of Florida oranges every month. I swear, those oranges all show up here on the same day. Hernia Monday, I call it." He flashed a toothy grin at her. "If nobody's home I try to stash the parcel out of the elements. Or bag it in plastic."

"Do you leave the truck unlocked while you're busy doing that?"

"Never. Not a chance. You never, ever leave your truck unlocked. "

"Do you drive the same truck every day?"

"Yeah, we all do."

"So your truck is *your* truck?"

"Well, it is but it isn't. It's not like they let us drive the danged LLVs home. We're not even allowed to keep a set of keys on our key rings. The truck keys and scanners spend the night in the safe in Paulette's office, along with any accountables that we weren't able to deliver. That's standard operating procedure. This is the U.S. Mail, Des. There's nothing slipshod or haphazard about anything. It's a secure operation. And this is a secure building. It's locked-down plenty tight at night." Hank glanced up at the clock on the wall. "Listen, I really should load up and run. How about we talk some more later?" He hesitated, his jaw working on the nicotine gum. "And also maybe? . . ."

"Maybe what, Hank?"

"Can we keep it just between the two of us?"

Des narrowed her gaze at him. He had something on his mind. Something that he wished to tell her in private. "Sure thing," she said, handing him one of her business cards. "Call me any time, day or night."

"I'll do that." He pocketed her card just as Paulette came striding toward them, a clipboard clutched to her chest. She raised her eyebrows at them curiously.

"Hank's going to contact me directly if he sees anything out of the ordinary," Des explained, showing her a smile.

Paulette showed her a smile right back. Or tried to. It came off more like a pained grimace. "Excellent. And I'm glad I caught you, Hank. I need to know how the transmission is doing on that old '94 of yours."

"The tranny on my LLV is okay."

"I thought you told me it was getting balky in the cold."

"It's okay," he repeated.

"Are you sure? Because I've been ordered to report on the mechanical status of all ten of our vehicles by the end of the year." She tapped at a form on her clipboard. "Money's tight. If yours needs retrofitting now's the time to speak up."

"It's okay," Hank barked at her. "How many times do I have to tell you?"

"Well, you don't have to bite my head off. I'm just doing my job."

"And now I'm doing mine." He rolled his cart off toward the loading dock.

Paulette watched him go, stung. "I'm afraid things are getting a little tense around here. Sorry."

"No need to apologize, Paulette. I've given some thought to your situation. Officially, my feeling is that we ought to notify the postal inspectors right away."

She looked at Des hopefully. "And unofficially? . . ."

"If you want to wait a day before you notify them I'll do some nosing around. Does that sound okay?"

Paulette let out a sigh of relief. "I don't know how to thank you, Des."

"No need to. I haven't done jack yet."

CHAPTER 6

ADD THIS TO THE list of 297 things that Mitch Berger, proud child of the streets of New York City, never thought he'd find himself doing: standing out on a rickety wooden causeway over the freezing waters of Long Island Sound in the middle of a blizzard pushing around a John Deere professional-grade snow thrower. The damned thing was a monster that had a fourteen-inch steel augur and a whopping thirty-eight-inch clearing width. Six forward speeds, two rear speeds, dual halogen headlights and a dash-mounted electric chute-rotation control. It even had heated handgrips. He could feel the warmth through his work gloves as he cut a swath across the causeway with grim determination. Mitch was dressed for outdoor labor. He wore his arctic-weight Eddie Bauer goose down parka over a wool fisherman's sweater, twenty-four-ounce wool field pants, merino wool long johns, insulated snow boots and his festive C.C. Filson red-and-black checked mackinaw wool hat with sheepskin earflaps, the one that made him look like a Jewish version of Percy Kilbride in a Ma and Pa Kettle movie. But, hey, he needed every layer. Not only was it snowing like crazy but it was starting to get really, really windy out there on that narrow causeway.

Mitch was a screening-room rat. A man who got paid to sit on his butt in the dark. Working a snow thrower? Not part of his normal job description. But this wasn't a normal day. His neighbor, Bryce Peck, was dead. A foot of snow had fallen. And someone had to get the causeway cleared so that the damned hearse from Dousson Mortuary in New London could pick up Bryce and deliver him to the Medical Examiner in Farmington. The hearse was hours late because of the storm and the poor guy was *still* lying there in his bed. It would have been comical if it weren't so ghastly.

Just an awkward stage.

Mitch had stayed there with a shaken Josie while a detective from the Troop F barracks conducted a follow-up interview with her about Bryce's state of mind and history of drug and alcohol abuse. Then a death investigator from the M.E.'s office had shown up to ask her pretty much the same questions all over again. It had been painful and tedious for Josie, but she'd remained calm and composed—despite the fact that the bald, middle-aged death investigator could not stop undressing her with his eyes. No wonder Des didn't get along with most of the men on her job.

Supposedly the hearse would be along shortly to pick up Bryce. Mitch told Josie he'd be happy to wait there if she wanted to attend to her clients. He thought it would be good for her to get out of that house.

"Mitch, I can't ask you to stay here with him."

"You're not asking me. Besides, I'm your naybs. This is what naybs do."

She'd gone into the bedroom to say good-bye to Bryce. Mitch heard her murmur some words to him before she came out of there, wiping tears from her eyes, and headed on out to meet her clients.

As soon as she left Mitch got right the hell out of there. No freaking way he was staying in that house by himself with a dead body. When the hearse arrived at the foot of the causeway he'd see it through his window and raise the barricade. Besides, he was on deadline and still hadn't posted his column on unheralded movie scores. By the time he'd sent it off the hearse still hadn't shown up—and Mitch was quite certain that the causeway was no longer passable. So he fired up the snow thrower and went to work out there. For company he had Leonard Cohen's haunting voice singing "The Stranger Song" from the opening credits of Robert Altman's *McCabe and Mrs. Miller*, which happened to be one of Mitch's favorite movies. Every single time he saw it he rooted for Warren Beatty to get up out of that deep snow and keep walking, gut shot or not. Every single time he was devastated when Beatty succumbed to the inevitable and settled down into the snow to die.

Just an awkward stage.

Mitch had nearly completed his third full swath when he saw a vehicle pull slowly up to the barricade. But it wasn't the hearse. It was Josie's Subaru. She didn't try to drive out. Just parked there and started toward him on foot in her ski parka and stocking cap. She looked pale. She looked terrible. Her left eye was swollen almost completely shut.

He set the snow thrower to idle, rushing to her. "Josie, what happened to your eye?"

"You didn't hear?" Her voice was low and morose. He'd never known her to sound that way before. "I figured Des would phone you."

He shook his head. "Not when she gets busy."

"Kylie Champlain lost control of her car and slammed into my building. It was . . . unreal. I was sitting there with a client and suddenly the front end of her car was *inside* my office."

"And what happened to your eye?"

"A ceiling tile fell and hit me. It looks a lot worse than it is."

"How about your client?"

"Just a scratch on the head. We were both lucky. The building inspector thinks the whole building may collapse. I had to beg him to let me back in for my files. He went in with me. Then he declared it off-limits—so I no longer have an office." She let out a hollow laugh. "When I decide to have a shitty day I don't mess around, do I?"

Now another vehicle was making its way through the Nature Preserve to the foot of the causeway. Again, not the hearse. It was a blue Toyota Tacoma pickup.

Josie let out a low groan. "Oh, God, I don't believe this."

The Tacoma pulled up next to her Subaru and Paulette Zander's son, Casey, climbed out and approached them, hands buried deep in the pockets of his jacket, a Red Sox cap pulled low over his close-set eyes. Casey wore a pouty expression on his chubby face. Not a brooding, sensitive sort of pouty. He looked more like he was pissed off because Dada was too busy to play catch with him. "I need to talk to you, Josie!" he called out.

"Casey, now is not a good time," she responded, politely but firmly.

He ducked under the barricade and started out onto the causeway anyway. "But we have to talk."

"Casey, I have a personal situation to deal with right now. I'll call you later, okay?"

"What time?"

"As soon as I can. I don't know when it'll be."

"I just want to talk. Why are you being such a bitch?"

"Casey, this isn't appropriate behavior. There are boundaries to our relationship."

"*Boundaries?* What does *that* mean?"

"You know perfectly well what it means," she said, maintaining that same polite, firm voice. "Now please leave."

Casey didn't budge. Just gaped at her in disbelief.

"Why don't you take off?" Mitch suggested. "Josie's had a hard morning."

"You shut up," Casey snarled in response.

"Mitch, please stay out of this."

"Yeah, *Mitch*, mind your own business."

"Actually, this is my business. You're trespassing on private property. *My* private property. There's a great big sign posted right over there, see it? Josie asked you to leave. Now I'm telling you to leave."

"But I want to talk to her!"

"She doesn't want to talk to you. That's kind of obvious, isn't it?"

Casey curled his lip at him. "Oh, sure, I get it now. You want to do her, don't you? Or are you already doing her?"

Josie let out a gasp. "Casey, you are way out of line."

Mitch started toward him. "What did you just say?"

"You heard me," he jeered.

"No, I'm not sure that I did. Would you like to repeat that?"

"Mitch, don't do this," Josie said pleadingly.

"I bet your girlfriend the trooper doesn't know about you two. She was asking me a million stupid questions in the ambulance. She's a total bitch."

"You really like that word, don't you?" Mitch stood face-to-face with Casey now. "You're on private property. Leave."

"Don't tell me what to do," Casey warned him.

"*Leave.*"

Casey shoved him. It wasn't much of a shove. He was all blubber. Mitch wasn't. He shoved Casey back and sent him tumbling onto his butt. Casey got right back up and came rushing at him. Mitch sidestepped him and shoved him to the causeway again, this time planting his work boot on Casey's neck and plastering his fat face to the snow-crusted wooden planks.

"Are you going to behave yourself or do I have to throw you in the water?"

Casey started squirming and whimpering like a little schoolkid. "Let me up, will ya?"

"Not until you promise to behave yourself."

Josie put her hand on Mitch's arm. "Mitch, his face is going to freeze to the causeway."

"Good, it'll be a vast improvement. Say you'll behave yourself!"

"Okay, okay. I'll . . . behave myself."

Mitch removed his foot from Casey's neck and helped him up. "Now get back in your truck and get the hell out of here."

"You'll be sorry you did that," Casey vowed, shaking his fist at him.

"Look at me—I'm quaking with fear."

Casey slunk back to his truck and drove off, his wheels spinning in the deep snow.

"Mitch, that wasn't necessary," Josie said scoldingly.

"I know, but it was fun."

"This is a side of you I've never seen before. You have anger issues."

"No, I don't. I wasn't the least bit angry." He looked at her curiously. "He's the client who you were with when Kylie went boom?"

"Yes."

"He seems to have a major crush on you."

"It happens. Some of my male clients, especially the younger ones, can get emotionally involved. Casey's lonely. He needs a girlfriend."

"He needs a new personality, too."

Another vehicle was approaching the causeway now. This one was the black Cadillac hearse from Dousson Mortuary.

"Oh, good, they're finally here." Mitch inserted his coded plastic card in the security slot to raise the barricade.

The driver, a young black guy, rolled down his window and said, "Sorry it took us so long, bro. It is some kind of a mess out there."

Josie drew in her breath. "Mitch, is Bryce *still* here?"

"I'm afraid so. That's why I've been clearing the causeway."

"Where do I go, bro?"

"Just follow the pathway that I've cleared to the big, natural-shingled house. He's in the downstairs bedroom. I'll be right behind you." Mitch stepped aside so that the hearse could start its way out to the island.

"I-I can't believe he's still . . ." Josie started to shake. Her breathing was shallow and rapid. "This whole day . . . it's some kind of a nightmare. I'm going to lose it, I swear."

"No, you're not. You're doing great."

"Mitch, I'm not doing great at all. My life is a total mess." She let out a grief-stricken sob and then threw herself into his arms.

Mitch put his arms around her as she cried and cried, hugging him tight. She was more compactly built than Des but strong for her size. It was like being hugged by a python. "I know it all seems overwhelming," he said. "But it'll work out. We'll work it out together. What you need right now, more than anything else, is a nice heaping bowl of Cocoa Puffs."

She pulled away from him, laughing through her tears. "You always know how to make me feel better. I don't know what I'd do without you, Mitch."

"You'd do fine. You *are* doing fine."

"No, I'm not. I'm going to be awfully clingy for the next few days."

"Be as clingy as you want."

"I won't send you running for the hills?"

"Not a chance. I'm your naybs, remember?"

She gazed at him with her one good eye, which was huge and shiny. Then she hugged him again, gently this time. "Mitch, you are so much more to me than the guy next door. Don't you know that?"

CHAPTER 7

WHAT IN THE HELL am I doing?

Des pulled around behind the firehouse and used her key to the back door. She went directly up the stairs to the meeting room, which had a window that offered a panoramic view of the entire Dorset Street Historic District buried under its blanket of pure white snow. The village's highest concentration of mailboxes was situated directly across from her—the boxes for the Captain Chadwick House condo colony and the four houses that adjoined it on Maple Lane. More than a dozen mailboxes bunched together right there. The flags on three of them were raised, meaning the residents had left something for Hank to take.

Des set a folding chair in front of the window and parked herself there, testing out the zoom lens on her Nikon D80. It was so powerful that she could make out the words *Approved by the Postmaster General* on the boxes halfway to Town Hall. She'd brought her lunch—a container of steaming-hot clam chowder from Mitzi's fish market. Des opened the container and helped herself to some. It was chilly in the firehouse. And the wind was starting to pick up, rattling the windows. She kept her jacket on as she settled in.

Why am I doing this?

Because this was her town. These were her people. If someone was preying on them then she wanted to be the one to handle it. True, the jurisdictional boundaries were pretty clear. If a crime involved the U.S. Postal Service then it was a job for the postal inspectors. If an illegal prescription drug ring was targeting Dorset, then that was a job for the state's Narcotics Task Force. But Des didn't like the idea of reaching out for help. So she was giving herself this day to see what she could see. If nothing jumped out at her then, okay, she'd play it by the book. But she needed to do this her way. If she didn't then she'd just be an empty uniform.

She spotted Hank as soon as his white Grumman LLV turned onto Dorset Street from Big Branch. The mail truck was pretty hard to miss with those red and blue stripes and postal insignias stamped all over it. Especially when it was the only vehicle out on the road. Through her zoom lens she watched Hank nose it slowly from curbside box to curbside box. The LLV's steering wheel was on the right-hand side. Hank used his right hand to open the mailbox, his left to grab the mail from the tray next to him. Then he reached across his body to stuff the mail in, closing the box with his right hand before he moved on. It was not an easy or natural repetitive motion. She wondered how many carriers developed rotator cuff problems from doing it hundreds of times every day. She also wondered how they dealt with the monotony of performing the same exact task the same exact way, day in and day out. Then again, she supposed that someone could say the same thing about her job or Mitch's or a brain surgeon's. Every job had its share of sameness. The challenge was to find a way to keep it fresh.

So what was Hank's way?

Now he pulled up directly across from her at the Captain Chadwick House. Her zoom lens gave her a straight-on close-up view of Hank filling the mailboxes with the catalogues, junk mail and packages that had arrived on the early truck from Norwich. As he inched his way forward, box by box, Des watched his every move, snapping pictures in case she needed them. When he reached a box with a raised flag he paused to remove two unstamped envelopes. One he held on to. His Christmas tip, Des figured. The other he returned to the box. Lem's plow money, she assumed. Maple Lane's residents were still leaving cash out, grinch or no grinch. That was Dorset. Cranky Yankees did not, would not, change their ways.

Now Hank stopped and got out and went around to the back of the truck. He opened it and removed a carton from L.L. Bean. A big one, at least two feet square, though it didn't weigh much judging by the way he was handling it. He locked the truck, just like he'd told Des he did, and clomped his way through the snow to Nan Sidell's little farmhouse next door to Rut Peck's. He set the box down on the front porch under the overhang and rang the bell. He was starting back to his truck when the front door opened and Nan, a middle-school teacher, called out to him. Hank stopped to accept a paper plate of cookies from her. They chatted there for a sec, both of them very animated.

Meanwhile, back at the Captain Chadwick House, one of its elderly residents was waddling through the deep snow down to the curb—none other than her good friend Bella Tillis, looking like Nanook of Nostrand Avenue in her hooded down jacket, fleece pants and duck boots equipped with bright orange Yaktrax snow grippers. The old girl must have been watching for Hank. Didn't want to give that damned grinch a chance to snatch her mail. She collected it and went tromping back inside, her precious bubble-wrapped packages of meds clutched to her chest. Des couldn't help smiling.

Hank had unlocked his truck and moved on. As he neared Town Hall a red Champlain Landscaping plow pickup turned onto Dorset Street from Big Branch and began working its way slowly along in Hank's wake. It wasn't there to plow—its blade was raised high up off of the ground. No, its driver was there to check out the contents of each and every mailbox, leafing carefully through the mail Hank had just delivered before returning it to the box. Sometimes all of it, sometimes not. Sometimes he held on to an envelope and took it with him back to his truck. Des sat there watching him through her zoom lens. He was incredibly calm as he stood there rummaging through other peoples' mail. So damned calm she almost couldn't believe what she was seeing.

She went back downstairs to her cruiser. Pulled it around to the street and caught up with the red truck, flashing her lights at him. When he came to a stop she got out, big Smokey hat planted firmly on her head, and approached him.

Pat Faulstich, the thick-necked young Swamp Yankee with the reddish see-through beard, sat there behind the wheel looking nervous. Same as he had at McGee's Diner earlier that morning.

"How's it going, Pat?" she asked, tipping her hat at him.

He cleared his throat, swallowing. "Was I speeding or something?"

"Nope."

"Then why'd you pull me over?"

"You tell me. What in the heck are you doing?"

"Picking up Lem's money." He grabbed a dozen or more envelopes from the seat next to him and showed them to her. "Lem's the one who usually picks 'em up but he's at the hospital on account of Kylie so he told me to. I didn't take anything. It's all there, I swear. And I don't have a thing in my pockets except my own money, which is like maybe seven dollars, okay?"

"You seem a bit defensive, Pat." Agitated was more like it. "Why is that?"

95

He colored slightly. "I'm not. I just . . . why are you hassling me?"

"Mind if I look behind your seat?"

He shrugged his big shoulders. "Go right ahead. I got nothing to hide."

The storage area behind his seat was a messy tangle of food wrappers, work gloves, sweatshirts, tools and jumper cables. She saw no U.S. Mail parcels back there. Nor on the floor beneath the dashboard. Nor on the seat next to him. There was a sheet of paper on the seat that appeared to be a computer printout of addresses. Several had been crossed out with a pen.

"Looking for something special, ma'am?"

Des showed him her smile. "Just looking."

"I do what Lem tells me to. Ask him if you don't believe me."

"Thank you, Pat. I just may do that."

"I got like forty-three driveways to do. Can I go now?"

"I don't see why not. Are you planning to visit Kylie?"

Pat frowned at her. "Why would I want to do that?"

"I heard you two were tight."

"We've hung out a few times. But she's the boss's daughter, you know? Plus Tina doesn't like me."

"Is Kylie tight with anyone else?"

"You'd know that better than me."

"Would I?"

"Well, yeah. Nothing goes on around here you don't know about, am I right?"

"Some days you are totally right, Pat. But then there are other days, days like today, when I realize that I haven't got the faintest idea what's happening." She tipped her hat at him again. "Drive safe, okay?"

———

It took her nearly an hour to make it to Lawrence and Memorial on I-95. The state's plow crews were doing their best to keep an emergency lane open in each direction, but a good fifteen inches of snow had fallen and the howling wind was starting to blow it right back into the freshly plowed and sanded lane. If she tried to push her cruiser up over twenty mph she could feel it start to fishtail on her.

She found Lem and Tina seated in the surgical waiting room, a big room that on most days was crammed with relatives and loved ones. Today there were only a few families there. When hospitals got advance warning of a major blizzard they postponed most elective procedures. The only patients who were in surgery right now were emergency cases like Kylie.

Tina's dark, protruding eyes grew wide when she saw Des approaching them. Quickly, she lowered her gaze and went back to doing what she'd been doing, which was texting. Lem sat and stared right at Des like a hulking, menacing bear. He must have rushed there straight from work. He was wearing a pair of filthy tan coveralls and oil-stained work boots.

"I'm probably the last person in the world you want to see right now."

"I'm not blaming you," he grumbled. "It was Kylie's own stupid fault."

"I tried to get her to stop. I got out of my car and begged her to stop."

"I'm sure you did," Lem said.

Tina said nothing at all. Just kept on texting.

"How is she doing?"

"Her ankle's busted into a million pieces," he replied, running a thick hand over his shiny shaved head. "The orthopedic surgeon said he'd have to insert titanium screws and plates and stuff like

97

that. She's only eighteen years old. This'll bother her for the rest of her life."

"I'm real sorry to hear that. Can the three of us talk somewhere for a few minutes?"

"Why not? She'll be in surgery for at least another hour." Lem got his huge self up out of the molded plastic chair and looked down at Tina, who was still sitting there texting. "Could you stop doing that for thirty goddamned seconds and come with us?"

"I'm telling my mom what's going on, you mind?" she huffed at him. But she did get up and join them.

Down the hall was a small room that used to be the smoking lounge. Now it was used for private conversations between physicians and families. Nobody was in there. There was a table with a half dozen chairs set around it. The three of them sat down. Tina immediately glanced down at the screen of her cell phone. Lem immediately glared at her. There was definite hostility between them. Part of it was the strain of Kylie's not-so-excellent adventure. Part of it was that same sour vibe that Des had picked up on at Rut's party.

Des took off her hat and set it on the table. "Talk to me. Why did Kylie try to steal those Ugg boots?"

"Because we took away her charge cards," Lem answered.

"We had to," Tina explained. "The girl's a shopaholic. She becomes totally obsessed with *this* jacket or *those* boots and she will not think about anything else. Or *do* anything else. She won't work. Won't go to college. She just sits around the house all day dreaming her stupid dreams. Wants to be like that Kim Kardashian or one of those 'Real Housewives' who lives in a big mansion somewhere and spends all day getting pedicures and planning fancy parties. I keep telling her, sweetie, that's television. It's not real.

You got to *work* for every little thing you get in life. But she doesn't want to hear that."

Lem tugged uneasily at his long beard. "Is she in bad trouble?"

"Possibly. There's the shoplifting charge. She also shoved Joanie Tooker to the ground and dislocated her elbow. Joanie can call that criminal assault if she chooses to. And then she fled the scene of a crime and engaged me in a pursuit that endangered the lives of several drivers before she plowed into that building. We're talking hit and run, reckless endangerment . . ."

"Are you saying she may go to *jail?*" Tina's dark eyes searched Des's face apprehensively.

"That'll be up to the district prosecutor."

Lem let the weight of this soak in for a moment. "We'll have to get her a lawyer, won't we? Damn, this is just what I don't need right now. I can barely make my payroll. You don't suppose if she apologized to Joanie and, say, we offered to repair the building that maybe that'd do the trick, do you?"

"Like I said, it'll be up to the district prosecutor."

Tina's cell phone vibrated on the table in front of her. She squinted at the screen and said, "It's my mother again. Back in a sec, okay?"

"Whatever," Lem growled.

She was already thumbing out a text as she took off down the hall.

Des sat there with Lem, growing increasingly aware of his powerful scent. The man smelled as if he'd been marinating in beef broth for a week.

"I ran into Pat Faulstich on Dorset Street before I came here. He was collecting your money from your customers' mailboxes."

"Yeah, I asked him to. Was he leaving those flyers, too?"

"I didn't see any flyers."

He looked at her in disbelief. "He didn't pick up the flyers? I told the damned mo-ron to get 'em from my house. They're right there on the dining table. Big stack of yellow flyers saying we got to tack on an ten extra bucks from now on. It's because my supplier keeps jacking up the price of road salt. Pat *promised* me he'd put 'em in the boxes. And he's my best man, can you imagine?"

"Does he have any money problems that you're aware of?"

"He hasn't got any of it, if that's what you mean."

"How about drugs? Is he into drugs?"

"Smokes a little weed now and then. All of those boys do. But he's never been in trouble with the law or had an accident on the job. And he shows up every morning, which is more than I can say for a lot of them. They stay up half of the night boozing at the Rustic and some of 'em are still so wasted when they show up that I have to send 'em home. You got to have your head on straight when you're manning a plow truck. If you don't you'll sideswipe a telephone pole. But those boys just don't give a damn. I call 'em boys but they're not. Pat's twenty-six. When I was his age I already had a wife and an eight-year-old daughter." He peered across the table at her. "Why are we talking about this?"

"You have routine access to the mailboxes on Hank Merrill's route."

"So? . . ."

"So someone's been stealing from those boxes. They've taken mail, small packages, Hank's tips . . ."

"And *my* money." He stabbed himself in the chest with a blunt thumb.

"Do you know anything about this, Lem?"

"You bet I do. I know that some bastard's taking food out of my mouth. I know that if I ever get my hands on him I'm going to-to . . ." Lem broke off, glowering at her. "You think *I'm* the thief? Why would I do something crazy like that? No, don't tell me. I already know the answer. You think I'm hiding money from Tina so I can spend it on Debbie, am I right? That is total bull. How does this stuff even start? I'll bet it's Rut Peck. That old geezer's always flapping his gums. Especially after he gets a glass of stout in him. Let me ask *you* something—why is my marriage any of your business?"

"It's not."

"Damned right it's not. Debbie's husband left her for a younger woman last summer, okay? And she called me out of the blue. I hadn't heard from her in ten, twelve years. Debbie was the first girl I was ever with. We were each other's first. And she was feeling kind of sad and sentimental, so I met her for lunch in Mystic. She's way out of my league now. All frosted and polished. Designer clothes, fancy perfume. She sure smells good. You know what Tina smells like? Tina smells like Windex. Anyhow, we ended up taking a room at the Mohegan Sun—strictly for old times' sake. It was just that one time, I swear. That one time and then another time two weeks later. But I'm not carrying on some kind of love affair with her. Us being together, it was just something Debbie needed. And I was happy to help her out. I mean, she and Tina are the only two women I've ever been with in my whole life. First Debbie, then Tina. There are still folks in Dorset who think Debbie was my true love and that I only married Tina because I knocked her up. That's bull. Tina and me have had a lot of good years together."

"And how are things between you right now?"

Lem narrowed his gaze at her. "Why are you asking?"

"You seem a bit snappish with each other."

"We've hit a rough patch," he acknowledged. "It happens. Hell, we've been together almost twenty years. And I still love that little peanut, too. Trouble is that she doesn't feel the same way about me. She used to call me her big poppa bear. Now I come home from work and she's on me, yap-yap-yap. Telling me I ought to lose weight, shave off my beard, grow my business, yap-yap-yap. She's just not happy anymore. I don't know why. Maybe her mom does. Tina's on that damned phone with her day and night." He glanced up at the doorway as Tina returned now. "I need a smoke," he said abruptly. "Do you mind?"

"Go right ahead," Des responded.

He got up and lumbered out of the lounge, digging a rumpled pack of Camels out of the pocket of his coveralls.

Tina sat back down and set her phone on the table in front of her, gazing down at its screen every few seconds. She couldn't keep her eyes off of it. "I guess you want to talk about Kylie."

"That would be great."

"I wish I could get through to her," Tina said with a shake of her frizzy head. "All she thinks about are clothes and boys. I keep telling her, sweetie, you have got to figure out who you want to be. Otherwise you'll end up like me—cleaning other people's toilets for a living. Mind you, I make as much in a week as a lot of my customers do. And I could tell you some things that *nobody* else knows. Trust me, if you really want to find out what's going on, ask a cleaning lady. But this isn't the life I wanted for myself. I wanted to be a nurse. I want Kylie to be a nurse. Now I don't know if that'll even be possible with her ankle all busted up like that. A nurse has to be on her feet all day." Tina looked at Des curiously. "What did you and Lem talk about?"

"He told me that you two have hit a rough patch."

Tina bristled, her nostrils flaring. "If by that he means he's mixed up again with that fancy tramp, Debbie, then I guess we have."

"He said he isn't mixed up with her."

"And you *believed* him? He's a man. Men lie."

"Are you seeing someone else, too?"

"What gives you the right to ask me that?"

"I'm trying to assess the stability of Kylie's home life for my report. My general impressions can be a determining factor in whether the district prosecutor decides to prosecute her case. But if you don't want to talk to me . . ."

"No, no, I'll talk to you." Tina shot a furtive glance over her shoulder at the door. Lem was still outside having a smoke. "Yes, I do have a male friend. He's sensitive and caring. He respects me. He *loves* me. Lem doesn't anymore."

"Want to tell me a little bit about him?"

"His name's Matt. He works for Verizon. He's married to someone else, too. A woman who doesn't love him or understand him. Matt is *here* for me emotionally. He listens to me. And he's incredibly affectionate. I don't just mean the physical part. Although that's been amazing. I swear, every time I think about him my heart starts beating *so* fast. Me and Lem haven't exactly been burning up the sheets lately. And even back when we were he never took *my* needs into consideration. Matt does. He's so romantic and nurturing."

"Where did you two meet?"

"On a dating site. It was like he was my best friend instantly. Right away, I was telling him things that I've never told anyone. And so was he. It was totally amazing. He's . . ." Tina hesitated, reddening. "Matt's my soul mate. I've never been this close with anyone in my whole life. We must text back and forth a hundred times a day. Lem thinks I'm texting my mom. I'm not. It's Matt. It's always Matt."

"Where does he live?"

"Just outside of Tacoma."

"Tacoma, *Washington*? How often are you able to be together?"

"We're together constantly."

"I mean in the flesh, Tina."

"We haven't been together that way yet. But real soon, we're hoping."

"Are you telling me you're in love with a man who you've never met?"

Tina sighed at her impatiently. "Matt and I have an intense bond."

"Meaning, what, you sext back and forth a lot?"

"You're making it sound smutty. It's not like that. What we have is romantic and intimate and *so* hot. I've done things with Matt that I've *never* done with Lem. He's just so loving and tender. Know what he said to me just now while I was out in the hall?"

"Really can't imagine."

"He said 'Every time I'm inside of you I feel like I'm where I was meant to be all along.' Lem's never felt that way about me. Not even when we were a couple of sex-crazed teenagers. And now he doesn't even want me. He wants Debbie, who's not even that good-looking anymore. Which Matt is, by the way. He's tall and slim with good shoulders and strong hands. He has the most amazing blue eyes."

"And you know this how?"

"He sends me pictures of himself."

"Nude pictures?"

Tina reddened again, nodding. "And I send him pictures of me. I take them in the bathroom mirror with my phone."

"You're not worried that he might show them to someone else?"

"Matt would never do that to me. Our relationship is built on trust."

"And what about Lem? Aren't you afraid he might find a nude photo of Matt on your computer?"

"Lem doesn't want me anymore, I told you."

"That's right, you did," Des said with a twinge of profound sadness. Not because what Tina Champlain was telling her was shocking, but because it wasn't. The Champlains were just a typical modern Dorset family. None of them were participating in their own lives. Instead of working toward a genuine career, Kylie wanted to be a reality TV star. Tina was more emotionally and sexually involved with her cell phone than with her husband. And Lem was reliving his glory days with his first girlfriend while Champlain Landscaping seemed to be circling the drain. Kylie had stolen a pair of four-hundred-dollar Ugg boots to keep her dream alive. Tina was sending and receiving pornographic text messages and photographs. What was Lem resorting to? Was he siphoning off money from his own business to pay for those trysts with Debbie at the Mohegan Sun? Was he stealing prescription meds, gift cards and Hank Merrill's Christmas tips? "Tina, this is the part where I have to tell you something you won't want to hear."

Tina frowned at her. "About Kylie?"

"About *Matt*. You have no idea who he really is, okay? *Matt* could be some sleaze in Croatia who's peddling those pictures of you on a porn site. *Matt* could be the online identity of a half-dozen horny sophomores in a frat house somewhere. *Matt* could be a predator who's looking to steal your identity or nuke your credit."

Tina's eyes hardened. "Why would you say something horrible like that?"

"Because it's my job to look out for you. I've seen what can happen. I've seen an innocent blond schoolgirl who thought she was meeting up at West Farms Mall with this nice high school boy she'd met on Facebook. There was no nice high school boy. She was abducted and gang raped by a wolf pack for forty-eight hours straight before they left her for dead."

"Des, I'm not fourteen years old. I know what I'm doing. But I get where you're coming from."

"Do you?"

"Absolutely. You think I'm stupid."

"No, I don't."

"Yeah, you do," Tina said angrily. "So stupid that I can't even tell what's real. What I have with Matt is *real*. The way we make each other feel is *real*. He's the best thing that's happened to me in years and don't you tell me otherwise. My daughter may never walk normal again. And she may go to jail. How dare you show up here and crap all over the one good thing I have going on in my life? Who in the hell do you think you are?"

CHAPTER 8

"I NEED A SECOND opinion here, doughboy. Is Tina just playing harmless X-rated cyber-games or is she cheating on her husband?"

"It's no game. She's totally cheating on Lem."

"Even though she and Matt have never actually bumped skin?"

"Tina's emotionally and sexually involved with the guy. That means she's having an affair with him."

They were snuggled together on the love seat in front of a roaring fire, sipping Chianti and enjoying the aroma of Mitch's meat loaf with pancetta and onions as it baked in the oven. He still had to mash the potatoes and sauté the chard. But he was in no hurry. He could sit here like this all night with Des, who had changed out of her uniform into the gray four-ply cashmere robe that he'd bought for her in Paris on his way home from the Cannes Film Festival. Clemmie and Quirt were nestled together in an easy chair. Des's yellow string bikini was back up on the Chanukah bush where it belonged. Outside, the snow had turned to frozen rain. He could hear it tapping on the roof and windows. On the stereo was *Everybody Knows This is Nowhere,* a highly addictive vintage album from Neil Young's Crazy Horse days.

"But, Mitch, it's not real."

"Beg to differ, little lady. How she feels about Matt is real. Her sexual responses are real. Therefore, the betrayal is real. We're living in a not-so brave new world now. The line between real and virtual has gotten really blurred. There are a lot of lonely, un-happy people out there. Many of them are married people who are desperate to become someone, anyone, else. Dating sites allow them to create a whole new identity. They meet new people, get involved, get laid. They even fall in love."

"That's not real love. And it's for damned sure not my idea of real sex." Des sipped her wine, staring into the fire. "Sometimes I get the feeling that things have stopped making sense."

"You're not alone. I get that feeling a lot."

"Does it scare you?"

"It can. But then I hug you and I'm not scared anymore."

She leaned over and kissed him softly. "I wish you wouldn't say things like that. I get all gooey inside and then I'm no good for anything."

"Oh, I wouldn't say that." He stroked her face, studying her with concern. "You look whipped."

"Only because I am. After I visited the Champlains I had to log face time with my troop commander in Westbrook. Explain to him up, down and sideways why I didn't just put out a BOLO on Kylie and let her go."

"Are you going to get in trouble over this?"

"I don't think so. I didn't provoke the chase. And I tried to talk her out of her car. I've got witnesses who'll corroborate that. But I had to file a detailed incident report. And it'll definitely be re-viewed by Internal Affairs."

"Sounds to me like we'd better watch *Palm Beach Story* after dinner."

"*Again?* I've already watched that damned movie three times."

"Is that all? Then we definitely need to see it. That sequence when Claudette Colbert escapes on the train with the Ale and Quail Club has to be the funniest ten minutes Preston Sturges ever filmed. Pure gold." He got up and put another log on the fire. "You have no idea how lucky you are."

She raised an eyebrow at him. "Is that right?"

"You could have gotten mixed up with a critic who's a Danny Kaye fan. Then you'd be sorry. He'd make you sit through *The Man From the Diner's Club* over and over and over again. No two ways about it—you dodged a bullet when you met me."

Des gazed out the bay window at the lights in the windows next door. "How's Josie holding up?"

"Amazingly well considering the day she's had. First Bryce, then Kylie. Plus Casey Zander showed up out here and got creepy on her."

"Creepy as in? . . ."

"He has a major crush on her. Josie asked him politely to go home. He refused. I had to encourage him. It got a little physical—nothing serious—before he finally left. After the funeral home people carted Bryce's body away she started right in on her to-do list. She's incredibly organized and take-charge. I guess it helps to be a professional life coach. When I left her she was already boxing up Bryce's possessions. She has to call his attorney, Glynis, to find out what to do with them." Mitch refilled their wineglasses and sat back down. "She and Casey were lucky they weren't seriously hurt when Kylie slammed into her office. She'll have a shiner from that ceiling tile whacking her in the eye but it could have been a lot worse."

Des pulled in her stomach muscles ever so slightly. So slightly that most people wouldn't have noticed it. Mitch wasn't most people.

He sipped his wine, studying her over his glass. "There's something you really want to avoid telling me. What is it?"

She looked at him in amazement. "I can't hide a thing from you, can I?"

"Don't even try."

"Look, this is kind of awkward for me. I know that you like Josie."

He nodded. "And I know that you don't."

"What makes you say that?"

"You get all stiff-necked whenever she's around."

"Is it that obvious?"

"Only to me. What do you want to tell me?"

"When I dashed into her office I found her having sex on the sofa with Casey. Rough sex. That's how she got the shiner. Casey hit her in the eye. When I spoke to her about it she insisted that it was strictly a role-playing exercise. Casey has confidence issues with women and she's been trying to help him out. I asked her point-blank if they're romantically involved. She told me point-blank that they aren't."

"But you didn't believe her."

"Mitch, I saw what I saw."

"She told me she got hit in the eye by a ceiling tile."

"Casey's the one who tangled with the ceiling tile. Josie lied to you."

He listened to the frozen rain tapping on the roof, frowning. "I've been around a lot of world-class liars. I'm talking about movie producers, agents. She's a damned good one."

"How much has she told you about her background?"

"Josie isn't someone who talks about her childhood. All I know is she grew up in Maine and graduated from Bates. She used to live with some guy up in Castine who liked to write sci-fi. After they broke up she moved down here and became a life coach."

"She has a Web site. Have you ever checked it out?"

"No, I haven't. Why?"

"Well, for starters her bio doesn't say she graduated from Bates.

It says she studied there. That's a classic resume padder. If you audit a summer school class somewhere you can say you studied there. Her bio also boasts that she's a fully accredited professional life coach. Remember how she mentioned that to us this morning?"

"I remember."

"Do you have any idea what it actually means?"

"Not really."

"It means that Josie completed an online degree program and then became officially certified by the American Life Coach Federation. Which sounds really impressive except, hello, it's not. The American Life Coach Federation and the online degree program are one and the same entity. The outfit that enrolls you in its degree program—at a cost of around three grand—also serves as its very own certifying agency. Josie hasn't been accredited by any official agency that's regulated by the State of Connecticut. She *bought* her accreditation from a for-profit outfit."

"So you think she's a scam artist?"

"I think I'm not so sure how qualified she is to be doing what she's doing. And after walking in on her and Casey getting sweaty, well, I'm not entirely sure *what* she's doing." Des trailed off into uncomfortable silence. "I'm not loving any of this. I know Josie's your friend, and I'm fine with that."

"Really? Because I'm not. I don't stay friends with people who lie to my face. That's generally a deal breaker for me." The rain on the roof sounded quieter now. It had switched from frozen to plain old rain. "Did you get anywhere with our grinch?"

"I found out that it's a whole lot bigger than some kids swiping Hank's Christmas cookies. Prescription meds are disappearing. That's serious business. I'm kicking it to the postal inspectors tomorrow. It's their case."

"Now that you bring it up something has occurred to me."

"Um, okay, *you* brought it up. And something *always* occurs to you." Des gazed at him sternly before she rolled her eyes and said, "What is it?"

"That the right answer's often the most obvious one."

"You mean that Hank's been stealing the stuff himself?"

"Exactly."

"That did occur to me," she conceded. "It would explain why Paulette's been acting so tense. Maybe she's been thinking it, too. Last thing in the world she'd want to do is bring down her own boyfriend. But answer me this—why would Hank resort to stealing his own mail?"

"He has big-time money problems. According to Rut Peck he owes his ex-wife a fortune."

"Paulette mentioned he'd had a personal setback. He even started smoking again. You do know who helped him quit, don't you?"

"Are we back to Josie again?"

"Does Rut think that Hank's capable of something that extreme?"

"Absolutely. Mind you, Rut's not exactly Hank's biggest fan."

"Why not?"

"Because he sees him a rival for Paulette's affections. Like I told you—Rut's real sweet on her."

"The only mail that's been disappearing is the mail on Hank's route," she said slowly. "If Hank has serious money problems then you'd have to take a good, hard look at him. I watched him deliver packages up and down Dorset Street today. Didn't see him do a thing that wasn't kosher. But I'd just spoken with him at the Post Office. Maybe he was just being careful."

"You'd have to catch him in the act, wouldn't you?"

"I'd have to catch him with other people's mail in his wrongful personal possession. Except it's not going to be me. It's the postal inspectors who'll go at him. And they'll go at him hard."

"There's no way around that?"

"If he turned himself in they might cut him a deal. He'd have to give up his buyer."

"What buyer?"

"Someone has been gobbling up those stolen prescription meds. Hank would have to finger that individual along with whoever else he's been doing business with. If he did that he'd have a chance. He's a solid career employee, active in the community."

"But he'd lose his job."

"Hell yes, he'd lose his job. But if Hank's our grinch then he'll have to pay the price." Her cell phone rang. Des reached for it on the coffee table and took the call, her face tightening as she listened. Then she rang off and started toward the bathroom. Her uniform was hanging on the back of the door in there. "You'd better eat dinner without me. I'm going to be gone for a while."

"What is it, Des?"

"Another suicide, that's what. Hank Merrill just took his own life."

CHAPTER 9

THE ROADS WERE ALL slushy and soupy now that so much wind-driven rain was coming down on top of all of that snow. Absolutely no one else was out as Des splish-splashed her way up Route 156, the narrow country road that twisted its way north of the village alongside of the Connecticut River into Dorset's rural farm country.

Her destination was Kinney Road, a remote little lane that ran straight down to the river. Two immense riverfront mansions had been built there a hundred or so years ago. Both places were dark and neither driveway had been plowed. Evidently their owners were spending the holiday season somewhere warm. The road itself had been plowed very recently. She knew this because the town's big orange plow truck was idling there in the rain when she pulled into the small parking lot at the foot of Kinney, which was a real happening place during the summer. Folks put their kayaks and canoes into the water there. This time of year no one came around.

Hank Merrill's black VW Passat was parked facing the river. A garden hose was attached to the Passat's tailpipe with silver duct tape. The other end of the hose was poking through the top of the driver's side window, which had been rolled up tight enough to hold it in place. The driver's door was open, the car's interior lights on. Madge Jewett was crouched there in the rain having a look at Hank while Mary talked to the town plowman, Paul

Fiore, who'd phoned it in. The girls' EMT van idled next to his plow truck.

Des buttoned her rain slicker and got out, tugging her big hat tight to her head. She started with Paul, a heavyset fellow who worked for the town full-time.

"I made one pass through here this afternoon," he informed her, running a hand over his face. The man was very upset. "It must have been about three o'clock. Nobody was here. When I came through again just now I noticed the Passat parked over there with its engine running. Didn't pay it much mind. Figured it was a couple of kids playing grab-ass. They like these out-of-the-way places, you know?"

"Sure, I know," Des said to him gently.

"I've been plowing nonstop since five o'clock this morning, so maybe I'm not as alert as I should be. I'd practically . . ." Paul broke off, gulping. "I did almost the whole parking lot before I noticed that hose sticking out of the tailpipe. When I realized what I was looking at I jumped right out and shut off his engine. But I knew I was too late soon as I got a good look at him. His eyes were . . . staring at me. And I've *never* seen anyone that color before."

"Paul, did you touch him or move him? It's okay if you did. I just need to know."

"No, ma'am. Just reached in and shut off the engine."

"Okay, thanks. We'll need a statement from you later, but you can take off now. I know you've still got work to do."

"Paul's going to hang out with me for a few more minutes," cautioned Mary. "He's had a bit of a shock."

Now Des splashed her way over to the Passat.

"Hello yet again," groused Marge. "Is it just me or is this turning into our worst day ever?"

"We've had better, that's for damned sure."

Hank was seated behind the wheel, eyes wide open, his face a bright cherry red—carbon monoxide poisoning turns the hemoglobin bright. He wore an L.L. Bean ski jacket, jeans and snow boots. His cell phone was on the passenger seat next to him, along with a roll of silver duct tape, a box cutter and a business card.

"That's your card," Marge mentioned to her.

It was the one she'd given Hank that morning at the Post Office. He'd wanted to talk to her in private. Had something he wanted to tell her. Now he was dead.

"Any sign of a suicide note?"

"Didn't see one. Maybe he left it at home before he drove out here."

Des moved in for a closer look—and smell. Hank reeked of whiskey. The whole interior of the car did. "Is that Scotch I'm smelling?"

"Smells like bourbon to me."

"It's really strong. Why is it so strong?" She sniffed here, there, everywhere. And discovered that Hank had spilled it here, there, everywhere. On his chest. On his pants. On the upholstery of his seat. "So, let's see, he drove up here and drank a whole lot. Rigged up the hose with the tape, got back in, closed the door and . . ." She was reaching for Hank's cell phone— maybe he'd called someone—when she suddenly noticed something and stopped herself, her heart beating faster now.

She fetched the big Maglite and a pair of latex gloves from her cruiser and came back, aiming the flashlight's beam at Hank's forehead. On his right temple, there was a highly distinctive purple bruise showing through the cherry red, a perfectly cylindrical ring that was about the diameter of a nickel. She'd seen a bruise just like it once before—when a very messed up Colchester man had pressed the muzzle of a Smith and Wesson .38 Special against his distraught wife's head and held it there for several minutes before he finally made the decision to use the gun on himself.

Des went looking farther now. Carefully, she turned down the collar of Hank's jacket. Found more purple bruising around the left side of his neck. Finger bruising, as if someone had gripped him and held him. There was also bruising beneath his lower lip just above his chin.

She stepped back out into the rain, her eyes flicking over Hank from head to toe. "He's not wearing a hat."

"A guy who's getting ready to do himself in doesn't usually worry about a wet head," Marge pointed out.

"But that's just it, Marge. His hair's dry. So are his hands and his sleeves. Look at his boots. They're dry. So is his floor mat. He's dry all over—except for the rain that's blown onto his leg because we have his door open."

"So? . . ."

"So the duct tape and box cutter on the passenger seat over there still have beads of water on them." She reached across Hank's body with her left hand. "The back of the passenger seat is damp. And, hello, the floor mat in front of the passenger seat is missing." She waved the Maglite behind the front seat, searching the floor in back. "I don't see a bottle. Do you see a bottle?"

"He must have tossed it."

Des went back to her ride for her Nikon D80 and photographed the wet items on the seat, along with Hank's dry hair and boots, the flooring, all of it. She also photographed the pavement around the car, snapping pic after pic of the puddles in the pavement. Not that the pics would reveal a damned thing. Between Paul's plowing and all of this damned rain coming down, any shoe prints or tire tracks that might have been left behind were history now—drowned, washed away, gone. But she took the photos anyway. Because there was no doubt in her mind that this was a crime scene. Hank Merrill hadn't been alone out here in this remote spot. Someone else had been riding in the passenger seat of the Passat. Someone who'd held that gun to his head. And gripped him by the throat. And rigged up that hose to the Passat's tailpipe to make it look as if Hank had committed suicide.

She phoned it in before she returned to Mary Jewett and Paul Fiore. "Paul, you don't remember seeing a whiskey bottle on the ground, do you? Or broken glass?"

"I'm afraid not," he replied.

She gazed over at the six-foot-high snowbanks that edged the parking lot. The plow truck could have shoved the shards of a broken bourbon bottle into any one of those banks. It would take an exhaustive daylight search to find them—assuming they were even there. "How about another car? When you turned onto Kinney Road did you notice someone else leaving this parking lot?"

"Trooper Des, I didn't see anyone else here. Just him."

Mary cleared Paul to take off now. Two troopers in cruisers arrived from Westbrook soon after that to secure the perimeter. Next came the crime-scene techies in their blue-and-white cube vans, grumbling about the rain. Then a death investigator from the medical examiner's office.

Lastly, a dark blue slick-top arrived from Meriden and out climbed Lt. Yolie Snipes of the Major Crime Squad, Central District, and Sgt. Toni Tedone. Yolie, who was half black, half Cuban and all pit bull, had escaped the Frog Hollow Projects to start at point guard for Coach Vivian Stringer at Rutgers before she joined the Connecticut State Police. She was street tough, street-smart and fierce. Back in Des's glory days, when it was *she* who was a hotshot lieutenant working homicides out of the Headmaster's House, Des's sergeant had been a Mr. Potato Head named Rico Tedone. The Tedones were big-time players in the Waterbury Mafia, the clan of Brass City Italian-American men that pretty much ran the state police. When they made Rico a lieutenant, the immensely capable Yolie had been chosen as his sergeant. And when Yolie moved up—a promotion that Des felt was long overdue—Rico's younger cousin, Toni, became her sergeant. Toni looked about thirteen but, unlike Rico, she was sharp. She was also the very first Brass City boy who happened to be a girl. Toni was a feisty, lippy little thing—seventy percent big hair, thirty percent hooters. The older detectives called her Toni the Tiger. The younger ones called her Snooki, though never, ever to her face.

Yolie smiled hugely when she saw Des standing there in the rain. "It's been too long, Miss Thing. Good to see you again."

"Same here, Yolie."

"What have you got for us?"

"Please say hello to Hank Merrill," Des said, leading them through the rain-soaked techies who surrounded the Passat. "Hank's my second suicide of the day. Except this one stinks out loud, as my grandma used to say. See these premortem bruises here, here and here? Somebody held a gun to this man's head and restrained him and, judging by that bruise under his lip, made him drink down a whole lot of bourbon. He reeks of it. The whole car does. But there's no bottle. He may have tossed it out the window—in which case the village plowman may have buried it under one of those man-sized snowbanks over there. A little something for us to deal with in daylight. Right now, let's talk about what we're supposed to be thinking."

Yolie frowned at her. "Which is? . . ."

"That Hank got himself drunk, rigged that hose to the tailpipe—in the pouring rain—got back inside his car and waited to

119

die. Except when I got here his hair and shoes were bone-dry. So was his floor mat. The duct tape and box cutters on that seat were wet. Still are, as you can see. The passenger seat's damp. And the floor mat over there is missing. In my opinion, somebody frog-marched him into this car while it was parked in a nice, dry garage somewhere. Drove him up here, got him drunk at gunpoint and rigged up that hose to the tailpipe. Make that two somebodys."

"Wait, why two?" Toni asked.

"There would have to be two," Yolie answered. "One to ride along with the victim. The other to follow in a second car."

"There had to be a second car," Des said, nodding her head. "That's how they fled the scene after they staged this. They picked themselves a perfect spot. No one around to see them drive away. I'd classify them as clever but not smart. They think they know what they're doing but they don't."

"A pair of real amateurs." Yolie glanced around at the wet pavement surrounding the Passat. "Were there any shoe prints or tire tracks when you got here?"

Des shook her head. "The rain washed them all away."

"Let's get us the hell out of it," Yolie said, starting back toward the shelter of their slick-top. She and Toni climbed into the front seat. Des got in back. "So talk to me, girl. Was Hank Merrill into anything stanky?"

Des was about to answer her when she felt a major sneezing fit coming on, the kind for which there was only one possible explanation. "I'm sorry, but is one of you wearing *patchouli*?"

"That would be me," Toni said. "Why?"

Yolie let out a laugh. "Girl, I have tried to set her straight but she won't listen to me. *You* tell her."

"I like patchouli," Toni said defensively. "It smells sexy."

"Actually, it smells like the lobby of a massage parlor," Des sniffled. "And I don't mean the day-spa kind. Will someone please crack a window so I can breathe?"

Yolie lowered the windows enough to let some fresh, cold air in.

"Hank Merrill was a postal carrier here in town," Des informed them as the rain beat down on the car's roof. "He was also assistant fire chief, coached the high school girls' basketball team and played tuba in the town band. He was divorced, no kids. Lived with the village postmaster, Paulette Zander."

"Have you notified her yet?" Yolie asked.

"Was just about to when you showed up."

"Why would anyone want to kill him?"

"Hank may have been mixed up in something. Stuff has been going missing on his route for the past couple of weeks. At first glance, it looked small-time. Someone swiping his Christmas cookies, tips and—"

"Wait, people in Dorset bake *cookies* for the mailman?" Toni shook her big hair in amazement. "Who lives here—the Keebler Elves?"

"But the deeper I got into it the more it started to smell like something for the postal inspectors. Items of real street value have been disappearing. We're talking about retail gift cards, DVDs, iPods and—brace yourself because this is going to hurt—shipments of prescription meds."

"Oh no, you didn't," Yolie groaned.

"Oh, yes, I did. Hank's route was the Historic District. That's the highest concentration of people in Dorset. A lot of them are older people who get all kinds of meds and those meds are being stolen."

Yolie took a deep breath, letting it out slowly. "The Narcotics

Task Force broke up a black-market meds ring in Bridgeport a few months back. It's big money stuff. You think he was into it?"

"Either that or he stumbled onto someone who is. I spoke to him at the Post Office this morning. He was very forthcoming and co-operative, but he also asked if we could speak later in private. I gave him my card. It's sitting right there on his passenger seat. He had something more he wanted to tell me, Yolie. And now he's dead."

"And we're going to be in a world-class pissing contest," Yolie fumed. "You do *not* bump off a mailman. By tomorrow morning the postal inspectors will be all up in my grille. So will the FBI. And you just know *they* have to be in charge because *they* are the FBI. Our Narcotics Task Force will want in, too. Plus it's the week before Christmas." She glowered across the seat at Des. "Thank you large for this."

Des smiled at her sweetly. "Yolie, I do what I can."

"Did the victim have any money troubles?" Toni asked.

"I hear he was into his ex-wife big-time. Mitch is the one who got wind of it—by way of a friend who didn't have much use for Hank."

"Any chance this friend might have killed him?"

"No, he's over eighty years old. Can barely get around." Then again, Des reflected, if Rut Park wanted someone to take care of Hank he had dozens of loyal friends who owed him favors. Would they do him this kind of a favor?

"Something's bothering me, Loo . . . ," Toni said slowly.

"Then spit it the hell out, Sergeant," Yolie barked. She rode the kid hard. Was supposed to. Plus it amused her. "*Don't* waste the resident trooper's valuable time by telling me you've got something to tell me. Just *say* it."

"Right, Loo. Sorry, Loo. If the victim brushed up against a

black-market meds ring then we are talking about some real bad boys. The kind of boys who'd put a bullet in your head. They wouldn't bother to stage a suicide. Someone went to a whole lot of extra trouble here. Why?"

"Good question, Sergeant," Des said. "I wish I had an answer for you. All I know is that Hank was one of my people and I let him down."

"You're taking this kind of personally, aren't you?" Toni said.

"Miss Desiree Mitry takes *everything* personally," Yolie lectured her. "Miss Desiree Mitry *cares*. That's why she's good at her job. You feeling me, Sergeant?"

Toni nodded her head convulsively. "Absolutely, Loo."

Yolie gazed at Des curiously. "Sorry, did you say this was your second suicide of the day?"

"First one was Bryce Peck, Mitch's neighbor out on Big Sister."

"Any chance that one wasn't a suicide either?"

"To me it played suicide all of the way. But given what's happened here we certainly ought to take a . . ." Des's cell phone interrupted her. She glanced down at its screen. "Paulette Zander's calling me. I'd better take this."

"Go for it."

"I'm so sorry to bother you, Des," Paulette said when Des answered. "But I-I'm a bit . . . I'm worried about Hank." Her voice was faint and halting. "He went out before dinner and he hasn't come back and I-I don't know where he is. This . . . isn't like him."

"What time did he leave, Paulette?"

"It was about 5:30, I think. But he doesn't have band practice tonight. It was cancelled. Everything's been cancelled. And he sent me the *strangest* text message. I was downstairs doing laundry and I didn't notice it until just now."

"What does his message say?"

"Here, I can read it to you . . . It says, *'It's all my fault. I messed up. Sorry for everything. Take care of yourself.'*"

"And what time did he send this?"

"I got it at 7:13."

About thirty minutes before Paul Fiore phoned 911 from Kinney Road.

"I'm probably overreacting," Paulette went on. "But I just wondered if there've been any accidents on the road tonight or-or . . .' She trailed off into uneasy silence. "Have there?"

Des didn't like to break this kind of bad news to a loved one over the phone. Doing it in person was much more humane. "Paulette, how about if I stop by and we talk about this, okay? I'll be there in ten minutes." Then she rang off and said, "That cell phone on the seat next to Hank just got a whole lot more interesting. He texted a suicide note to his girlfriend."

Yolie frowned at her. "So maybe it *is* a suicide."

"Or maybe he texted her at gunpoint. Then again, maybe *he* didn't text her. Maybe one of his killers did."

"We don't usually have much luck getting developed prints off of those teeny-tiny buttons. But we might get one off of the phone itself." Yolie sat there in brooding silence for a moment. "Damn, where were we? . . ."

"Today's first suicide, Loo," Toni reminded her.

"For breakfast in bed this morning Bryce Peck washed down a boatload of Vicodin, Xanax and Ambien with a fifth of Cuervo Gold. I saw no sign of a struggle. No bruises. No scratches. Nothing in the room was disturbed. Bryce had a long history of depression and substance abuse. He left a handwritten note. And he died out on Big Sister. It's a private island. No one else was out there this morning besides Bryce, Mitch and Bryce's live-in girl-

124

friend, Josie Cantro. Josie and Mitch went out running together for about an hour. She found Bryce when she got home. Like I said, to me it played suicide. But I could have missed something. You may want to fast track his autopsy. The M.E. doesn't usually get around to suicides for days."

"I'll take care of it," Yolie said, shoving her lower lip in and out. "Bryce Peck OD'd on prescription meds. Any chance he was mixed up in stealing the meds from Hank Merrill's route?"

"Anything's possible, but I kind of doubt it. Bryce was a loner."

"Well, is there any connection at all between the two men?"

"Josie Cantro. Both men were clients of hers. She's a life coach."

Yolie raised her eyebrows. "She's a what?"

"Life coach. One of those gung-ho types who help you to lose weight or whatever."

"Oh, is that what those bitches are calling themselves now?"

"Before Josie moved in with Bryce she was helping him get off of the Vicodin and Xanax. She helped Hank quit smoking. It so happens she's also treating Paulette's twenty-eight-year-old son, Casey."

"Wheels within wheels," Yolie said with a shake of her head. "Next I suppose you're going to tell us Casey's a mail carrier, too."

Des nodded. "Part-time."

"Shut up!" Toni exclaimed.

"And I haven't even brought out the real funk. I walked in on Casey and Josie getting busy on her office sofa this morning. They like it rough."

"Shut *up*!"

"Would you stop that?" Yolie roared at Toni. "This is a murder investigation, not a slumber party!"

"Mind you, Josie assured me that it absolutely, positively wasn't what it looked like. That she was simply helping Casey with his self-esteem issues. All I know is I found them buck naked together not two hours after her boyfriend did himself in."

"She sounds like a real slice," Yolie said.

"She's a real *something*."

Yolie peered at her curiously. "Have you got more on her?"

"Nothing solid, but something about her feels wrong."

"I hear you. She one of those perky girl types?"

"Real perky."

"I hate perky. Always want to punch perky. Why else don't you like her? Aside from the fact that she's a blonde, I mean."

"I don't recall saying she was a blonde."

"You didn't have to. Your neck muscles gave you away."

"Okay, that's it. I have to start working on my body language."

"Is Josie hot?" Toni asked.

"Plenty hot. Although her butt's kind of big."

"I thought black people liked big butts."

"She ain't black," Yolie pointed out gruffly.

Des heard a truck pulling up behind them. She turned and looked out of the car's rear window. "Well, lookie-lookie. This same bad penny just keeps turning up. Excuse me for a sec, will you?"

She got out and strode across the parking lot in the rain. A red Champlain Landscaping plow pickup was idling just beyond the perimeter of the crime scene with its window rolled down so that the driver could get a better look at what was going on.

"Evening, Pat," she said, tipping her big hat at him. "Anything I can do for you?"

"No, ma'am," Pat Faulstich said, then gulped nervously. "Just came out this way to plow the Beckman and Sherman places. Saw all of these lights and everything. What's going on?"

"Someone did himself in, it appears."

Pat's eyes widened. "Another suicide? Who is it?"

"Can't share that information with you, Pat. I haven't informed the next of kin yet. Did you see that black Passat parked here when you came through earlier?"

"This is my first pass. I don't usually do Kinney Road at all. Lem does. He asked me to on account of he's still at the hospital with Kylie."

"How is Kylie doing?"

"She's out of surgery but she'll have to stay there for a couple of days."

"Take her some flowers. She'll really appreciate it."

He considered this, his brow furrowing. "You think?"

"I know. I'm a woman, remember? Are the Beckmans in town?"

"No, they winter over in Bermuda. When I cleared their leaves last month they were getting ready to take off."

"Do they have a housekeeper or caretaker? Anyone staying there?"

"No, ma'am. They shut off the water, bleed their pipes, all of that. So do the Shermans, who've got like five, six other houses around the world. But these rich types still want their driveways plowed regular even when they aren't around. Well, I'd better get to it," he said wearily. "Still got seventeen more driveways to do before I can hit the Rustic. I need a beerski so bad I can practically taste it."

Des watched Pat back up his truck and angle it around so that he was facing the Beckmans' driveway. Then she started her way back to Yolie and Toni, who were over by the Passat now, getting wet and cold with the techies.

"Who was that?" Yolie asked her.

"Plow boy named Pat Faulstich. I spotted him rummaging through Hank's mailboxes this afternoon. Thought maybe I had me something until I checked with his boss, Lem Champlain, who confirmed that he'd asked Pat to check the mailboxes."

"Check them for what?" asked Toni.

"People leave Lem's money out in their boxes for him. It's been disappearing along with everything else."

"They leave *money* in their mailboxes? Seriously, do they know what century this is?"

Yolie watched the lights of Pat's truck as he plowed his way up the driveway, powering back and forth, back and forth. "I'm thinking it's funny him turning up here right now."

Des nodded her head. "Downright hilarious."

CHAPTER 10

THOSE GLEEFULLY MADCAP *PALM Beach Story* opening credits were just starting to roll when she knocked on his door.

"Come on in, naybs!" Mitch called out, his mouth stuffed full of meat loaf and mashed potatoes.

Josie came in out of the rain wearing a bright yellow hooded slicker and matching yellow rain boots, a plastic bag tucked under one arm. She looked tired and defeated, which wasn't at all typical of the Josie Cantro Mitch knew. But Josie hadn't exactly had a typical day. Plus that swollen left eye of hers was turning into a real shiner.

Mitch set his dinner plate down on the coffee table and hit the pause button on his DVD remote. "How's your eye doing?"

"It's fine," she said quietly. "It's nothing."

"Still, those ceiling tiles can do a lot of damage. You're lucky you weren't blinded."

She studied him a bit curiously. "I guess."

"Have you eaten? I made lots."

"I'm not hungry, thanks. But, please, you go right ahead."

"Okay, you talked me into it. Have you ever seen *Palm Beach Story*?"

"I don't think so."

"Then you absolutely must. Have a seat."

Josie just stood there, swallowing uneasily. Which, again, wasn't at all typical of her. "Mitch, could we talk instead?"

He flicked off the TV and said, "Sure thing. How about a glass of wine?"

"A glass of wine would be great."

He went into the kitchen to fetch it for her. By the time he returned she'd taken off her wet slicker and boots and settled herself on the loveseat next to Clemmie and Quirt. She wore an oversized charcoal-gray sweater of Bryce's, jeans and thick wool socks. Her long, shiny mane of blond hair was pulled back in a ponytail. Mitch put another log on the fire, then sat back down with his dinner and resumed shoveling.

Josie sipped her wine. "Are you sure I'm not interrupting anything?"

"Positive. Des had to duck out on an emergency call."

"I noticed that her car was gone. Otherwise I wouldn't have barged in on you like this. Was it anything serious?"

"I'm afraid it was. Hank Merrill committed suicide tonight. Attached a hose to the tailpipe of his car."

She gaped at him in shock. "God, I can't *believe* it. Hank was such a nice man. And he seemed so happy at Rut's party. Do they have any idea why he? . . ."

"You know as much as I do."

"Damn . . ." Josie slumped against the back of the sofa. "I guess this makes it official—I totally and completely suck at my job."

"No, you don't."

"Mitch, two of my clients have committed suicide in the same day. That's not exactly something I'll be posting on my Web site." She shook herself and reached for the plastic bag she'd brought. "I wanted to return the Randolph Scott movies you loaned us. Also your collection of Manny Farber essays."

"Okay . . ." Mitch cleaned his plate and sat back on the loveseat. The cats rearranged themselves around him for warmth.

"Talk to me, naybs. Is returning my stuff item sixteen on your to-do list or is something else going on?"

Josie took another sip of wine, gazing down into her glass. "I had it on my list to call Bryce's lawyer, Glynis, but she beat me to it. I just got off the phone with her."

"What did she have to say?"

"Something kind of . . . stunning. It seems that Bryce paid her a visit last week."

This much Mitch already knew. Rut had told him. "Any particular reason?"

"He wanted her to draw up his will for him."

"Bryce didn't have a will?"

"Not until last week, according to Glynis."

"I wonder if that means he was, you know, planning to do what he did."

"I wondered about that, too," Josie said.

"Why did Glynis call you tonight?"

"To let me know that Bryce left the house on Big Sister to me. It's mine, Mitch, free and clear. Or it will be as soon as his estate clears probate. She also wanted to warn me that I'm going to have a nasty fight on my hands."

"What kind of a nasty fight?"

"Apparently, as soon as Des notified Preston Peck that Bryce was dead Preston phoned Glynis to inform her he'd be on the next plane out of Chicago to come here and kick me the hell out. She had to tell him not so fast, cowboy. And Preston went absolutely ballistic. As far as he's concerned the Big Sister house belongs to the Peck family and it's going to stay in the Peck family. Glynis thinks he'll contest the will. Fight me in court over it, knowing that I'm not someone who can afford a long, drawn-out legal battle."

"That sounds really pleasant."

"Doesn't it? Glynis wants me to stand my ground. She gave me the names of two lawyers who she said are very good."

Mitch sipped his wine, peering at her. "You didn't know anything about this?"

"I had no idea."

"Bryce didn't tell you that he'd drawn up his will?"

"No."

"Did he tell you that he'd been to see Glynis?"

"*No*. And please stop interrogating me, will you?"

"Sorry, I guess I've been around Des too long." Mitch listened to the rain pounding on the roof. "I wonder why he didn't tell you."

"It doesn't surprise me in the least. Bryce could be very secretive. The weird thing is I don't even want the damned house."

"Why not?"

"Because it's not mine. It'll never feel like mine."

"If that's the case then your lawyer can probably make a deal with the Peck family."

Josie stared into the fire. "Glynis did mention something like that. Reaching a financial settlement, I mean. It just . . . It seems so crass and disgusting to be talking about money while Bryce is still lying in a body bag somewhere. As far as I'm concerned Preston can just *take* the damned place. I don't belong out here. And I for damned sure have no business being a life coach. I've messed up everyone who I've come in contact with. Bryce chose death over sharing his life with me. Casey is a clinging nutso. And now Hank is gone, too. I'm no good at what I do, Mitch. I'm no good, period."

"That's not true, Josie. You've helped a lot of people. They count on you. I know I do. I'd miss you if you weren't around."

She looked at him searchingly. "Do you really mean that?"

"I really do. Who'll run with me every morning if you leave?"

She was still looking at him. "Des told you, didn't she? About finding me on the sofa with Casey. I can see it in your eyes."

Mitch reached over and stroked Clemmie, who stirred from her nap and began to make small motorboat noises. "See what, Josie?"

"That you're wondering about me now. Trying to figure out if I'm a scheming, money-grubbing slut. I'm not, Mitch. And I'm sorry I lied to you about what happened. Friends shouldn't do that to each other."

"You're right, they shouldn't. So why did you?"

"Because I didn't want you to think less of me. You have no idea how much I look up to you. Mitch, if I lose you I'll never make it through this. Are you still my friend?"

"Sure, I am," he said, because it was what she needed to hear. "Don't sweat it. You've got enough to worry about. Seriously, are you thinking about leaving town?"

She nodded her head. "It's time for me to move on."

"Will you go back to Maine?"

She glanced at him sharply. "Why would I want to do that?"

"It's where you're from, isn't it?"

"Why are you suddenly asking me about Maine?"

"Just curious. You don't talk much about your childhood."

"So?"

"So most people do. Have you got any brothers or sisters?"

"I had a father," she said quietly. "He was a logger and a mean drunk. Used to beat the crap out of my mother and me every Saturday night. He took off for good when I was twelve. After that, it was just mom and me freezing our asses off in a drafty trailer. I'm trailer-park trash through and through, Mitch. I ran away when I was sixteen. I've been on my own ever since. I put myself through school. I've never had anyone to look after me—especially a big brother."

"Meaning what?"

"Meaning you're the first male friend I've ever had who hasn't tried to get in my pants. You don't even joke about it."

"I'm in a committed relationship, remember?"

"Yeah, like that's ever stopped any of you."

"You haven't met many nice Jewish boys, have you?"

"I haven't met many nice boys, period."

"So how do you like it? Having a big brother, I mean."

"I'm not sure. I still can't decide whether I should be insulted or flattered."

"Try flattered. I've never had a kid sister. And I don't want you to leave. Please stay, Josie. If you go away then I'll have Preston Peck for a neighbor and that would be too heinous to contemplate. Promise me you'll think about staying, okay?"

"Okay," she conceded reluctantly. "I'll think about it."

"Good. Now how about watching *Palm Beach Story* with me? I promise that you'll laugh nonstop."

"No, thanks. I have a ton of stuff to do." She got up and retrieved her rain slicker and boots, smiling that great big smile of hers. "But thanks, naybs. For everything."

"Any time, naybs," he said, thinking that she seemed much more like her usual sunny, upbeat self again.

Unless, of course, it was all an act. Which he had to admit was entirely possible. Because it was becoming more and more obvious to Mitch with each passing hour that he really didn't know Josie Cantro at all.

CHAPTER 11

PAULETTE ZANDER'S HOUSE WAS a dreary little raised ranch, just like a lot of the other houses on Grassy Hill Road, a blue-collar enclave up near Uncas Lake. The door of her two-car garage was open. Her Nissan Pathfinder was parked in one space. The other space was empty. No cars were parked in the driveway.

Des rang the doorbell and stood in the rain listening to the thudding of footsteps as Paulette came to the door. She did not relish this. Delivering bad news to loved ones was the hardest thing she had to do—especially when the circumstances called for her to be less than completely candid. At this stage of the investigation she had to paint Hank's death as the suicide that it was meant to look like. She couldn't let on that they felt sure he'd been murdered. Not when there was a chance, however remote, that Paulette was mixed up in it herself.

When Paulette opened the door she had on the same sweater and slacks that she'd been wearing at the Post Office that morning. "He still hasn't shown up," she told Des warily. "Have you heard anything?"

"May I come in, Paulette?"

The house was even drearier on the inside—the ceilings low, the harvest gold shag carpeting worn and dingy. The stale, overheated air smelled like dirty laundry. Des removed her wet slicker and hat and hung them on a peg rack by the front door. The living room, which was right off of the entry hall, was crowded full of Hank's tubas—three of them, to be exact—a Christmas tree and an elaborate electric train set that looked as if it dated back to the 1950s. Paulette led Des down a short hallway to the dining room, which had been converted into a TV room. A matched pair of huge plush recliners sat parked in front of a sixty-inch flat-screen TV. Paulette seemed to be watching a reality show about hoarders. Des had always wondered who watched such shows. Now she knew. On an end table between the giant recliners there was a gallon jug of Carlo Rossi Chablis, a half-empty wineglass, an ashtray and a pack of Marlboros. Des could smell spaghetti sauce simmering through the open kitchen doorway. And see that the kitchen table was set for two. The lady was still waiting for her man to come home for dinner.

Paulette flicked off the TV and flopped down in one of the recliners, motioning Des toward the other one. "Can I get you anything?"

"I'm all set, thanks." Des perched on the edge of the recliner while Paulette took a big gulp of wine, then lit a cigarette, pulling on it deeply. "I don't recall seeing you smoke before."

"I quit two years ago," she said with a casual wave of her hand. The lady was more than a bit tipsy, Des realized. "Found these down in Casey's room. Not my old brand, but who gives a crap. You don't mind if I smoke, do you?"

"It's your house, Paulette. Where is Casey?"

"At the Rustic, same as every night. He and all of the other boys. It's their little clubhouse."

"When did he leave?"

"After dinner, same as always."

"You were saying on the phone that Hank didn't come home from work?"

"No, he came straight home." She flicked her cigarette ash in the general direction of the ashtray. "Fiddled around with his train set for a while. He drags the silly thing out of the attic every Christmas and sets it up and watches it go around and around. He's had it ever since he was a little boy. You wouldn't believe how happy it makes him. Then he put on his coat and told me he had to check on something at the firehouse before dinner."

"Such as what?"

Paulette let out a hollow laugh. "How would I know? He's in and out of there all of the time. They all are. The firehouse is *their* little clubhouse. It's where they go when they want to get away from us. That's how men are. But Hank's Mr. Reliable. He's always back in time for dinner. You can set your watch by Hank." She stubbed out her cigarette, her face tightening. "I gave Casey his dinner at 6:30 so he could take off for the Rustic. When Hank still wasn't back by 7:00, I started to get ticked off. It's a rotten night out there and I'm sitting here all by myself. I tried his cell phone, but it was turned off."

"Did you leave him a voice message?"

"I sure did. And when he didn't call me back I started getting worried. I was going to try him again when I noticed the text message that he'd sent me. It sounded *so* unlike him. Also kind of . . . scary. That's why I called you. Maybe I'm making something out of nothing. If I am I'm sorry to drag you out like this."

Des cleared her throat. "Actually, you didn't. I was already out. There's no easy way to say this, Paulette, but we've found Hank's Passat by the boat launch at the end of Kinney Road. He hooked up one end of a garden hose to the tailpipe, stuck the other end through his window and—"

"Oh, no . . ." Paulette's eyes bulged with fright. "Are you telling me he's *dead*?"

"I'm afraid so. I'm sorry."

Paulette groped for another cigarette and lit it, her hands trembling. "That's why you didn't say anything on the phone, isn't it? I knew it. As soon as you told me you were coming by I knew it was going to be bad news. I-I thought maybe he'd been in an accident. The roads being so bad and all. But not something like-like *this*." She shook her head slowly from side to side. "That text message . . . that was his suicide note, wasn't it?"

"It certainly appears that way. Shall I call Casey for you at the Rustic? Have him come home?"

"No, I'm fine," Paulette said softly, reaching for her wineglass.

"Was Hank acting unusual this evening? Did he seem depressed?"

"He's been upset about those thefts on his route. I wouldn't say he was depressed. Hank doesn't . . . didn't get depressed. He was real even tempered."

"And how were things going between you two? Were you happy?"

Paulette stared at her blankly. "*Happy*? You're kidding me, right? I haven't met anyone who's *happy* in a really, really long time. But I thought we were doing okay. We enjoyed each other's company. Laughed a little. Made love a little. Not as much as we used to but that's to be expected, right?"

"Was Hank a big drinker?"

"He liked his beer."

"How about bourbon?"

"Not real often. Why?"

"He smelled strongly of it when we found him."

Paulette furrowed her brow. "There's a half-bottle of Jack Daniel's in the kitchen cupboard, I think. It's been in there for at least a year."

"Would you mind checking to see if it's still there?"

Paulette got up out of her recliner and went into the kitchen. "Still here," she called out, returning with it. "I guess . . . he must have bought a bottle somewhere."

"Must have."

Paulette put the bottle of Jack Daniel's down on the kitchen table and retrieved her wineglass, swaying slightly as she stood there. "Hank was the grinch, wasn't he? That's why he did himself in—because you were closing in on him. That text he sent me, when he said, '*It's all my fault. I messed up.*' That was him confessing."

"It's too soon to know at this point. Anything I say would be speculation, and I don't like to speculate. May I see the text message?"

Paulette fetched her cell from the arm of her recliner, found Hank's text message and held it out to her. Des studied it carefully. It was just as Paulette had reported it, word for word. "*It's all my fault. I messed up. Sorry for everything. Take care of yourself.*" All very neat and correct. No typos. No text speak. And she'd received it when she'd said she had—at 7:13.

"You said you left him a voice message?"

Paulette nodded. "It should be on my call log. There it is, see? I called him at 7:07."

"Paulette, I'm going to need to borrow your phone for a day or two."

"Fine." She sat back down in her recliner, sighing morosely. "It's not much to grab on to, is it? He didn't say he loved me or he'd miss me. He just said '*Take care.*' Like I was one of his firehouse buddies." Paulette gulped down some more wine. "What happens now?"

"The postal inspectors will be contacting you in the morning, I imagine. They'll no doubt want to look into what's been happening on Hank's route. Try to determine if, say, he had money troubles."

"Tell them to talk to his bitch of an ex-wife," Paulette said angrily. "Her and that lawyer of hers. They tormented the poor man constantly about money. All because his mother committed the cardinal sin of dying. He sold her house and made a few dollars. Worked day and night and made a few dollars more. And for that they hounded him and hounded him. . . ."

"Paulette, do *you* think Hank was stealing his own mail?"

Dorset's postmaster considered her reply for a long moment. "It wasn't like him to pull something sneaky. Hank was the ultimate Boy Scout. His friends and neighbors felt safe having him coach their teenaged daughters. That's saying something, isn't it?"

"Yes, it is."

"But it sure looks like he was up to no good," Paulette admitted. "I'd have to be an idiot not to see that. I just find it hard to believe, that's all."

"If Hank was stealing prescription meds then he must have had a buyer. Do you have any idea who he might have been dealing with? Did he make regular trips to New Haven or New London during the course of the week? Mention a friend who he visited? Anything like that?"

Paulette shook her head. "Nothing like that. But he did know a lot of people here in town. Maybe one of his firehouse or marching-band buddies put him in touch with someone. And he worked at John's barber shop every Saturday. God only knows what sort of riffraff slithers in and out of there." She heaved a pained sigh. "We could have licked it together. Taken out a second mortgage on this place. Sold one of our cars. Who cares? It's only money. But Hank wouldn't let me help him. He just kept saying, 'It's my baggage, not yours.' He was a stubborn bastard. They're *all* stubborn bastards."

"Paulette, are you positive you don't want me to call Casey for you? I'm sure he'll want to come straight home."

"The Rustic *is* his home. This is just where he sleeps."

"Is there anybody I can call for you?"

"Why would you want to do that?"

"So someone can be with you. You shouldn't be alone at a time like this."

"I *am* alone," she said, reaching for her wineglass. "I'm going to be alone for the whole rest of my life. I may as well start getting used to it."

"So how's my good friend Yolie Snipes?"

"She's been happier. An entire boxed set of Feds will be swarming all over this by tomorrow morning. Yolie doesn't play well with others."

"Is she still partnered with Toni the Tiger?"

"She is."

"Which one of them has started wearing patchouli?"

"Mitch, how on earth did? . . ."

"You reeked of it when you walked in that door. And I happen to know that there are no head shops in Dorset."

Des shook her head at him. "I swear, sometimes you terrify me."

All she'd wanted to do when she walked in that door was shuck her wet uni, jump into a hot shower and then into Mitch's nice, warm bed. But Mitch, who was seven-tenths Jewish mother, had insisted she eat a late supper after her shower. So now she was seated on a blanket in front of the fire stuffing herself on the world's most gigantic, delicious meat loaf sandwich. Clemmie and Quirt were crouched next to her, sniffing at her plate with keen, busy-nosed interest. Outside, the rain was still coming down. It was good to be warm and dry in front of this fire with Mitch and the cats. It was good to be Des Mitry tonight—as opposed to

141

Paulette Zander, who was sitting in that dingy house with only a gallon jug of cheap Chablis and her dead boyfriend's electric train set for company.

"You're positive that Hank's death wasn't a suicide?"

"Couldn't be more positive." Des set aside the remains of her sandwich and took a sip from her glass of milk. "Someone staged the suicide scene, sent Paulette that text message and then took off in a second car. Whoever did it had a partner. We're looking for two people."

Mitch gazed thoughtfully into the fire for a long moment before he said, "Are you going to finish that sandwich?"

"It's all yours."

He dove in, continuing to stare into the fire. She knew that stare. His wheels were turning.

"What are you thinking, doughboy?"

"That I should have put some of Sheila Enman's bread-and-butter pickles on this. Also something truly crazy. What if Bryce's suicide was staged, too?"

"That's not crazy at all. Yolie's already fast-tracking Bryce's autopsy. Although I don't understand why someone would want to kill Bryce."

"Why *Josie* would want to kill him, you mean."

She frowned at him. "Josie?"

"No one else was out here this morning when he died. There were no tire tracks in the snow, no footprints."

"Okay, let's say you're right about that. . . ."

"Oh, I'm right."

"Why would Josie do it?"

"I can help you when it comes to a motive," he said, shoving the last of her sandwich into his mouth. "Mighty big one, too."

"Well, don't be bashful. Let's hear it."

"Josie showed up here not long after you left with some very interesting news—Bryce asked Glynis Fairchild-Forniaux to draw up his will for him last week. He hadn't had one before, apparently. Guess who he left his house to? Go ahead, take a wild guess."

"Um, okay, somebody who has long blond hair and isn't named Preston?"

"Bingo. Glynis phoned Josie to warn her that Preston totally freaked when he found out. Glynis thinks Preston will contest it in court. She wants Josie to hire a lawyer and stand her ground."

"Is she going to?"

"Too soon to tell. Josie seemed genuinely stunned by the whole thing. Swore to me that she didn't know a thing about what Bryce had done."

"Did you believe her?"

"Honestly? When it comes to Josie I'm not sure what to believe." Mitch gulped down what was left of Des's milk. The man did not know how to leave any food or beverage untouched. "Let's just riff here for a sec. Let's say Josie killed Bryce so that she could score his megamillions house, okay?"

"Okay . . ."

"Why would she need to kill Hank, too?"

Des settled back against a big throw pillow. It had been a long, grueling day. Her body was starting to relax. Not her head though. "We know that Hank was a client of hers a couple of months back."

Mitch nodded. "And let's say Hank *was* stealing that stuff from his route. What if *he* supplied Josie with the prescription meds that killed Bryce?"

"Bryce had perfectly legit prescription bottles."

"That Josie told us were full at the time of his death. Let's say she lied about that. Let's say those bottles of Vicodin, Xanax and

Ambien were actually empty. For all we know, Bryce was still using them on a daily basis. We only have Josie's word for it that he was drug free these past weeks. Besides, we don't know that those are the actual drugs he swallowed this morning."

"Agreed. That's why we need his toxicology results. We also need to take a good, hard look at that suicide Post-it of his."

"What about it?"

"Josie told us that *'Just an awkward stage'* was a pet phrase of Bryce's. That he used it a lot."

"So? . . ."

"So we've been assuming that Bryce wrote it this morning when he was preparing to do himself in. But he could have written it days or even weeks ago. Stuck it on the fridge or the bathroom mirror. Our lab people can determine how long the ink's been drying on the Post-it. If that ink's more than twenty-four hours old, then right away this gets way more interesting."

Mitch looked at her in astonishment. "I didn't know they could do that."

"Maybe Josie doesn't either." Des lay there, her mind working through it. "Let's say you're right. Let's say Josie convinced Hank to supply her with some of his stolen prescription meds. Hell, let's go all the way in and say she's the one who convinced him to steal the damned stuff in the first place. How did she manage that? We talking about role-playing exercises on her office sofa again?"

"She could have offered Hank something a lot more enticing than her body."

"Like what?"

"Like a healthy share of the proceeds once she sold Bryce's house. More than enough money for him to get out of the mess he was in with his ex-wife. He and Josie no doubt talked about his financial problems when she was helping him quit smoking.

Mind you, that would mean she knew weeks ago that Bryce intended to leave her his house *and* that she lied to me about it tonight to cover her tracks. But I have no problem believing that."

"I don't either. I also have no problem believing she was doing Hank just for good measure. It's still the world's best form of persuasion."

"Then she bumped him off tonight because he could implicate her in Bryce's death."

"And because she didn't need him anymore," Des said. "It's nice and neat. Appallingly so."

"Wait, I just thought of something. Josie never left the island tonight. I would have heard her car."

"What if she walked across the causeway and got picked up? Hank's killer had a partner, remember? Someone else was waiting in a getaway car."

He tilted his head at her. "Someone like Casey Zander?"

"He's certainly a likely candidate. I also have my eye on Pat Faulstich. Everywhere I go I keep tripping over him. He was rummaging through the mailboxes when I had Dorset Street staked out this afternoon. And tonight he showed up on Kinney Road— supposedly to plow the neighboring driveways."

"That's interesting. I wonder if he has a connection to Josie."

"So do I."

"Any idea where Casey was tonight?"

"Paulette told me he was at the Rustic, same as every night. I offered to call him for her but she didn't want me to call anyone. The woman went totally Garbo on me."

Mitch beamed at her. "That was totally an old movie reference. I'm rubbing off on you, admit it."

"It's true, you are." She sighed. "Won't be long now before I'm

145

talking for hours on end about the pulsing cinematic muscularity of Mr. Stan Fuller."

"It's *Sam* Fuller. And just for that I'm going to make you watch *The Steel Helmet*."

"Yum, can't wait. What was she wearing?"

"Who?"

"Josie. You said she showed up here not long after I left. Just wondered if she was wet or muddy or whatever."

"Her slicker and rain boots were wet. Her hair was dry. So were her jeans and her socks."

"She could have changed clothes before she came over here. She didn't happen to smell of whiskey, did she?"

"No, she didn't. I pumped her a bit about her childhood in Maine."

"And? . . ."

"She got surprisingly defensive, bordering on hostile."

"Mitch, we have to take a good, hard look at her. Will you be okay with that?"

"Sure I will. Do what you have to do. I just have one small problem."

"What is it?"

"Think about where we're going with this. We're suggesting that Josie Cantro is a cold, calculating predator who's been using her life-coaching practice to troll for juicy prey. That she targeted Bryce, bedded him, killed him and picked him clean. That she's the proverbial black widow—an evil bitch who has no sense of morality and zero conscience. I've spent a decent amount of time around Josie and, well, I'm not there yet. Are you? Do you really think that's who she is?"

"I don't know. But I can guarantee you this—starting first thing tomorrow morning, we sure as hell are going to find out."

CHAPTER 12

"AWFULLY DARNED NICE OF you to do this, Mitch."

"My pleasure, Rut. Well, not a pleasure. But I'm happy to do it."

The old postmaster was riding next to him in the Studey. Rut had spent another night in his house on Maple Lane, what with the torrents of rain falling on top of all of that snow. Mitch was driving him back to his room at Essex Meadows, with a stopover to pay a call on Paulette, his grieving protégé.

"Don't know what to say to her," Rut grumbled. "I never know what to say after somebody's gone."

"You don't have to say a thing. It's enough that you're showing up."

It was a bright, beautiful morning. The air was incredibly fresh. But it was also chilly enough that last night's rain had frozen over in the hours before dawn, leaving a gleaming coat of ice behind. Mitch had to take a scraper to his pickup's windshield and spray its door handles with WD-40 before he could pry the doors open. Frozen puddles remained here and there on the plowed road surfaces, although those would be thawing soon. It was supposed to climb into the toasty upper thirties by the afternoon.

He'd expected to find many cars parked outside of Paulette's raised ranch on Grassy Hill Road. This was Dorset. Friends and neighbors always showed up when you were hurting. Yet only Casey's blue Toyota Tacoma was parked in the driveway.

Rut sat in his heavy wool coat staring at the house. "She doesn't have any family to be with her. Her parents are dead. And the folks at the Post Office need to get their work done. They'll stop by later to pay their respects, I imagine. Paulette isn't the sort who makes a lot of friends. But Hank had a million of them." The old man heaved a reluctant sigh. "Guess we'd better go on in. It's not getting any warmer in this here truck. You should have the heater looked at, young fella."

"Rut, there is no heater."

"Well then, that explains it."

Paulette's front walk and steps hadn't been salted or sanded. The brick pavers were perilously slick.

"You'd better hold on to me, Rut. I don't want you to fall."

"I don't want me to fall either," Rut said, grabbing hold of Mitch's arm with a grip of iron.

They made it up the steps to the frozen welcome mat. Mitch rang the bell.

Paulette opened the door, smelling strongly of wine and cigarettes. Her face softened when she saw Rut standing there. "Hello, Rutherford," she murmured, blinking back tears.

"Hey there, young lady," he said gently, stepping inside to give her a hug. "Anybody else here?"

"Not right now. A bunch of neighbors came by with casserole dishes but I sent them packing. Why do people always bring casserole dishes when somebody dies? Hank's dead and so, what, I'm suddenly supposed to be in the mood for ham and scalloped potatoes?"

Mitch stood there salivating. Maybe she wasn't, but he sure was. He had a nice big hunk of Harrington's ham in the fridge, too. Plenty of Yukon Golds. Assorted bits of stinky Cato Corner Farm cheeses. Yummy.

"I didn't feel like talking to anyone," Paulette added, leading them inside past her cluttered living room, which Mitch noticed had a really cool vintage Lionel train set all laid out and ready to go. "Besides, a postal inspector from New York City showed up here at the crack of dawn and grilled me for a solid hour. Get this, will you? They're bringing in a temporary supervisor from Norwich. I have to stay home for a few days."

"That's because you're grieving," Rut said to her. "You *should* take some time off. And I'm sure he wasn't grilling you. Just following procedure."

"No, he was definitely grilling me. Treated me like I don't know how to do my job. He was a nasty little man. I didn't care for his tone at all."

There were two big recliners in the TV room, which smelled of cigarette smoke and dirty laundry. The television was turned off but Mitch could hear a TV blaring from somewhere else in the house. Paulette sat down in one of the recliners and lit a cigarette. A half-empty gallon jug of cheap Chablis and a wineglass were on the end table next to her.

She poured some wine into the glass. "Care for any?"

Rut said, "Kind of early in the day, isn't it?"

"I'm taking a *personal* day. That means I can do anything I *personally* feel like doing, which happens to be getting slightly blitzed." She gazed up at the old man, her eyes crinkling. "Why did he do it, Rutherford?"

"I don't know the answer to that, hon."

"I would have helped him. I would have done anything for him. He didn't have to *steal*."

"Slow yourself down. You don't know for a fact that Hank was stealing."

"He texted me. He said it was all his fault."

"The man was preparing to take his own life. There's no telling what he meant by that. He could have been referring to how unhappy he was. Trying to let you know that it was his own doing, as opposed to something you might have said or done. That makes sense, doesn't it, Mitch?"

"Yes, it does."

"Sure it does. So don't get out ahead of yourself, okay?"

"I just wish . . . If Hank felt cornered and desperate he should have told me."

"You're right, he should have. But fellas aren't made that way. We don't go crying to mommy."

Mitch nodded. "We're taught from a very early age that it's a sign of weakness."

"Is that right?" Paulette shot back. "Tell me, what's weaker than *killing* yourself?"

Mitch had no answer for that. "Do you mind if I get a glass of water?"

"Go right ahead."

He went into the kitchen, where the counter was crowded with those casserole dishes from Paulette's neighbors. He could hear the TV louder from in here—it was coming from down in the basement. The door to the basement stairs was open. A plastic laundry basket heaped with dirty clothes was parked there, which explained the ripe aroma. Mitch nudged the basket aside with his foot and started down the steep wooden stairs.

A lot of people who owned raised ranches made an effort to convert the basement into an extra room. They installed paneling and flooring. Dropped a ceiling to cover the electrical conduits and copper pipes that ran along the joists overhead. Not Paulette and Hank. Theirs was strictly a bare-bones, cement-floored basement. For décor there was a Kenmore washer-dryer and a clothesline with sheets and towels hanging from it. An electric space heater was doing what it could to fight the chill down there, and a towel had been shoved under the door to the garage to keep the draft out. But it was cold in the basement that Casey Zander called home. Also messy. There was a Ping-Pong table heaped with sports magazines and newspapers. A convertible sofa bed, which was open and unmade. Dirty clothes were heaped everywhere. A sprung easy chair was set before the TV in the corner.

Here Paulette's pale, jiggly son sat in a flannel bathrobe watching last night's NBA highlights on ESPN and eating a bowl of what appeared to be Cocoa Puffs. At least he had good taste in breakfast cereals. What he didn't have was good taste in hair. His henna-tinted mop top made him look like a colorized member of The Three Stooges. He still had a bandage on his forehead from his unfortunate encounter yesterday with Kylie Champlain's Honda Civic. There was a card table next to the TV that had a computer and printer on it. Stacked on the floor next to Casey's chair were computer printouts of NFL game stats. Team stats, individual player stats. Mitch had never seen so many stats in his life. Many of the pages had been circled or flagged with Post-its.

"You sure are into stats," Mitch observed. "Are you in a fantasy football league?"

"Fantasy football leagues are for assholes," Casey replied coldly.

"I'm in a fantasy football league."

"Gee, there's a surprise." He glanced up at Mitch, his surly gaze narrowing. "What do *you* want?"

"I brought Rut by to visit your mom."

"No, I mean what do you want from *me*?"

"To tell you that I was sorry about Hank."

"Okay, you told me," he said, turning back to the TV.

"Also sorry about what happened yesterday on the causeway."

Casey didn't respond. Just sat there eating his cereal and watching the succession of slam dunks that passed for highlights.

"This is the part where you say you're sorry, too, and then we shake hands."

Casey heaved a sigh of annoyance. "Why don't you go back upstairs and leave me alone?"

"Your mom's pretty deep into the Chablis this morning. Is she okay?"

"How the hell would I know?"

"You two are tight, aren't you?"

"She's my mom. It's not like we hang together."

"Did you hang with Hank?"

He let out a derisive snort. "Hank played the *tuba*."

"Meaning what, he flunked your coolness test?"

"We lived in the same house—period."

"You also worked together, didn't you?"

"We didn't work *together*. I'm only there on Saturdays or if somebody's sick or on vacation."

"Are you hoping to become a full-time carrier?"

"I'm hoping you'll go back upstairs and leave me the hell alone."

"Suit yourself. Nice talking to you. Actually, I lied. No, it wasn't." Mitch started back toward the stairs.

"Wait a sec," Casey said, allowing a tiny trace of hopefulness to creep into his voice. "Did Josie give you a message for me?"

"No, she didn't. But I haven't spoken to her today."

"Yeah, you have."

"So now you're calling me a liar?"

"I'm betting a million bucks she asked you to tell me something. And *that's* why you came down here."

"Don't ever bet with real money, Casey. You suck as a gambler."

"Tell me something I don't already know." He peered at Mitch with those nonpenetrating eyes of his. "Are you two getting it on?"

"Josie and I are nothing more than friends. I told you that yesterday."

"I didn't believe you yesterday. Still don't."

"That's fine. I won't bother to set you straight. There's no point, since you've already got life all figured out. Hell, you're sitting here in your mom's basement watching TV in your jammies and you're, what, twenty-six?"

"Twenty-eight."

"When I was twenty-eight I was freelancing for two different magazines, teaching a class at NYU and finishing up my first movie encyclopedia."

"Goodie for you, asshole."

"I'm not bragging. I'm just saying that there was so much I wanted to do every single hour of every single day. Isn't there anything you'd like to do?"

"Yeah, there is. I'd like to sit here without you hassling me. Jesus, you're as bad as Hank. He was always on me about how I should be *applying* myself. Like I'd take advice from that clown."

"You take advice from Josie, don't you? What does she tell you to do?"

Casey reached for a pack of Marlboros and found it empty. Crumpled it and tossed it aside. "She doesn't *tell* me to do anything. She encourages me."

"To do what?"

He shrugged. "Be more assertive."

"Is that why you gave her a black eye?"

"That was an accident. And I can't believe she told you about it."

"She didn't."

"Who did?"

"You did," Mitch replied. "Just now."

For a second, Casey looked as if he wanted to tear Mitch's head off. But he'd already tried that yesterday and ended up with his face frozen to the causeway. So instead he stuck out his chin and said, "I guess you think you're pretty smart. Trust me, you don't know shit."

"I know that you're in love with Josie."

"I *don't* want to talk about Josie!"

"Then why did you ask me about her?"

Casey said nothing to that. Just sat there in petulant silence.

Mitch glanced back down at the pile of NFL stats next to his chair. "Are you into the Patriots or the Giants?" Since Dorset was situated halfway between Boston and New York, its residents' team loyalties were divided right down the middle.

"Patriots," Casey grunted. "The Giants play down to the level of their competition. Hardly ever cover the spread."

"It sounds like you're in an office betting pool. Am I right?"

Casey had had enough. He got up out of the sagging chair and took off his robe. He wore an ancient Metallica T-shirt and long johns under it. He dug a Patriots hoodie and a pair of sweatpants out of a rumpled pile of clothing on the floor and put them on. Then he made his way upstairs to the TV room, where Paulette and Rut sat talking quietly. Mitch followed him.

"I'm going out for a while, Mom."

Paulette frowned at him. "Where to?"

"Got some errands to run. I'm out of smokes, for one thing."

"Okay, son. Would you mind getting me two packs of Merits?"

"Are you going to give me some money?"

Paulette fetched her wallet from the kitchen table and removed a twenty-dollar bill from it. "Just do me one small favor, will you?"

He rolled his eyes. "What is it?"

"Don't spend the whole afternoon at the Rustic. I need you here, okay?"

"Whatever." He snatched the money from her and stormed out of the house.

Paulette sat back down, a distraught expression on her face as she listened to Casey start up his pickup and go roaring off.

Rut reached over from the recliner next to hers and patted her hand. "Hank was a real fine fellow. Try to remember the good times you two had together."

She glanced at him curiously. "I always thought you didn't approve of Hank."

"That's not true at all. Hank was okay. I was just jealous. I'd be jealous of any man who's lucky enough to wake up and see your shining face right there next to him every morning."

"You're a silly old man, Rutherford."

Rut smiled faintly, his eighty-two-year-old heart overflowing with the hopeless, unrequited love that he'd kept to himself for all of these years. Briefly, Mitch thought he might tell Paulette how he genuinely felt. But Rut didn't, couldn't. Just nodded his tufty white head and said, "That's me, all right—silly."

CHAPTER 13

THE WORLD-CLASS PISSING CONTEST—more commonly known as a team meeting—was held in the auxiliary conference room of Dorset's Town Hall, a stately white-columned edifice that smelled all year round of mothballs, musty carpeting and Ben-Gay. Everyone was there at nine o'clock sharp with the noticeable exception of the agent from the FBI, who Des had no doubt would start throwing his weight around as soon as he walked in. The bureau was incredibly dependable that way.

Four members of the Connecticut State Police were in attendance: Des, Yolie, Toni and Capt. Joey Amalfitano, a rumpled old-timer who was with the Narcotics Task Force. Des had worked a drug case with Amalfitano on Sour Cherry Lane last spring. Everyone called him The Aardvark due to his huge, down-turned snout of a nose. Des thought of him more as a weasel.

The U.S. Postal Service had sent Inspector Sam Questa from New York City. Questa was in his late forties and bore a startling resemblance to Fred Flintstone. His huge, blunt featured head was set directly atop a massive torso with almost a complete absence of anything resembling a neck. Seated there at the conference table, Questa gave the impression of being a large man. Yet Des doubted he stood much taller than five-feet-four. He had the stubbiest little arms and legs she'd ever seen. She could not imagine how the man found clothing to fit him. He wore a plain gray suit, white shirt and muted tie. Kept his gleaming black hair combed carefully in place, but didn't do nearly as good a job of keeping his emotions in check. He glanced repeatedly at his watch, growing more and more pissed as the minutes ticked by. The man didn't like to be kept waiting by the FBI. The man was feeling disrespected.

And, at precisely 9:17, the man decided he'd had enough. "What do you say we get started here?" he growled. "I got a full plate and I can't sit around all morning waiting for the god-damned bureau to grace us with its presence."

"Okay by me," said The Aardark, slurping loudly from his container of coffee.

Yolie nodded her head in agreement.

Questa glanced down at a yellow legal pad. "Fine, then let's get down to business here. . . ."

That was when the conference room door burst open and in strutted a twenty-something testosterone jarhead wearing a pair of aviator shades and a snug-fitting red ski jacket. He whipped off his shades, then off came the jacket, too. Underneath it he had on a white merino wool turtleneck that was stretched so tight across his pumped-up muscles that Des swore she could make out his entire six-pack of abs as he stood there styling self-importantly for everyone's benefit, his granite jaw working on a piece of chewing gum.

"Lord help us, they've stuck us with Maverick again," Yolie groaned under her breath. "Did we piss somebody off?"

"Possibly in a previous life," Des murmured unhappily.

"You *know* him?" whispered Toni, who was positively goggle-eyed.

Yolie looked at her, aghast. "Don't tell me you *want* that," she whispered in response.

157

"Loo, I swear I've just laid eyes on the father of my children."

"Trust me, you won't feel that way once it opens its mouth."

Toni continued to gape at him. "Oh, it doesn't have to talk."

"Oh, yes it does. And every single word that comes out of its mouth rhymes with 'asshole.'"

"Sorry I'm late, people," he declared in a booming, authoritative voice. "They closed I-95 because of a jackknifed tractor trailor and I had to make it out here on Route 1. I've never seen so many muffler shops in my life. Seriously, how do folks out here afford to eat three meals a day if they're always buying so many mufflers? Am I right or am I right?" He went around the table and shook hands. First with Sam Questa. "Grisky, FBI, how are you? Then with Joey Amalfitano. "It's Grisky."

"We've already met, Agent Grisky," The Aardvark pointed out. "We worked the Sour Cherry Lane case last spring."

"Sure, we did." Grisky's eyes said he didn't remember The Aardvark at all.

But he did remember Des. "Hey there, girlfriend," he exclaimed, grinning at her wolfishly. "Sure never thought I'd find myself back in your sleepy little hamlet again."

"It's not sleepy and I'm still not your girlfriend," Des said. "You remember Yolie Snipes of the Major Crime Squad, don't you?"

"You kidding me? How could I forget a sweet-looking sister like Miss Yo-lan-da Snipes. How goes it, Sarge?"

"It's lieutenant now," Yolie informed him between gritted teeth.

"Moving on up, hunh? Good for you. And, whoa, look who they gave you for a sergeant—it's *Snooki*. Are we on MTV right now? Seriously, am I or am I not standing in the presence of Miss . . . Nicole . . . Polizzi?"

"Actually, my name's Toni Tedone," she simpered breathlessly.

This qualified as a major departure for Toni the Tiger. The last time someone at the Headmaster's House dared to call her Snooki he got a knee in the *cojones*.

"Real glad to know you. And, hey, lovin' the patchouli," he said as he made his way to the other end of the conference table.

Toni gaped at him, awestruck. "I'm going to marry that man."

Des and Yolie exchanged a horrified look before Des said, "Toni, there are two very important words you need to know about a man like Grisky."

"What are they?"

"*Premature* and *ejaculation*."

Toni frowned at her. "You say that like there's some other kind."

Grisky parked himself in a chair and said, "I just heard that the DEA's jonesing to get in on this, too. That means they'll be crawling up our butts if we don't nail it in the next thirty-six hours—which I've assured my boss we will. We have to. I'm flying to Cancún late tomorrow night to hook up with my Quantico buds for a *sacred* ritual. We spend the week before Christmas down there every year and I cannot, will not, miss it. So let's hit this out of the park and I mean *now*. So far it looks to me like we've got ourselves quite a little shitstorm. Possible organized drug activity, theft of the U.S. Mail, a dead mailman . . ."

"Postal carrier," Questa grunted.

Grisky raised his chin at him. "Sorry?"

"They're known as postal carriers, Agent Grisky. I thought you'd like to know since you seem to think you're in charge of my investigation. What we've *got* here is a matter for the U.S. Postal Inspectors to deal with."

"Well, that's a big no," Grisky fired back cheerfully. "Otherwise, we wouldn't all be sitting here at this large table with you.

We're all working together on this one, Inspector. And we need to share what we know. So how about you put your dick in a box and tell us what you've got, okay?"

Questa shifted around unhappily in his chair. "I've had two teams of investigators on the ground since approximately nine o'clock last evening," he said grudgingly. "One of my teams is presently up in Norwich working the supply chain. The other's at the Dorset Post Office conducting interviews. I personally interviewed Postmaster Zander at her home early this morning. The victim, Hank Merrill, was her live-in lover. She's grieving and extremely upset. I also spoke with her son, Casey, who's a part-time carrier. I found him to be reasonably cooperative, although I did think he gave me an attitude."

"It was nothing personal," Des said. "He gives that to everyone."

"At the present time," Questa continued, "there is no reason to suspect Postmaster Zander has been complicit in any wrongdoing. But, based on my experience, the odds are good that she knows more than she was willing to admit about what's been going on."

"Which is what?" Grisky asked.

"High-value parcels have been disappearing from Hank Merrill's route for the past two weeks—retail gift cards, choice little Christmas presents from the likes of Amazon and, most notably, prescription meds."

"How much are we talking about? Can you give us a dollar figure?"

Questa shook his giant head. "We'll have to canvass each resident on his route before we know that. Frankly, I'm still not entirely certain why Postmaster Zander didn't contact us immediately when she became aware of the situation."

"I may be able to help you with that," Des said. "Dorset's a small town with small-town traditions."

Questa stared across the table at her. "What kind of traditions?"

"Folks put Christmas tips in their mailboxes for Hank. Some of them bake cookies, others leave him cash. Hank donated the cash to the Food Pantry."

"I don't care *who* he donated it to," Questa blustered. "Mail carriers are prohibited from accepting holiday gratuities."

"I know this. I also know that the boxes aren't supposed to be used for anything other than official U.S. Mail. But in Dorset they are. Lem Champlain, our busiest private plowman, conducts his business by mailbox. That's how he bills his customers and that's how they pay him—mostly in cash. Lem told me he's short about two thousand dollars this month in payments that his customers swear they put out for him, although I'm not one hundred percent sold on his credibility."

Questa gazed at her sternly. "Sounds to me like you know an awful lot about this case. Was Postmaster Zander in contact with you?"

"Let's just say I got wind of it, okay?"

"Homegirl keeps her ear to the ground," Grisky said admiringly.

"*When* did you get wind of it?"

"Yesterday. I spoke to Hank Merrill about it at the Post Office."

"That's not your job," Questa fumed. "It's mine."

"I'm aware of the protocol, Inspector. But Paulette was highly resistant to contacting you. She was worried about how it would look. I told her that I'd be willing to make some informal inquiries on the matter *if* she'd agree to contact you. I was making a concerted effort to move the investigative process your way. She promised me she'd reach out to you."

"Well, she didn't."

"Well, that's not my fault."

"Well, it's *somebody's* fault."

Des let out a sigh. "Inspector, do you want to throw down or do you want to figure out what happened to Hank Merrill?"

Questa didn't respond. Just glowered at her.

"So you spoke with the victim yesterday?" Grisky asked Des.

"Informally," Des reiterated.

"And now he's formally dead. What do we know about this gee?"

"We know that he had financial problems stemming from his divorce," she replied. "We know that he texted Paulette a suicide note in which he appeared to confess to stealing the mail himself. The trouble is . . ."

"Okay, I need for you to stop talking now," Grisky broke in. To Questa he said, "Tell us what you're doing about this."

"We've brought in a temporary supervisor from Norwich to take over for Postmaster Zander. He'll assign a part-time carrier to Hank Merrill's route until this matter resolves itself. We have to keep the mail moving. That is, and always will be, job one for the USPS. Meanwhile, we work our fundies."

Grisky peered at him curiously. "Work your *what*?"

"Our fundamentals," Questa said, louder this time. "We acquaint ourselves with every aspect of the operation at this individual branch. Interview each and every carrier and clerk. Determine if anyone has recently transferred, retired or been terminated. Determine when the keypad lock in the office was most recently updated. We undertake a top-to-bottom investigation of the security procedures that are in place. Check the padlocks and deadbolts, the safe where the scanners and vehicle keys are kept. According to Postmaster Zander, only she and her senior clerk know the combination to that safe. We'll have to see about that. We've encountered these types of thefts numerous times before. Maybe we're looking at a dirty carrier. Maybe not. There are other possible scenarios. One is that the theft of these valuables occurred *before* they got to the carrier. A dirty clerk or clerks can divert them as soon as they come off of the truck, repackage them and send them on to a complicit third party. I've seen it happen."

Des considered this, wondering if Hank had accidentally seen something going on in the back room. Wondering if this was what he'd wanted to talk to her about.

"If that's how it went down," Toni said, "then wouldn't parcels have been disappearing from more than just Hank Merrill's route?"

Grisky raised his eyebrows, impressed. "Snooki makes an excellent point."

"Thank you, Agent," she said, blushing. The poor girl was totally gaga. A temporary and treatable affliction, Des hoped and prayed.

"Not necessarily," Questa responded. "Hank Merrill had the choicest route in Dorset. And if stuff from all over town started disappearing that would have set off too many alarm bells. Besides, that's just *one* possible scenario. Another is the supply train, by which I mean the trucks that bring the mail to this branch from the distribution hub in Norwich. The postal service outsources the trucking to private contractors these days. We perform background checks on all of the drivers, but that doesn't mean we don't have ourselves a bad apple. So we work that, too. Interview each and every driver who comes in contact with the Dorset-bound mail. Review the security procedures that are in place in Norwich, then keep on backtracking from there. The Norwich hub gets its mail from Hartford and Wallingford. If mail comes into this state by air it arrives at Bradley International and is trucked to Hartford. We'll follow it every step of the way. And if we turn up a bad apple I assure you we will prosecute him to the full extent of the law. We're the US Postal Service. We take our responsibilities seriously. We were on the front lines in the War Against Terror from day one, in case you've forgotten the anthrax scare. Because we haven't. We're professional investigators who do a professional job. We're not clowns."

"It never occurred to any of us that you were," The Aardvark assured him.

"What he said," Yolie agreed, nodding his head.

"Kind of thin-skinned, aren't you, Inspector?" Grisky asked.

"Maybe I'm just sick of you gung-ho frat boys from the bureau taking over our cases."

Des found herself starting to like little Sam Questa, even if she did keep expecting him to let loose with a *yabba-dabba-doo.*

Grisky ratcheted down his hard-charging tone a bit. "No one here is doubting that you know how to do your job. And I'm not trying to muscle you. I just do what I'm told, same as you."

"We all do what we're told," The Aarvark agreed. "So let's just get it done, okay?"

"Fine," Questa growled.

Grisky looked across the table at Des. "The trouble is? . . ."

"Excuse me, Agent?"

"You were saying that Hank Merrill had money problems stemming from his divorce. That he texted Paulette Zander a suicide note in which he appeared to confess to stealing his own mail. But that the trouble is . . ."

"That he didn't commit suicide," Yolie spoke up. "Hank Merrill was murdered last night on Kinney Road. There was a cylindrical bruise on his right temple. Early this morning our medical examiner confirmed that it matches the nose of a .38 caliber Smith and Wesson Special. The victim didn't have a gun permit for any such weapon. We're checking to see if any of his close friends or coworkers do. There were bruises on the left side of his neck that indicate he was physically coerced. Also bruising beneath his lower lip that suggests he was forced to drink the large quantity of the bourbon that he ingested shortly before his death. His blood alcohol level was .26—more than three times the legal limit to drive in this state. No way he drove his Passat to such a remote locale in that condition. He drank it after he got there. Had to. Yet we can't find a bottle. If he tossed it out the window then the town plowman most likely shoved it into the snowbanks surrounding the parking lot. I've got eight trainees from the academy digging their way through those snowbanks as we speak. If there's broken glass they'll find it. We're also canvassing Hank's neighbors on Grassy Hill Road to determine if any of them saw him drive away last evening and if so what time. One more thing—when we searched Hank's jacket pockets we found an unmarked prescription bottle with a half dozen pills in it. The M.E. identified them as ten-milligram doses of diazepam, better known as Valium. Hank had what they estimate to be twenty milligrams of diazepam in his bloodstream when he died. He still had traces in his stomach. We just checked with his personal physician. Hank had never been prescribed diazepam."

"Sounds to me like he was pacified into submission," Des said.

"I hear you," Yolie agreed.

"Were his fingerprints on that pill bottle?" The Aardvark asked her.

Yolie shook her head. "It was wiped clean. The passenger seat floor mat was removed. The passenger seat was moist. The duct tape and box cutter on the seat were wet. Yet when Resident Trooper Mitry found Hank, his hair and shoulders were dry. So were his shoes and the floor mat under them. The man never got out of that car. Someone else duct taped the garden hose to the tailpipe. We found Hank's fingerprints on the hose. No prints on the duct tape that was wrapped around the tailpipe. Not that we would. The car's exhaust heated the tailpipe enough to evaporate any fingerprint residue on the tape. We're continuing to search the car and its contents for prints. We still have to take fingerprint samples from Paulette and Casey Zander, who've doubtless ridden in that car a million times and probably driven it, too. We need to eliminate their prints so we can isolate any others that don't belong. Although I'm guessing that these people were careful enough to wear gloves. And I do mean *people*. We believe we're looking for a pair. One drove up there with the victim. The other followed in a getaway car."

"That's good work," Grisky concluded. "Sounds like you're right on top of this case."

"We may be talking *two* cases. Resident Trooper Mitry caught another suicide earlier in the day—a man named Bryce Peck who lived out on Big Sister Island."

"Are you telling us Bryce Peck was murdered, too?"

"I'm telling you we're looking into it."

"Initially, Bryce's death played suicide all of the way," Des explained. "He was someone who had a long history of depression and substance abuse. And I found nothing at the scene to suggest a struggle."

"How did he die?" Questa asked her.

"By washing down a one-month supply of Vicodin, Xanax and Ambien with a bottle of Jose Cuervo Gold."

"Prescription meds again," The Aardvark reflected, slurping his coffee.

"Bryce had legitimate prescriptions for the pills. And his live-

166

in girlfriend, Josie Cantro, swears that all three bottles were full last time she looked. But we only have her word for that. And we won't know for a fact *what* Bryce swallowed until we get his toxicology results, which Lieutenant Snipes fast-tracked last night, right after Hank Merrill's death."

Grisky furrowed his brow. "Have you got reason to believe that this Josie Cantro might have been less than truthful with you?"

"Let's say I have more information about her today than I did yesterday."

"What kind of information?"

"Bryce Peck's attorney drew up his will for him last week. It seems that he left Josie his house on Big Sister, which he owned free and clear. It's worth in the neighborhood of five million."

Sam Questa let out a low whistle. "Nice neighborhood."

"Josie's a life coach who has a thriving little practice around town. She had a professional relationship with Hank Merrill. And she currently has one with Paulette Zander's son, Casey, who she also happens to be sleeping with. I know this because I walked in on them getting busy yesterday, less than two hours after Bryce Peck was pronounced dead."

Now it was Grisky who let out a low whistle. "Josie's a baad girl. Is she a babe?"

Des nodded. "She's a babe."

"Sounds to me like she's up to her pretty eyeballs in this thing."

"Whatever this thing is," Des acknowledged.

Now Grisky turned to The Aardvark. "Okay, what does the Narcotics Task Force have for us?"

Joey Amalfitano took another loud slurp of his coffee before he said, "What this *thing* is, maybe. We're spending more and more of our time going after dealers of stolen prescription meds. They sell them at a cut-rate price to low-wage working people who have no access to health insurance—diabetics, asthmatics, women who need birth control pills and so on. I'm not talking about a couple of skeejie characters peddling Oxy in a dark alley. These are organized, highly profitable black-market pharmacies that are operating under the protection of the Castagno crime family. Last summer we busted an operation in Bridgeport that was selling meds in broad daylight out of ice cream trucks at the playgrounds. The kids were buying Rocky Road. The grown-ups were buying Celebrex."

"And this wasn't counterfeit stuff from China or whatever?" Grisky asked.

"The real stuff," The Aardvark assured him. "It's turning into a huge problem for us. There is absolutely no way we can choke off the demand. Not when so many people are barely scraping by. So we're attacking it from the supply end. We have an ongoing investigation into a gang that exists for the sole purpose of stealing prescription drugs for these black-market pharmacies. Some of these guys were connected with the gang we took down in Bridgeport. They're still operating—with the blessing of the Castagnos—in places like New Haven, New London and Norwich. And they have a million different ways of getting what they need. The big-timers go after drug warehouses and delivery trucks. I'm talking armed, serious pros. Lower down on the food chain you've got hundreds of hustlers who gobble it up wherever they can find it. They steal it from the curbside mailboxes in wealthy rural towns like this one. And they have legions of little people who do their dirty work for them. Some of these people are pharmacy cashiers, motel chambermaids, cleaning ladies and the like. A lot of them are ordinary high school kids who're just looking to score some pot or coke. You wouldn't believe what these kids are lifting from their parents' medicine chests. They swap it for their own drug of choice, legal or illegal, or for just plain old cash—which, as we know, never goes out of style. None of it's real flashy, but it's very profitable and it's *everywhere*." He glanced over at Questa. "If you discover that the postal service has some bad apples diverting prescription meds from the supply trucks into the hands of these guys then we may be able to bring down some major players. These are nasty boys, Inspector."

Questa considered this for a moment. "Maybe Hank Merrill got in over his head with them."

"If that's the case," Des said, "then he must have had a contact. Someone who was buying the stuff off of him."

"And we need to have a conversation with that someone," Yolie said. "Captain, I'd like to put some names and faces to the operation in this part of the state. Who the players are, where they hang out. We need to grab somebody and throw him in an interview room. He doesn't have to be a big-timer. Just someone who we can pry open."

"I'll put my people to work on it," The Aardvark said.

"Whoa, I feel like we're really getting somewhere here," Grisky exclaimed, rubbing his hands together. "You see what happens when we all pull together as a team? Okay, let's slice this bad boy up. Inspector Questa and his people will work the postal side. Captain Amalfitano and his task force have got the prescription meds angle. The girls will run their investigation into the murder itself. Or *murders*, if that's how it plays out. Resident Trooper Mitry will continue to assist as needed. Sound good?"

"All except for one small detail," Yolie said coolly. "Sergeant Tedone and myself are homicide investigators attached to the Central District branch of the Connecticut State Police's Major Crime Squad."

He frowned at her. "Okay, really not following you."

"She means we're not 'the girls,'" Toni explained.

"Gotcha. My bad, Snooki."

"And my name's not Snooki."

"Whatever you say. Questions?"

Toni raised her chin at him. "Yeah, I have one."

Grisky flashed her a grin. "You keep right on coming. I like that. Okay, what is it?"

"Exactly what are *you* going to be doing?"

He blinked at her, taken aback. "I'm sorry, you were sitting here at this large table just now, weren't you? Paying attention to what was going on?"

Toni nodded her head slowly. "Yeah? . . ."

"That was me doing it."

Kylie was in a third-floor room for two that she had all to herself. Bright sunlight streamed in through the window.

She lay propped up in bed with her surgically repaired right ankle in traction. They had her on a morphine drip for the pain and she seemed to be in a semi-zonked state when Des walked in. There were abrasions on her lips and forehead from the Honda's air bag, and her hair lay limp and flat on her head. But she was still a cutie in the way that so many big-eyed, soft-mouthed little eighteen-year-old girls are cuties. There was no telling what Kylie Champlain would look like in ten years when she lost her baby fat and the bones in her face started to become more pronounced. She might resemble her father more than her mother, though Des certainly hoped not, for her sake.

"Hey, Trooper Des," she said groggily. "I must have dozed off for a sec. Are my folks here?"

"Don't appear to be."

"They went out for coffee awhile ago. Guess they're not back yet."

"That's okay, Kylie. I came to see you."

Kylie lowered her gaze, swallowing. "I'm really sorry about what happened. It was all my fault. I told him that."

"Told who?"

"The policeman who was here this morning."

"Someone came here to talk to you?"

"Uh-huh. I don't remember his name. He said he was with . . . it sounded like the IRS, except not. Internal *something*."

Des felt her abdominal muscles tighten involuntarily. "Internal Affairs?"

"That's it."

"What did he ask you?"

"Whether you made me drive faster than I wanted to."

"Did I?"

Kylie let out a weak laugh. "No way. I'm the one who's stupid, not you." Then she looked up at Des, frowning. "*You're* not in trouble, too, are you?"

"No. It's routine procedure any time there's an accident of this type."

"I panicked, Trooper Des. Totally lost it. You must hate me. Everyone must."

"No one hates you, Kylie. I certainly don't. But do you mind if I ask you something, girl to girl?"

"I don't mind. What is it?"

"Why did you try to steal those boots?"

"Because I have to look nice. Guys don't notice me otherwise."

"Sure, they do."

"No, they don't. Trust me, there's girls who guys notice and then there's girls like me—sort of okay looking except not really. My legs are too short and I have these thick calves and fat little toes. I look like a *troll* in shorts and flip-flops. Plus I'm a total dimwit."

"No, you're not. You're eighteen. Believe me, I screwed up a lot when I was your age. We all do."

Kylie let out a sigh. "I don't even know *why* I keep screwing up. Except sometimes I just feel like I'm going to explode, you know?"

"I know."

"How did . . . I mean, what did you do?"

"Figured out who I really wanted to be. And then came up with a plan. As long as I stayed focused on my plan I was okay."

"I've tried doing that but I always . . . I-I daydream."

"What do you daydream about?"

"Being tall and skinny like you. Looking good in a bikini. Lying on a beach in Malibu with a really cute guy who's rich and nice and totally into me. We have a house right there on the beach. Everything in it's new and clean. I have my own walk-in closet with a hundred pairs of shoes. And I have a dog. I love dogs. Big, slobbery ones."

"Kylie, do you ever daydream about working?"

She looked at Des blankly. "Why would I want to do that?"

"No reason. I just wondered."

"My mom wants me to be a nurse. I've been watching the nurses since I got here. They're so smart and together. I don't think I could be that way all day long."

"Sure, you could—if you really wanted to. It does help if you have someone else in your corner."

"You mean like my parents? No way. They are *so* screwed up and miserable."

"I didn't mean your parents."

"Oh, you mean like a guy." She shook her head. "Not going to happen."

"Why not?"

"I just told you—I'm a dimwit. They only want me for sex. Not one of them is willing to just chill with me. Go for walks on the beach. *Talk* to me."

"I know a guy just like that."

"Sure, because you're tall and skinny and gorgeous."

"No, I mean a guy who'd walk on the beach with you."

Kylie tilted her head at Des quizzically. "Who are we talking about?"

"Pat."

"The Pat who works for my dad? No way. I mean, yeah, we hung out a couple of times, but he's not into me. He didn't even try to kiss me."

"He's shy."

"Shy around *me*?"

"What I'm saying."

Kylie thought this over. "That red beard of his . . . it looks itchy."

"Tell him to shave it off."

"He'd do that for me?"

"He'd jumped off of the Baldwin Bridge for you," Des said, wondering what else Pat would do for her. Would he steal? Would he kill?

"Trooper Des, I'm kind of zonked right now. Are you chumping me?"

"I'm not chumping you."

Kylie gazed glumly at her elevated ankle. "I don't know if I'll ever be able to walk on the beach like a normal person again."

"Sure you will. Let's not turn this into an old Bette Davis . . ." Des drew in her breath. "Damn, I almost did it again."

"Did what?"

"Kylie, you *will* walk like a normal person again. You're young. You're getting excellent care. And you'll be a beast when it comes to rehab."

"No, I won't. I'm incredibly lazy on top of everything else."

"You *used* to be lazy. You're not anymore."

"What makes you say that?"

"I have a feeling about these things."

Des heard a noise out in the hall and Kylie's mammoth, bearded father appeared in the doorway, glowering at her. She stepped out of the room and joined him.

"What do you want now?" demanded Lem, who wasn't in a particularly friendly mood today.

"Just came by to see how you folks are holding up," she said, glancing around for Tina.

"My wife's in the ladies room. Anything *I* can do for you?"

"Actually, there is something I wanted to ask you. Did you tell Pat Faulstich to plow the driveways on Kinney Road last evening?"

"Kinney Road?" Lem scratched at his long, not-so-clean beard. "I've only got two customers up there, the Beckmans and the Shermans. I usually handle 'em myself. Don't recall telling Pat to go up there. Slipped my mind, I guess, what with Kylie and all. But it wouldn't surprise me if he did. He has a lot of initiative. Well, *some* initiative. I hear that's where you found Hank Merrill."

"You hear right. I ran into Pat while I was at the scene. He told me he was making his first pass of the day through there. I wondered if you might have sent one of your other drivers to Kinney

Road earlier. Someone who could help us verify what time Hank arrived there."

"That's a no. I didn't even talk to any of my other men yesterday. Just Pat." Lem glanced down the hallway at the sound of approaching footsteps. "Well, well, speak of the devil . . ."

Pat Faulstich was trudging his way toward them carrying a bunch of tulips and looking extremely uneasy.

Lem noticed how uncomfortable his young driver seemed. "What's the trouble, Pat? Did one of our trucks screw the pooch?"

"No, sir," Pat said. "Everything's fine. Just came by to, you know, pay my respects."

"Aw, hey, that's awful nice of you. I'll be sure to give those to Kylie."

"Maybe Pat would like to give them to her himself," Des suggested.

"Why, sure. What am I thinking? Go right on in, son."

Pat studied the floor bashfully. "You don't think she'd mind?"

"You kidding me?" Lem said. "She'll be happy for the company."

Pat squared his shoulders and went on in.

"I suppose she could do worse," Lem said with a shrug.

Tina came darting down the hall toward them now, looking bug-eyed with fright at the sight of Des standing there. "What is it now?" she demanded.

"It's nothing, hon," Lem assured her. "Relax, will you?"

"I *am* relaxed. I want to know why she's—"

"I just stopped by to look in on Kylie," Des said.

Lem's cell phone rang. He glanced down at the screen. "It's one of my men. I got nothing but headaches this season, I swear." He went off down the hall, grumbling into the phone.

"One of his men, my ass," Tina said sourly. "It's that tramp Debbie."

"Could be. Then again, we did have a blizzard yesterday."

Tina glared at her. "Did you come here just to be nasty again?"

"I'm sorry if that's how I came across. I was just doing my job. And I wondered how you were doing."

"I'm doing *lousy*, okay?" Tina shot a glance over her shoulder to make sure Lem was out of earshot. "Matt left for Cabo San Lucas this morning with his wife. They'll be there straight on through Christmas. Together in the same hotel room, day and night. My Matt and that cold bitch. I *need* him right now and I can't contact him. She watches him like a hawk."

"She's his wife, Tina."

"Matt doesn't love her. He loves me. I don't know what to do."

"You could try using this as an opportunity to reconnect with Lem. You two will be taking Kylie home soon. Maybe this is a chance for you to regroup as a family. Maybe something positive can come out of this."

"And maybe you are totally full of crap. Did that ever occur to you?" Tina looked at Kylie's doorway, frowning. "Is that her surgeon in there with her?"

"No, it's Pat Faulstich."

"What does *he* want?"

"He brought her some flowers." Des moved farther away from the room, motioning for Tina to join her. "You told me yesterday that if I really want to know what's what I should ask a cleaning lady. So I'm asking. What do you know about Pat?"

"I know I don't like him."

"Why not?"

Tina hesitated. "Look, his parents are decent, hard-working

people. But he's got this older brother, Mickey, who he really looks up to, okay? And Mickey's absolutely no good."

"Don't think I've run across him."

"That's because he's been in prison in Virginia for the past couple of years. He got pulled over down there with something like three hundred pounds of marijuana in the trunk of his Camaro."

"Do you know if Pat hangs with Casey Zander?"

"*Nobody* hangs with Casey. He's a total mama's boy. Not to mention just plain weird. Have you *seen* that haircut of his? I swear, Paulette must have dropped him on his head when he was a baby."

"What's Casey's deal with Gigi Garanski?"

Tina's face fell. "There's no deal. Gigi's just a pathetic, drugged-out mess. She was such a sweet little girl, too. Her folks lived next door to mine. I used to baby-sit her when she was a kid. It makes me sick what's happened to her."

"Tommy Stratton's her boyfriend?"

"Pimp is more like it. He passes her around to those horny losers at the Rustic like she's a bowl of peanuts. She'll do anyone Tommy tells her to as long as he keeps her supplied with dope. Tommy the Pinhead is total trash."

Total trash, Des reflected, who happened to have low-level ties to the Castagno crime family.

"He gave Kylie the eye when were at the supermarket together last week. I said to him, 'What are you looking at, you piece of filth?' He just blew me a kiss and went sauntering off like he thinks he's some big shot." Tina peered at Des curiously. "Why are you asking me all of this?"

"Just trying to figure something out. I have an itch I can't scratch." Des's cell phone rang. She glanced down at it before she excused herself and took the call. "What's up, Yolie?"

"Grisky wants to hold another team meeting at two o'clock."

"What for?"

"He told me that he likes to touch base regularly with his quarterbacks."

"I see myself more as a shifty wide receiver."

"Real? I see myself placekicking that man's buns of steel all the way out to Block Island."

"What have you got that you didn't have this morning?"

"Plenty. I'll fill you in when I see you." Then Yolie rang off.

Des was alone in the hospital hallway. Tina had gone into Kylie's room to hurl herself between Kylie and Pat. Lem was still off somewhere talking on the phone to whomever he was talking to. Maybe Debbie. Des couldn't imagine him talking to one of his men for this long. She stood there for a moment before she found herself speed dialing Mitch for no reason other than that she needed to hear his voice right now. Needed a brief moment where everything and everyone in the world didn't feel completely dysfunctional and insane. Because it wasn't an itch she was feeling. It was pure dread. She didn't know why. Just knew that she felt it. And needed a dose of Mitch's sunny, calming self.

Except he wasn't answering his cell or his home phone. Mitch had been planning to take Rut Peck over to visit Paulette. Then he was going to drive Rut back to Essex Meadows and head on home. He ought to be there by now, she figured, glancing at her watch. Ought to be parked squarely in front of his computer writing crazy, funny, brilliant things about his all-time favorite Christmas movies. But he wasn't. He hadn't checked in either. Hadn't called her. Hadn't texted her.

Honestly? Des couldn't help wondering where in the hell her doughboy was.

CHAPTER 14

"SURE YOU DON'T MIND if we stop off for a quick glass of beer?"

"Young fella, you never have to talk me into a glass of beer," Rut replied as they bounced along in Mitch's Studey. "Quick or otherwise. Besides, I don't care if I *never* make it back to Essex Meadows."

Mitch was piloting his way up Old Boston Post Road toward Cardiff, Dorset's landlocked neighbor to the north. If Dorset possessed what could be truly classified as a seedy side of town it was this stretch of the Post Road north of Uncas Lake. Here, a tattered strip of businesses operated out of old wood-framed houses that seemed to be sagging even more than usual under the weight of so much snow and ice. If you wanted your sofa reupholstered or your unwanted facial hair removed then this was where you came. If you wished to engage in some illicit humpage then this is where you came—Dorset's designated hot-sheet motel, the Yankee Doodle Motor Court, was located here. So was the Rustic Inn, the beer joint that was a second home to Dorset's indigenous population of young male Swamp Yankees.

Mitch didn't phone Des to tell her that he was stopping off at the Rustic. He didn't tell the woman in his life every single thing he did. Plus he knew she'd tell him not to go. But he had a hunch—a good, solid one—and when Mitch Berger had a hunch he played it all of the way. He wasn't hamstrung by legal constraints the way Des was. He could go places she couldn't go, do things she couldn't do. He'd helped her on numerous cases, whether she cared to admit it or not. Mostly not. Actually, Des tended to get downright furious when Mitch played one of his hunches. But he couldn't sit idly by when bad things were happening to people who he knew and liked. This was what it meant to live in a small town. You got involved.

"I sure do feel badly for that tall, beautiful young thing."

"This would be Paulette?" Mitch asked Rut, who'd sat there in her TV room talking quietly with her for nearly two hours.

"She's so angry and alone. That's no way for a good woman to be."

"I'm sure you were a real comfort to her, Rut."

"You think so?" He shook his head sadly. "I don't think she'll even remember I was there."

The Rustic Inn was a log cabin of a place with illuminated Bud Light and Miller beer signs in its front windows and a satellite dish perched on its roof. The afternoon sun had gotten warm enough that the snow on the roof was starting to melt and rain down from the frozen rain gutters. The slushy parking lot was filled with pickups and dented old muscle cars. A sleek new silver Cadillac Coupe de Ville was parked there, looking distinctly out of place.

Inside, a wood stove kept the Rustic warm and cozy. There was a horseshoe-shaped bar, a big-screen TV and a pool table. It was crowded in there for a workday. The dozen or so tables were all filled, mostly by bearded young guys in flannel shirts who were hunched over beers and bowls of chili. There wasn't one woman in the place. And the mood wasn't what Mitch would call festive. A lot of these guys were construction workers who'd been idled by the sucky weather and even suckier economy. Times were hard for them. Mitch could feel their despair as soon as he walked in the door. Rut paused on his way to the bar to pat several of them on the shoulder and say hello.

The man behind the bar was a strapping fellow in his forties who seemed to have a hard time moving around. He had a definite limp. His face was etched in a permanent grimace. There were dark bags under his eyes and his complexion was sallow. He didn't look well.

But he brightened considerably when he spotted Rut easing himself into one of the two vacant bar stools. "Man, I haven't seen you in ages, you old peckerwood," he exclaimed. "How the hell are you?"

"I'm aboveground and the sun is shining. What more could I ask for? Steve Starkey, I want you to say hello to my friend Mitch Berger."

"Glad to know you, Mitch. Any friend of Rut's is a friend of mine. You're the one who dates our resident trooper, right? The movie guy?"

"That's me—the movie guy."

"Nice lady, our resident trooper. She knows what's what. Mostly, I keep the peace around here myself," Steve explained, pulling a baseball bat out from under the bar. "But every once in a while I need her help. And, let me tell you, Resident Trooper Mitry is no one to mess with."

"Believe me, I know."

Steve turned back to Rut, his face darkening. "How's Paulette?"

"Real broken up."

"I was awful sorry to hear about Hank. He was a good guy."

"He had a lot of friends," Rut agreed. "Did he stop in here a lot?"

"Maybe once every couple of weeks with the guys from the

firehouse. Not like that boy Casey of hers. He's in here every single night."

"He was here last night?" Mitch asked.

Steve nodded. "Came in about seven, same as always. Sat by himself on that same stool over there so he could watch the games on TV. He's a strange one. Never talks to a soul—except for Gigi when she's feeling, you know, charitable. What can I get you gentlemen?"

"*Excellent* question." Rut smacked his lips, his eyes gleaming with anticipation. He reminded Mitch of Harold Russell ordering his first beer at Uncle Butch's in *The Best Years of Our Lives*. "What's on draft?"

"On draft I've got Bud and Bud Light."

Rut's face fell. "No real beer?"

"Not too many of these boys go for the premium stuff. I do have a few bottles of Guinness in the cooler."

"You talked me into it. And one for my young friend here."

"Care for anything to eat?"

"I could go for one of your world-famous chili dogs."

"Make it two," Mitch said.

Steve hobbled off to take care of their order.

"His daddy, Jim, was my best friend in the whole world back when I was a boy," Rut recalled. "Jim got a degree in forestry and started a tree-cutting business when he got home from Korea. Did real well at it and passed it on to Steve, but a big oak limb broke loose on Steve when he was up in the bucket truck right after Hurricane Bob. Knocked him all of the way to the ground. Shattered his left hip, a whole bunch of ribs. He recovered but he couldn't do that kind of work anymore, so he opened this place."

Steve returned with their beers and went off to make their chili dogs.

Rut took a thirsty gulp, sighing contentedly. "Thanks for bringing me here, Mitch. It's been a long time. I used to stop in pretty regular when I was still working for a living."

"Has it changed much?"

"Not a bit."

Mitch glanced around, noticing two guys who were drinking coffee together at a table in the corner by the window. They didn't exactly blend in with the crowd. One was an enormous twenty-something body builder who looked as if he devoted most of his time to trying to look scary—which, in Mitch's opinion, he succeeded at quite admirably. The other guy was older, in his fifties, and nattily attired in a yellow turtleneck sweater, gray flannel slacks and a tan Kangol cap. He had an intense, focused air about him and was on his cell phone nonstop. A customer moseyed by and murmured something to him. He nodded and the customer walked away.

"Rut, who's that guy over there in the tan cap?"

Rut peered at him through his thick black-framed glasses. "Don't know him. But the big gorilla's Tommy Stratton. That one's as mean as a snake. Used to throw raw eggs at Sheila Enman when he was a little kid."

"Why'd he do that?"

"Well, sir, every day after school Tommy liked to beat the living daylights out of the little boy who lived next door to Sheila. One day she told him to pick on someone his own size. So he started throwing eggs at her every time she set foot outside her door. She had to call the resident trooper on him. They call him Tommy the Pinhead on account of he's built so thick through the neck— *and* he's a pinhead. Barely finished high school. Washed out of the U.S. Army. Now it looks to me like he's hired muscle for that there shady character in the tan cap. Want me to find out who he is?"

"I wouldn't say no."

Steve came back with their chili dogs. "Here you go, gentlemen," he said, setting paper plates before them.

Rut took a bite of his, munching on it appreciatively. "Steve, who's that fellow sitting there with Tommy the Pinhead?"

Steve's mouth tightened. "Rick Fontanella. They call him Slick Rick."

"Bookie, isn't he?" Rut asked him.

Steve glanced uneasily over at Mitch. "You trying to get me into trouble, Rut?"

"How long have you known me, Steve?"

"My whole life. But I've known your friend Mitch less than ten minutes."

"You don't have to worry about Mitch. He goes his way and Des goes hers. It's the secret to a successful relationship. Isn't that right, Mitch?"

"That's right," agreed Mitch, who couldn't help thinking that a man with Rut Peck's natural-born gifts had been wasted in the U.S. Postal Service. He was such a consummate bullshit artist that he should have gone into politics.

Rut peered over at Slick Rick again. "Is he a local fella? I don't recognize him."

"Rick has a condo in Mystic, I think," Steve said.

"I'm guessing that fancy Coupe de Ville parked outside is his."

"Yup."

"Does he operate on his own or is he hooked up?"

Steve leaned in a bit closer, lowering his voice. "He stops in and does a little business here, okay? Who he is or isn't hooked up with is none of my concern. Why are you so curious anyhow?"

"Because my friend Mitch and I we were both looking to place a wager on this Sunday's Patriots-Giants game. What's the spread?"

"Last I heard it was Pats by seven points."

Rut gawked at Steve in disbelief. "At home against the G-men? Why, the Pats are a lock to beat that."

Steve raised an eyebrow at the old fellow. "What kind of wager are you talking about, Rut?"

Rut took a sip of his Guinness. "A hundred on the Pats. How about you, Mitch?"

"I can't bet against my Giants. I'll ride them for a hundred."

"That's a sucker's bet," Rut informed him. "You're a born pigeon."

Steve said, "I can place your bets with Rick for you if you'd like."

"That'd be great, Steve." Rut took another bite of his chili dog. "What do you get out of it?"

Steve frowned at him. "What do you mean?"

"You allow the fella to operate in here. What's in it for you?"

Steve turned cold on him. "Why would you ask me something like that?"

Rut shrugged his soft shoulders. "Just curious."

Mitch said, "Is he into anything else?"

Steve stared across the bar at Mitch. "I don't allow any drugs in here, if that's what you're asking. Your girlfriend would shut me right down. The guys like to bet on football. I figure they may as well do it here. Nobody gets hurt and it's good for business."

"It wasn't," Mitch said, munching on his chili dog.

Steve shook his head. "Wasn't *what*?"

"What I was asking you. Does Slick Rick also extend credit to guys who come up a little bit short?"

185

"Well, yeah," Steve allowed. "If somebody needs a few bucks until payday or whatever."

"So he's a loan shark?"

"To my mind he's simply providing a service. His vig's a little high but, hey, it's not much higher than what the big boys nail you for when you fall behind on your credit cards. And them bastards have got the full faith and credit of the U.S. government behind them."

The door to the Rustic opened now and in barged Casey Zander in his Patriots hoodie and sweatpants, looking frazzled and agitated. Also not particularly happy to see Mitch and Rut.

"What are *you* doing here?" he demanded.

"You had a rough night, son," Rut responded soothingly. "You and your mom both. We'd like to buy you a beer. Have a seat."

"Not right now," Casey snapped, looking around the place. "Hey, Steve, where's Gigi?"

"She was here earlier, Casey. Went out."

"Who with?"

"No idea. Gigi goes her own way. You know that."

"Well, when's she coming back?"

"When she decides to come back," Steve answered patiently, as if he were speaking to a whiny, annoying child. Which he basically was. "Here she is now," he informed Casey as the door opened again. "Are you happy?"

Gigi Garanski looked as if she'd just wandered in from a Def Leppard video. She was an absolute vision of unloveliness in a torn denim jacket, hot pink spandex tights and snakeskin cowboy boots. Gigi had big, sticky-looking hair that was dyed a garish shade of yellow and she looked as if she'd applied her eye makeup with a trowel. She was pale and extremely skinny. Not a glam kind of skinny. A malnourished kind. Mitch doubted

Gigi was more than twenty-five but she had a lot of hard miles on her.

Casey reached over and grabbed her. "Where have you been?"

"What do *you* care?" she answered in a raspy voice.

"I was looking all over for you."

"I was right here, asshole. Where were *you*? Told me you were going to take me out for breakfast."

"I had to hang with my mom on account of Hank."

Gigi made a face at him. "Your mom. With other guys it's their wife or their girlfriend. With you it's always your mom."

"Shut up about my mom!"

"*Don't* tell me to shut up. And let go of my arm, will ya?"

"Seems like a stable, mature relationship built on mutual respect," Mitch observed.

"And common interests," Rut agreed, nodding his tufty white head. "Politics, religion, the theater . . ."

Gigi moved away from Casey now and sidled over to the corner table where Tommy the Pinhead sat with Slick Rick. She bent over, taunting Casey with a defiant gaze, and gave Tommy a wet, slurpy kiss. Casey watched the two of them, red faced. When they were done sucking face, Tommy spoke to Gigi in a quiet voice. She nodded her sticky blond head, then made her way slowly back to Casey, Tommy watching her with cool-eyed detachment.

"How about we go for a drive someplace, babe?" she asked sweetly, cradling Casey's chubby cheeks in her pale, taloned hands.

Casey shrugged his shoulders. "Why not?"

"Hey, don't do me any favors."

"I'm not, Gigi. I want to go with you. Really, I do. Just give me a couple of minutes, okay? There's something I have to take care of first."

Gigi rolled her eyes at him. "Whatever."

Casey started toward the door, shooting a glance over at Tommy the Pinhead and Slick Rick. As he went outside, the two of them put their heads together and conferred. Then Tommy got his huge self to his feet and went out the door, too.

Gigi parked herself at the bar next to Mitch. Steve brought her a glass of white wine. She took a small sip, looking Mitch up and down with frank curiosity.

He smiled at her and said, "How are you?"

"Compared to what?"

"Is it just me or does Casey seem kind of antsy?"

"He's always antsy," she sniffed. "That one was *born* antsy." And with that she took her wine down to the other end of the bar.

"Nice girl," Mitch observed.

"Trust me, she's more popular around here than Casey is," Steve said.

"I can believe that." Rut drank down the last of his Guinness. "That boy is awful hard to warm up to."

"Does he place a lot of bets with Slick Rick?" Mitch asked Steve.

"Why are you asking?"

"When I was over at his place this morning I saw a ton of NFL stats lying around. Couldn't help wondering if he was a bit of a gambler."

"I wouldn't call what Casey does gambling," Steve said in a low voice.

"What would you call it?"

"A disease."

"He has a problem?"

"A big problem."

"Well, now," Rut murmured. "Ain't that a fine how do ya do?"

"I need to get something out of my truck," Mitch informed the old postmaster. "I'll be back in a sec, okay?"

"Okay by me." Rut tapped his empty Guinness bottle. "But it'll cost you."

"Another round, Steve. And it's my tab, okay?"

"In that case," Rut said, "I'll have another chili dog, too."

Mitch went out of the Rustic's front door, his eyes adjusting to the sunlight in the parking lot. Casey and Tommy the Pinhead were having words over by Casey's blue Tacoma pickup. Mitch inched his way over behind the fenced enclosure where Steve kept his firewood, snow shovel and sacks of rock salt. From there he could watch the two of them without being seen. Could even hear Casey's whiny voice, although he couldn't make out what he was saying.

Casey opened the door to his Tacoma and removed a pair of large, heavy shopping bags with handles. Tommy took them from him and headed over toward a beat-up old black Pontiac Trans Am. He popped the trunk and deposited the bags in there. Casey followed him, yapping all of the way. Now he was holding a fat, letter-sized envelope out to Tommy. Tommy took it and said something to Casey, smiling broadly at him. Then he punched Casey in the stomach really hard. Casey doubled over in pain, his eyes bulging, before he proceeded to gaack up his entire breakfast of Cocoa Puffs. Not a pretty sight.

Okay, that settles it. I have officially eaten my last bowl of Cocoa Puffs.

Casey fell to his knees, gasping and heaving, then toppled slowly over onto the slushy gravel, a low, animal moan coming from him.

Tommy was not without mercy. He helped Casey back up onto his feet, patting him gently on the shoulder. Then he steered him back toward the front door of the Rustic, Casey looking none too steady on his feet.

Mitch stayed where he was, safely hidden behind the woodpile as they made their way inside. He continued to stay there, waiting. Sure enough, Casey came back outside a moment later—this time with Gigi clutching him by the arm. He still wasn't moving real well. The two of them got into his Tacoma, Gigi behind the wheel, and started out of the parking lot. Mitch wanted to see which way they turned when they pulled out of the driveway. As he stood there, waiting, a shadow fell across his face. Then he heard a flurry of movement. He started to turn around but wasn't nearly fast enough—something had already smashed him on the back of his head.

And then everything went black.

CHAPTER 15

GRISKY WAS PACING THE conference room and flexing his biceps. Pacing and flexing. The G-Man was impatient. The G-Man was amped. Partly, this had to do with his sacred Christmas travel plans. "Every damned flight out of JFK tomorrow night has been scrambled because of the damned blizzard," he blustered. Mostly it had to do with the fact that Postal Inspector Sam Questa had failed to show up on time for Grisky's two o'clock quarterbacks meeting.

Yolie and Toni were there. Des was there. Capt. Joey Amalfitano of the Narcotics Task Force, aka The Aardvark, was there. The sandwiches and coffee from McGee's Diner were there. But Questa was a no-show. And would be one, Des felt certain, until precisely 2:17. Grisky would be kept waiting the same exact number of minutes that he'd kept Questa waiting earlier that morning. Boys. They could be so pissy.

"Do you realize I may actually have to spend Christmas *here* instead of in Cancún?" Grisky raged on, pacing and flexing.

"Boo-freaking-hoo," Yolie growled.

Des glanced at her watch. It was 2:16.

Sam Questa came bustling through the door ten seconds later—smack-dab on pissy man-time. Questa removed his coat and sat down at the table, reaching for a sandwich and a container of coffee. "Sorry I'm late," he said, biting into his sandwich. "Got held up in an interview."

Grisky narrowed his gaze before he sat down, too. "Okay, let's see where we're at," he said, rubbing his hands together briskly. He really liked to do that, and it was really starting to get on Des's nerves. "Resident Trooper Mitry? The ball's yours."

"Pat Faulstich's story didn't exactly check out," she reported. "Lem Champlain didn't send him to plow those driveways on Kinney Road last night."

Grisky shook his head at her. "And this is important because? . . ."

"Everywhere I go I keep tripping over him. He's clean, but he has an older brother, Mickey, who's doing a nickel at the Baskerville Correctional Center in Mecklenburg County, Virginia, for transporting three hundred pounds of marijuana. And he's a Rustic Inn regular, same as Casey Zander."

The Aarvark shifted uncomfortably in his chair at her mention of the Rustic, though he said nothing.

"What does all of this add up to?" Grisky demanded.

"Maybe something, maybe nothing. But I'm keeping my eye on him."

"Fair enough. Snooki, you're next."

Toni the Tiger stared across the table at him in silence.

He tilted his jarhead at her curiously. "Snooki? . . ."

"My name is Toni," she said to him between gritted teeth. "I also answer to Sargeant Tedone. But if you call me Snooki one more time I am going to make a bow tie out of your balls. Got it?"

Grisky held up his hands in a gesture of surrender. "Got it."

"Good," she said, slamming the door on what had to be the shortest crush on record. There truly was hope for this girl—even if she was a Tedone. "I've just spent several hours at the Headmaster's House with the geek squad looking into Josie Cantro." Toni leafed through her notepad. "Our local life coach has what

I'd classify as a lively bio. For starters, her birth name isn't Cantro. It's Hoyt. Josie Ann Hoyt was born on August 1, 1981 in Augusta, Maine. Cantro is her mother's maiden name. We found this out when we deepened our search into the details surrounding her father's shooting death."

Des blinked at her in surprise. "Josie's father was shot to death?"

Toni nodded. "When Josie was twelve. Officially, it was closed out as a hunting accident, shooter unknown. Unofficially, the Maine State Police didn't view it as an accident. The shooting took place in a wooded area less than a quarter mile from Hoyt's home. No hunters admitted to being in the area at the time. *And* Hoyt was shot from close range."

"How close?" Grisky asked.

"Less than ten feet."

"Yeah, down here in the Nutmeg State we don't generally call that a hunting accident," Yolie said. "We call it murder."

"They looked very hard at Josie's mother for it," Toni said. "It was commonly known that he'd been beating the crap out of her for years. But they had no weapon, no witness, no case. So they wrote it off and moved on. The next time Josie pops up on our radar screen is six years later in Lewiston when she applies for a Maine driver's license as Josie Ann Cantro, age eighteen. Her life on paper officially starts here—Social Security records, credit cards and so on. She rented an apartment in Lewiston. To support herself Josie Cantro was employed at the Down East Bar and Grill and at a Snap Fitness Center. Meanwhile, under the name Adele Slade, she was also employed as a pole dancer at a club called the Matrix, where she was arrested on numerous occasions for soliciting prostitution and lewd public behavior."

"Girl, you haven't lost your edge," Yolie said to Des admiringly.

"What edge?" Grisky asked.

"The Resident Trooper told us last night that Josie smelled wrong."

"She never served any time," Toni pointed out. "Just got slaps on the wrist. I spoke to an old-timer on the Lewiston PD who remembers her. He told me she'd been out on the streets, hooking and using drugs, ever since she was sixteen. But that she was a smart, scrappy kid who cleaned up her act. She even enrolled at Bates College. Studied there for one semester, according to her transcripts. Then she left town one day and was never heard from again. According to her Social Security records, she relocated to Castine, home to the Maine Maritime Academy, where she worked as a waitress and chambermaid at the Castine Inn. She lived on the premises until 2005 when she filed for a change of address to the home of one James Allen Miller—better known as J.A. Miller, the author of a series of bestselling science fiction novels featuring someone called Torbor the Reclaimer. Do we have any sci-fi fans in the house? No? Anyway, Josie was twenty-four at the time. Miller, age fifty-six, was a widower with two children who were both older than Josie. I spoke to someone on the local PD. It seems that Miller used to eat dinner at the Castine Inn every night. He and Josie struck up an acquaintanceship and eventually it led to something more. He taught marine systems engineering at the academy before he became a bestselling author and bought himself the historic waterfront home that he invited Josie to share with him." Toni paused to gulp down some coffee. "James Allen Miller died of an overdose of the prescription sleep aid Ambien in 2007. A therapist had been treating him for anxiety-related depression. They closed it out as a suicide."

"Damn, this is starting to sound familiar," Yolie said. "Did the local PD have any reason to suspect it *wasn't* suicide?"

"None. Miller was seeing a therapist, like I said. Had been increasingly despondent in the days leading up to his death, and he left a suicide note."

"What did it say?" asked Des.

"It said, *'Forgive me, Torbor.'* But guess what Miller did two weeks before he died: He changed his will. Left his waterfront home to Josie instead of to his two kids."

Des shoved her heavy horn-rimmed glasses up her nose. "God, maybe she *is* a black widow."

"What's a black widow?" Sam Questa wanted to know.

"An attractive young woman who snags rich, lonely men, picks them clean and kills them before she moves on."

"I never heard of one of those," The Aardvark said.

"Maybe they only exist in the movies," Des conceded.

"Maybe not," Yolie said.

"Miller was well liked in Castine. Josie was regarded as a scheming little tramp. His children contested the will. Threatened to fight her in court if they had to. She accepted a cash settlement of $100,000 and left town." Toni glanced down at her notes again. "She shows up briefly on our radar screen next in Portland, Maine, then in Cambridge, Massachusetts, where she rented an apartment for a few months before she moved to New Haven. When she got to New Haven she enrolled in an online life-coach program. After that she rented a cottage here in Dorset, set up her practice and eventually met Bryce Peck. You know the rest."

"That's good work, Sergeant," Yolie said.

"Real good," echoed Grisky. "Aside from the fact that we *don't* know the rest. Is she or isn't she responsible for the deaths of Bryce Peck and Hank Merrill?"

"And what, if anything, does she have to do with our stolen mail?" Questa wondered.

"Maybe she and Hank were in on it together," Des said. "The

two of them had mutual interests. Hank had serious money problems. And Josie needed drugs—the drugs that she used to kill Bryce. We know that she's a clever girl. Clever enough to cook up this grinch smoke screen. Clever enough to persuade Hank to steal for her by promising him that when she got hold of Bryce's house she'd bail him out with his ex-wife."

"That plays pretty sweet," Grisky said. "Keep talking."

"When the grinch thing started setting off alarm bells Josie went proactive. First, she took care of Bryce the same way she took care of J.A. Miller in Castine. Then, last night, she eliminated Hank because he was the one man, the only man, who could link her to Bryce's death."

"It was a two-person job," Toni pointed out. "Who helped her?"

"Casey Zander, who else? That's why she's been sleeping with him. She's got Casey wrapped around her little finger. He'd do anything for her—including help her do away with his own mother's boyfriend."

"I'm liking this more and more," Grisky said. "We'd better make sure baad Josie doesn't leave town."

"She's not going anywhere," Des assured him. "Bryce's half-brother, Preston, is on his way here from Chicago to contest Bryce's will. Odds are she'll accept a financial settlement just like she did in Castine. But she'll stay put until then."

Grisky turned his attention to Yolie. "Please tell me you've come up with some forensics that actually tie her to these deaths."

"The M.E.'s office fast-tracked Bryce Peck's autopsy," she responded. "Bearing in mind that it takes them longer to find what they *aren't* looking for than what they *are,* the toxicology so far confirms that it went down exactly as it appeared—Bryce washed down massive doses of Vicodin, Xanax and Ambien with a bottle of tequila. They've found no bruising. His skin and fingernails have yielded nothing. It still looks like a straight suicide."

Grisky frowned at her. "Then how'd she do it?"

"Maybe she forced him to swallow the pills at gunpoint," Des suggested. "There's a .38 in the mix, remember?"

"Maybe," Grisky allowed. "But good luck proving that. How about the Kinney Road crime scene, Lieutenant? You find the missing bourbon bottle?"

"I've had eight trainees digging through the snowbanks around that parking lot for six solid hours. And more men searching the woods seventy-five feet in every direction just in case Hank got out of the car and heaved it. So far we haven't found so much as a shard of broken glass. There are no fingerprints on Hank's cell phone. No partials or smears, no nothing. It was wiped clean. We tracked the so-called suicide text message that he sent to Paulette Zander. It did originate from that locale on Kinney Road. And when Paulette received it she was in the vicinity of her home on Grassy Hill Road."

"She told me she was downstairs doing laundry," Des said. "Didn't notice she'd gotten it until a few minutes later."

"We had troopers canvass her neighbors up and down Grassy Hill Road. A woman who lives across the street, two houses down, said she saw Hank's Passat go out at about 5:30, which confirms what Paulette Zander told Master Sergeant Mitry. He headed off in the direction of Frederick Lane, which would be the way he'd go if his destination was Kinney Road. She also saw Casey's Toyota Tacoma go out an hour or so later. Casey went the opposite way—toward the Old Boston Post Road, which is where the Rustic Inn is located."

"Could the neighbor confirm that Hank was alone in his car?" Des asked.

Yolie shook her head. "Couldn't even confirm that it was Hank behind the wheel. Just Hank's car. Same goes for Casey's Tacoma."

Grisky frowned at Des. "Where the hell are you going with this?"

"Just playing out the what-ifs."

"We can't build a case on what-ifs," he said pointedly.

"My bad, Agent Grisky. Next time I have a question I'll raise my hand. Will that make you happy?"

"*Results* will make me happy," he barked, swiveling his jarhead back to Yolie. "Did you get anything from Hank Merrill's autopsy?"

She glanced down at her notepad. "The M.E. confirmed that the cylindrical bruise on his forehead is a dead-nuts match for the nose of a Smith and Wesson .38 Special. Hank didn't have a permit for any such weapon. No handgun permit at all. But he did have a coworker who owns one. A carrier at the Dorset Post Office named Abe Monahan."

"Monahan, Monahan . . ." Sam Questa leafed through his own notes. "Here we are: Abe's been at the Dorset branch for seven years. His wife's a Realtor with Coldwell Banker. They have two kids, ages ten and twelve. Own a home on Bittersweet Lane. Abe keeps the .38 Special on a shelf in his bedroom closet."

"How in the hell do you know that?" Grisky asked him.

"After Lieutenant Snipes mentioned the bruise this morning, I instructed my people to ask each and every employee if they own a .38 Special." Questa's eyes hardened at him. "Like I told you— we're professionals."

"We'd better take a good look at this Abe Monahan," Grisky said.

"He's in Boca Raton with his family," Questa said. "Has been

198

for the past three days. We had to interview him by phone. It was a planned vacation. He bought the travel package two months ago."

"His neighbor on Bittersweet has a key to the house," Yolie reported. "She let us in so we could determine if his .38 Special was still in his bedroom closet—which it was. There's always a chance it was removed and then put back, so we're having our people examine it for prints and skin residue."

"Do we know if anyone has been inside of that house since the Monahans left for Boca?" Des asked.

"Yeah, we do." Questa stuck out his lower lip as he scanned his notes. "A lady who cleans for them once a week—Tina Champlain."

Grisky looked at Des curiously. "Is she related to Lem Champlain?"

"She's his wife. Hmm . . ."

"What's that supposed to mean?"

Des smiled at him sweetly. "Not a thing, Agent."

"The .38 Special's a common weapon," Yolie pointed out. "Someone else who Hank knew could have purchased one illegally."

"Or someone who he *didn't* know," Toni said.

"Could be," Yolie acknowledged.

"*Could be* won't get me to Cancún," Grisky huffed. "That's not good enough. The ball's yours, Inspector Questa. What have *you* got?"

Questa took another bite of his sandwich, chewing on it thoughtfully. "A very well-run branch office of the U.S. Postal Service. The building security is excellent. The keypad code has been updated according to proper procedure. All keys to the deadbolts are accounted for. All vehicle keys and scanners are stored overnight in the safe. Only Postmaster Zander and her senior clerk know the combination to the safe. The U.S. Postal Service isn't perfect. We encounter branches that are sloppily run. Branches where the employees take liberties. This isn't one of those. Postmaster Zander's people respect the job and they respect her. These are all first-rate employees—with the possible exception of that son of hers, Casey, who comes across like a bit of a whiner."

"Only because he is one," Des said.

"Bottom line? The only blemish on Postmaster Zander's record is that she didn't report these mailbox thefts to us in a timely fashion. But I think it's obvious to everyone at this table why she didn't. We're continuing to explore every possible avenue. Delving into the bank records and spending patterns of every driver, loader and clerk in Norwich who comes in contact with the Dorset-bound trucks. My opinion? We won't turn up a thing. It looks to me like Postmaster Zander's boyfriend, Hank Merrill, by all accounts an otherwise decent guy, got into financial trouble with his ex-wife and resorted to stealing his own mail in order to pay her back. When he realized he was going to be subjected to the public humiliation of a criminal investigation he decided to take his own life."

"Makes sense," Yolie said. "Except we're positive he *didn't* take his own life."

Questa nodded his huge head. "Which means we're back to looking at Josie Cantro, his alleged partner in crime. She killed him and tried to make it look like a suicide. That's the only way it makes sense to me."

Grisky turned to The Aardvark now. "Do you have anything new? Please, God, say yes."

"I have a name," he answered, slurping loudly from his coffee container. "Richard Paul Fontanella, age fifty-four. Better known as Slick Rick."

"He deals in black-market meds?" Grisky asked.

"Not exactly. He's a bookie and loan shark." The Aardvark passed around copies of a surveillance photo of the man getting out of a silver Cadillac Coupe de Ville. Slick Rick had gray hair and wore a Kangol cap. "He operates out of a dozen or so bars, clubs, and VFW halls in Southeastern Connecticut under the protection of the Castagnos. Not a big player, but a good, steady earner. As I mentioned this morning, the black-market meds gang that we took down in Bridgeport was operating under the protection of the Castagnos, too. There are still plenty of those bastards out there doing their thing. And, according to our contacts, there's a direct link between them and Slick Rick."

"What kind of a link?" Grisky asked.

"Slick Rick has a muscle man who goes everywhere with him just in case anyone needs to be persuaded to pay up. A fellow who grew up here in Dorset by the name of Thomas Burke Stratton, better known as—"

"Tommy the Pinhead," Des said, nodding.

"You know him?" he asked her.

"We've tussled. He's a local lout. Low-level muscle, like you said."

"He also does a spot of pimping on the side," The Aardvark said. "Runs a girl named Gigi Garanski who has herself a serious heroin habit. Tommy keeps Gigi supplied with smack in exchange for which she does guys out of a motel called the Yankee Doodle Motor Court. But it's not just a business arrangement between these two. This is a truly heartwarming love story. They live together and everything. Most days and nights, Gigi can be found at a bar on the Old Boston Post Road called the Rustic Inn. The Rustic's owner, Steve Starkey, lets Slick Rick set up shop there two afternoons a week in exchange for a sweet discount on his beer from the regional distributor, which happens to be owned by the Castagnos. If anyone falls behind to Slick Rick, Tommy the Pinhead takes a mighty dim view of it. We know that Tommy's supplying Gigi with heroin. That means he has drug contacts. We also know that Hank Merrill used to drop in at the Rustic from time to time. So put two and two together. If Hank was stealing prescription meds from his postal route then it stands to reason that his local buyer was Slick Rick and/or Tommy."

Des considered this for a moment, frowning. "Captain, how is it that you know so much about the Rustic?"

The Aardvark cleared his throat uneasily. "The Narcotics Task Force put a man in there undercover last week."

She glared across the table at him. "You have a man operating undercover in my town and you don't tell me?"

"It was strictly a need-to-know matter, Master Sergeant."

"We needed to know about it this morning!"

"I wanted to touch base with my man first," he responded calmly.

Des shook her head at him angrily. "This is the same crap that you pulled on me before on Sour Cherry Lane. You come sneaking into my town, make a mess, and then stick me with the job of cleaning up after you."

"Look, I understand your frustration. . . ."

"No, I don't think you do, Captain."

"But we've had leaks on our undercover operations."

"I don't leak!"

"I'm not saying that you do. But I'm under strict orders, from the top, to tell no one."

"I don't like the way you weasels operate," Des fumed.

"It's not your job to like it. And don't call me a weasel."

"Is your man still there?"

"No."

"Would you tell me if he was?"

"Uh, excuse me for getting in the way of this little love fest," Grisky interjected, "but did your man have anything for us, Captain?"

"Possibly," The Aardvark replied. "Paulette Zander's son Casey is a heavy, heavy sports bettor. Football's his game. He's lousy at it. And Gigi knows how to play him like a fiddle. She eggs him on, gives him a little taste now and then. The end result, according to my man, is that Casey Zander's into Slick Rick for a whopping twenty large."

"Okay, now we're getting somewhere," Grisky said eagerly. "Let's play this out. Casey Zander has to raise twenty large to pay off Slick Rick. He's a part-time mail carrier. He's involved with Josie Cantro. We know that Josie's a naughty little girl. We know that valuable mail on Hank Merrill's route was disappearing in the weeks prior to his death."

"And we know that Casey can't be the brains behind this," Des said. "He's not bright enough—especially if the security at the Post Office is tight."

"It's very tight," Questa said. "Plus he only drives on Saturdays."

"So what does that make him?" Grisky wondered aloud.

"The weak link in the chain," Yolie answered. "Let's find him and break him."

"He's a U.S. Postal Service employee," Questa said. "I'll be the one to talk to him."

Yolie shook her head. "He's a person of interest in our homicide investigation. We're talking to him."

"We'll *all* talk to him, okay?" Grisky said. "Any idea where he is?"

"At home with his mother, I assume," Des said as her cell phone rang. She peered down at the screen. It was the Rustic Inn calling. She stepped out into the hallway to take the call. "This is Resident Trooper Mitry."

She heard heavy wheezing at the other end before a voice said, "Des, this here's Rutherford Peck calling."

"What can I do for you, Rut?"

"Well, it's like this. I'm at the Rustic and I don't have any way of getting home."

"Not a problem. I can arrange a ride for you. How did you get up there in the first place?"

"Your friend and mine Mitch Berger brought me up here for a friendly glass of beer."

"Did that old Studey truck of his break down again?"

"Not exactly. Although he did say that he wanted to get something out of his truck. He went out to the parking lot, oh, maybe a half hour ago or so."

"And? . . ."

"And he never came back."

Des felt her pulse quicken. "Where is he, Rut?"

"That's just it, young lady. Nobody seems to know. His truck's here but Mitch isn't. And I can't find anyone who knows what happened to him."

"Rut, are you okay?"

"Fine and dandy. It's Mitch who I'm worried about."

"Stay put. I'll be there in five minutes."

She rang off and turned to discover Yolie and Toni standing there in the hallway with her.

"What's going down?" Yolie wanted to know.

Des shook her head in amazement. "He did it to me again."

"Did what?"

"Went barging into the middle of things like Robert Mitchum on a bad-hair day. I'm going to kill him, I swear. But first I have to find him. I can't *believe* he . . ." She broke off, her stomach in knots. "Want to get in some trouble?"

"You know me, girl. I'm up for anything. Let's roll."

"You could end up back in a gunnysack like me," Des cautioned her.

"Not a problem. I look hot in gray. Whatever it is, I'm in."

"Me, too," Toni said.

"This ain't your fight," Yolie told her. "Besides, I need you holding down the fort here."

"No way, Loo. I've been chained to a computer all day. And if I have to spend five more minutes in a room with Grisky I'm going to shoot him. Enough with the talking thing, okay? Let's get out of here and break bad."

Yolie's fierce face broke into a smile. "Good answer, Sergeant."

Mitch's dear old truck was parked in the slushy lot just as Rut had said it was. Unlocked, with nothing and no one inside. Quite a few other pickups were crowded into the lot. There was no sign of Mr. Slick Rick Fontanella's silver Coupe de Ville.

Des could feel the tension inside the Rustic the second that she and Yolie walked in the door. The sight of two very large sisters, one of them in uniform, tends to do that in a bar that is frequented by pigment-challenged workingmen. Toni stayed outside to conduct a thorough search of the parking lot and the area out back.

Des's eyes scanned the room. She saw no sign of Tommy the Pinhead or Gigi Garanski. No sign of Rut Peck either, for that matter. She made her way over to Steve Starkey, who stood behind the bar with a wary look on his face.

"Afternoon, Des," he said, forcing up some good cheer. "What can I do for you today?"

"I got a call from Rut Peck a few minutes ago. He wanted a ride home."

Steve's face fell. "He told me he was calling the Jewett sisters. I didn't realize he called you."

"He seemed a little confused about a few things. Thought I'd better check them out. Steve, say hello to Lieutenant Yolanda Snipes of the Major Crimes Squad."

"Major Crimes?" Steve's eyes widened. "Hey, what's going on here?"

"That's what we'd like to know," Yolie growled.

"Where is Rut, Steve?"

"Lying down in my back room. He had one beer too many and got a little light-headed. Come on around, I'll take you to him."

Steve's back room was a combination kitchen, storeroom and office. Chili bubbled in a huge pot on the stove. Cases of beer were stacked practically to the ceiling. There was a desk cluttered with papers. Also a beat-up old sofa where the occasional Rustic regular had been known to spend the night if he'd had one or seven too many. Rut lay stretched out on it with a blanket thrown over him. He was awake but looked a bit wan.

"Are you okay, Rut?" Des asked him.

"I'm fine, young lady. Sure didn't mean to kick up a fuss. I'm just having a little bit of trouble sorting things out. Plus I think I ate one too many of Steve's chili dogs," he confessed, belching discreetly. "I feel like a fool for putting you to so much trouble."

"No need to. There's only one fool in this picture and it's not you. Where is he?"

"That's what I can't sort out. Mitch asked me if I'd mind stopping off here for a beer on our way to Essex Meadows."

"Did he say why?"

"No, he didn't. And I didn't care why. It was fine by me. Except now he's gone and I don't know where."

Des glanced over at Steve. "What can you tell us?"

"Not a whole lot. Rut popped in a couple of hours ago with a young guy who he introduced to me as your friend Mitch Berger."

"Mitch's truck is still here," Des said. "Where's Mitch?"

Steve hesitated, licking his lips. "Look, I run a friendly bar. A place where regular guys can hang out and relax."

"I'm going to keep this real simple, Steve. I'm not holding you personally responsible for anything that's happened here today—*unless* you start playing games with me. Then I promise that you'll be sorry this day ever happened."

Steve let out a sigh, then opened the bottom drawer of his desk and removed a half-empty bottle of Wild Turkey. He poured a stiff slug into a not-very-clean-looking glass, drank it down, and then poured himself another slug. "Des, you're going to get sore no matter what I say."

She stood there in silence, clenching and unclenching her fists.

"Rut and your friend Mitch were sitting at the bar enjoying a Guinness and a chili dog, okay?"

"Best chili dog in town," Rut said. "I had two."

"And Casey Zander showed up looking for Gigi. Casey wasn't in a friendly mood. When Rut offered to buy him a beer he gave Rut the brush-off."

"And he was downright rude about it," Rut said. "How a fine woman like Paulette could raise such a no-good louse I have never understood."

"Then Gigi sashayed in and right away those two are snarling at each other. She told Casey to get lost and went over to talk to Tommy."

"This would be Tommy the Pinhead?" Yolie demanded.

Steve blinked at her. "Yeah. He was sitting in the corner with a fellow who he sort of associates with."

Yolie nodded. "Slick Rick Fontanella. We know all about him. And we're not interested in that right now. We're interested in what happened to Mitch."

Steve took another swallow of Wild Turkey. "Gigi does pretty much whatever, *whoever*, Tommy tells her to. He beats her if she doesn't. I've seen her in here with a fat lip, bruises all over her arms. It's not pretty. Anyhow, after she talked to Tommy she came right back to Casey and started acting all nice. The two of them made a date. Casey told her he just had to take care of some business first. He went outside to the parking lot. Tommy followed him out there."

"That's when Mitch told me he had to get something out of his truck," Rut recalled. "I told him it would cost him another chili dog, which is how it came to pass that I ate two of them."

"So Mitch went outside just after Casey and Tommy did?" Des asked.

Rut nodded his tufty white head. "Correct."

I'm going to kill him. First I have to find him, then I'll kill him.

"Keep talking," Yolie ordered Steve.

"Tommy and Casey came back inside a few minutes later. Casey had a real sick look on his face. Was kind of bent over, too. He and Gigi took off together right after that."

"And what about Tommy?"

"He sat back down with Slick Rick. They talked for a sec and then he left, too. Slick Rick stuck around for another fifteen minutes. And that was that."

"*Except* for the part where Mitch never came back inside," Des said. "Stupid question, Steve. What do you think happened to him?"

Steve looked down into his glass. "It's not my business to say."

"I'm making it your business."

"I figured he took off to party with Casey and Gigi. She'll do that. Two guys at once, I mean. I just . . . I assumed he went out there to find out if he could get in on the action."

"And, what, he just ditched Rut here?"

Steve shrugged his shoulders helplessly. "Happens all of the time, Des. I don't mean to throw stones. Guys are going to do what they're going to do."

"Rut, is that what *you* think happened?"

"Never," the old man answered with total certainty. "Mitch is true-blue. He'd cut off his own foot before he'd cheat on you—especially with *that* one. Why in the heck do you think I called you? I'm worried."

Des bent over and kissed him on the forehead. Couldn't help herself.

"Steve, you were saying Tommy left right after Casey and Gigi did," Yolie put in. "What does Tommy drive?"

"A black '98 Trans Am, Loo," Toni answered as she came through the doorway from the bar. "I just ran his plate and texted it to you along with his last known address." She paused, her face tightening. "I found something outside that you need to look at."

Toni led them back through the bar and out the front door into the waning afternoon sunlight, Des moving on legs that felt numb. There was a fenced enclosure near the front door where Steve kept a stack of firewood and bags of rock salt.

"I found some fresh drops of blood in the snow right over here," Toni reported. "And some blood on that snow shovel, see?"

Yolie stared down at the blood drops in the snow. "Sergeant, here's what I want you to—"

"The cruisers from Troop F are already on their way," Toni assured her. "I made sure that one of them has a K-9 partner. A Troop F detective will be here in ten minutes. And I've called for a tech crew to take blood samples and dust the shovel for prints. Also Mitch's truck."

"Good work." Yolie peered over at Des. "What are you thinking?"

"He went Bulldog Drummond. He was hiding here watching the action in the parking lot—until someone sneaked up behind him and brained him with that shovel. Someone named Tommy the Pinhead."

"Sergeant, no one leaves this place without showing proper ID. I want the name of every man who was in here in the past two hours. I want every car in that lot searched. We have less than an hour of good sunlight left. As soon as the K-9 unit gets here make sure the woods surrounding this place are—"

"He's not in the woods," Des said softly. "He's not here at all."

"What makes you say that?" Toni asked her.

"Because if he was here I'd know."

"Have them undertake the search anyway," Yolie ordered Toni. "You're in charge here until you've brought the detective up to speed. Then I want you to catch up with us, got it?"

"Got it, Loo, except . . ."

"Except *what*?"

"I don't know where you're going."

Yolie glanced inquiringly at Des. "Do you?"

Mostly, the Yankee Doodle Motor Court offered privacy. Its decaying circa-1957 bungalows were spaced a discreet distance apart, and the parking spaces were around in back so that no one driving by could see who was getting busy there.

Danny Rochin, the manager, was a cadaverous Swamp Yankee whose jet-black Grecian Formula hair contrasted sharply with his two-day growth of white stubble. The plaid wool shirt that Danny had on was a couple of sizes too large and made him look shrunken. His bony hands trembled slightly as Des stood across the counter from him in the office bungalow, Yolie by her side.

"Gigi showed up in a blue Tacoma about an hour ago," he confirmed, his Adam's apple bobbing up and down. "I rented them Bungalow Six."

"Who was she with, Danny?"

"Don't know his name."

"Have you seen him here before with Gigi?"

"Oh, sure. He's one of her regulars. Odd-looking sort of guy. Real pale and soft. Colors his hair red. Wears it like one of the Beatles."

"How did Gigi seem to you?"

"She was high, same as always. Sloppy high. Fell halfway over this counter, slurred her words. She's a mess, that one. If she lives to be thirty I'll be surprised."

"How about the fifth Beatle?" Yolie asked him. "Was he high, too?"

"He was *something*. Like he was in pain."

"And how about the other guy?" Des asked.

Danny peered at her in confusion. "What other guy?"

"The other guy who was in the truck with them. Big fellow with curly black hair, eyes like a sad cocker spaniel."

"I didn't see anyone like that. Just them two. I rented them Bungalow Six. They parked in back and went in and then . . ." Danny hesitated, his grayish tongue flicking over his dry lips. "Tommy the Pinhead rolled in a few minutes after that."

"So you know Tommy?"

"I've known that bastard since he was a little kid. He used to beat up my nephew because the kid stuttered. Gave him a bruised kidney once in the fifth grade. Poor kid pissed blood for a week."

"What happened after he showed up, Danny?"

"He barged in here demanding to know which bungalow Gigi was in."

"Did you tell him?"

"Damned straight I told him. You think I want to piss blood? He pulled in front of Bungalow Six, got out and started pounding on the door, acting like he was all crazy with jealousy or something. Can't imagine how he could be, the way that girl sleeps around. She opened the door and they stood out there jawing at each other."

"Could you hear anything they said?"

Danny shook his head.

"Is anyone staying in the adjacent bungalows?"

He shook his head again. "Afternoons are quiet here during Christmas season. Business will pick up again soon as New Year's gets here."

"What happened after that, Danny?"

"He went inside of the bungalow with her and closed the door."

"And then? . . ."

"A nice, clean-cut young couple showed up. Couple of college kids home for the holiday is my guess. I got them settled into Bungalow One, good and comfy. A few minutes later I noticed Tommy and Gigi pulling out of the driveway in his Trans Am and heading off together."

"How long ago was this?"

"An hour ago, maybe."

"And what happened to the fifth Beatle?"

"Still there, as far as I know. Sleeping one off or whatever. The Tacoma's still parked around back."

Yolie headed right out the door to have a look at Casey's pickup.

"Danny, I'm going to need the key to Bungalow Six."

"I run a decent place here. I respect the privacy of my guests."

"I'm not saying otherwise. But I still need that key."

He let his breath out slowly. "Yes, ma'am."

She strode across the plowed gravel parking lot, the shadows growing long in the weak late-day sun. It got dark early in the days leading up to Christmas. They were the shortest days of the year. The chill of night was already settling in.

Yolie met her outside of the bungalow. "There's nobody in the Tacoma."

And nobody was home in Bungalow Six, which was small and sparely furnished. All of the bungalows were small and sparely furnished. People didn't come to the Yankee Doodle for the ambiance. They were strictly interested in a bed. The bed in Bungalow Six hadn't been used. A pair of men's scuffed Wolverine work boots were on the floor at the foot of it, where the covers were slightly rumpled. Otherwise, the quilt was smooth, the pillows plumped, sheets and blanket freshly made. Aside from the boots, no trace of Gigi, Casey or Tommy had been left behind. The ashtrays on the nightstands were clean. The wastebasket was empty. The closet was empty. The bedroom was spotless.

The same could not be said for the bathroom.

Blood was spattered all over the floor, sink and walls. More blood was smeared in the bathtub. The shower curtain was gone. So were all of the towels.

"You just relax, girl," Yolie said to her as they backed their way carefully out of the bungalow. They didn't want to compromise any trace evidence. "Don't jump to any conclusions, hear?"

Des said nothing in response. Couldn't speak. Couldn't breathe. *I will die. If anything has happened to Mitch I will curl up and die.*

Toni pulled into the parking lot now, hopped out and came charging toward them. "Detective Kinsler's taken charge of the Rustic Inn crime scene, Loo," she reported. "Techies just got there."

"We have another crime scene in Bungalow Six, Sergeant," Yolie informed her quietly.

Toni's eyes widened. "Is there a body?"

"Just blood. Lots of it. In fact, here's a couple of drops right here," she said, noticing them in the gravel just outside of the bungalow. "There's no trail though. Just the drops. Sergeant, this entire motel needs to be secured. And we need to find out if this blood's a match for what's on that snow shovel at the Rustic."

"On it, Loo," Toni said, reaching for her cell phone.

"Danny didn't say nothing to us about any gunshots," Yolie mused aloud. "Sure didn't smell like somebody fired off any rounds in there."

"No, it didn't."

"So Tommy must have gutted Casey with a knife."

"Must have."

"And then, let's see, Danny said Tommy parked his Trans Am out front here, didn't he?"

"Yes, he did."

"I'm guessing he wrapped Casey up in the shower curtain, popped his trunk and threw Casey's body in there before he and Gigi took off. That would explain the blood drops in the gravel.

Danny never saw it happen—the open trunk blocked his view from the office. Plus he told us he was busy with another couple, didn't he?"

"Yes, he did."

"That make sense to you?"

"Perfect sense, Yolie. All except for one thing. Where's Mitch?"

"Don't you worry about him. I won't let *nothing* happen to your boy." Yolie reached for her cell and started thumbing away. "Okay, here's Tommy's address. It's in Cardiff—Dunn's Lane, number 10A. Know where that is?"

"I know where it is."

"I'll follow you." She turned to Toni and said, "Sergeant, this is now a Major Crime Squad case. I need you to coordinate both crime scenes. I'll be back for you just as soon as I can."

"Sure thing, Loo."

They started toward their cruisers, moving quickly.

Danny Rochin came out of the office, his shoulders hunched. "Everything okay?" he asked nervously.

"Afraid not, Danny," Yolie replied. "Sergent Tedone has to search all of the other bungalows. Also your grounds and the woods surrounding the grounds. Oh, and Danny?"

"Yes, ma'am?"

"You're going to need a new shower curtain."

Des floored it up the Post Road into Cardiff with her hands gripping the wheel tight and Yolie hugging her tail. Cardiff wasn't nearly as affluent a town as Dorset. It had no beaches or marinas. No picture-postcard Historic District. Just a shuttered GM assembly plant, an abandoned thread mill, assorted fast-food franchises and a lot of rundown houses filled with rundown people who couldn't find work. The roads weren't nearly as well plowed as they

215

were in Dorset, and the countryside wasn't nearly as bucolic. Bleak was more like it.

At Upper Pattaganset Road she made a left and sped past an apartment complex, then a neighborhood of vinyl-sided starter Capes before she passed a frozen lake. Beyond it, the houses were older and saggier. Kids were having a snowball fight out in front of an abandoned farmhouse. The zoning became jumbled after that, which is to say nonexistent. There was a plumbing supply warehouse next to a mobile home park next to an auto wrecking yard. Dunn's Lane, which was just past that, was a cul-de-sac of tract homes for GM workers that had been built on the cheap in the 1970s before the plant closed down. Now, in what was rapidly becoming Not-the-American Century, it qualified as a Swamp Yankee slum. Junked cars sat on blocks in more than one of the driveways. Plywood boards covered broken windows. And the street was still buried under deep snow. Des doubted that the town plow had made more than one pass through here yesterday. She inched her way slowly along as she looked for street addresses. Behind her, Yolie had killed her headlights. In this sort of neighborhood the sight of two cruisers arriving together would send off silent alarm bells up and down the block.

There were no lights on at number 10. No cars parked out front. As Des eased on by she saw that 10A was around in back—an apartment over the garage at the end of the driveway. There were lights on in those windows, and a car was parked there. She drove two houses farther down the block before she edged over to the snowbank and parked, Yolie right behind her. They got out, closing their doors quietly. A dog barked at them from across the street. They stayed where they were until it fell silent, then made their way quietly up the driveway. As they got closer to the garage they could hear heavy metal music coming from the upstairs apartment. And make out that the parked car was a black Trans Am.

Des pressed her hand against its tailpipe. It felt warm.

The wooden staircase up to Tommy the Pinhead's apartment was on the outside of the garage. It was icy-slick and creaky as hell, but the music was plenty loud and the hand railing held them steady as they inched their way up. When they reached the landing they drew their SIGs and exchanged eye contact in the light from Tommy's front window. Yolie's gaze was steady and fearless.

Quietly, Des tried the doorknob. No good. Locked.

Yolie, who outweighed her by a solid thirty pounds of muscle, nudged her to one side. Then she took a deep breath and kicked the whole freaking door in. They went in low, guns drawn as "Welcome to the Jungle" greeted them on Tommy's stereo.

He and the girl were naked in the bed, Gigi on top, riding him. Tommy's eyes bulged as he saw them burst through the door. He tossed Gigi aside like a small child and started to reach for the Glock on his nightstand.

"Go for it," Yolie urged him as they stood at the foot of the bed with their SIGs pointed right at him. "You'll be doing the whole world a favor."

He froze, then lay back against the pillows with his hands up, his eyes narrow, hostile slits.

Des turned off the music, her nostrils twitching. It stank in the one-room apartment, a musky smell that was equal parts marijuana smoke, soiled bedsheets and soiled people. A half-eaten pepperoni pizza sat in an open box on the dinette table in what passed for a kitchen. There was a microwave and a minifridge. A work sink filled with dirty dishes. No stove. And not much furniture other than the bed and a beat-up old dresser. Des had seen nicer fleabag motel rooms. Hell, she'd just been in one. It wasn't particularly warm in there. In fact, it was downright cold. Tommy had nothing more than a kerosene space heater.

He and Gigi continued to lie there naked. Tommy appeared to spend a lot of his free time in a tanning salon. He also waxed his huge, rippling chest—the better to show off his tasteful swastika and Iron Cross tats. Gigi was so pallid and gaunt it was painful to look at her. Her arms and legs were barely more than sticks. Her skin was blotchy and covered with bruises. She wore a nipple ring in her right nipple. Beneath her belly button she had a tattoo of a cupcake with a glistening cherry on top.

Her eyes were huge and she was shaking. "I'm f-freezing. You mind if I cover myself up?"

"Please do," Yolie said to her with obvious distaste.

Gigi pulled the top sheet and blanket over them, shivering.

"What do you bitches want?" Tommy demanded, folding his body builder arms in front of his chest.

"Where is he?" Des asked.

"Where's *who*?"

"Mitch Berger."

"Don't know who you're talking about. This must be some kind of mistake. Me and Gigi haven't been out all day, except to get a pizza."

Yolie aimed her SIG directly in between his eyes. "Try again, Pinhead."

He bristled at her. "I don't like that name."

"And I don't like being jerked around, *Pinhead*."

"Like I just said, we been here all day. Smoked us a little weed, made love. I don't know what you want from me."

"Then let me put it in a language you can understand," Yolie said. "If you tell us right goddamned now what went down at the Yankee Doodle then I promise we won't shoot both of you dead."

He let out a laugh. "You can't lay a finger on us. That there's Resident Trooper Mitry. She has to play by the rules. I don't know who you are. . . ."

"I'm your worst nightmare. An angry black bitch with a loaded gun. You have three seconds to tell us what went down or I start shooting."

"I got nothing to tell you. Me and Gigi have been here all—"

Yolie fired at the wall right next to his head—once, twice, three times.

Gigi screamed. Tommy just lay there, glowering.

"Next one goes in your shoulder," Yolie promised him. "Where is he?"

"*Tell* her, Tommy."

"Shut up!"

"Tommy, I swear I-I'm gonna piss myself if you don't."

"And I said shut up," he snarled, his jaw muscles clenching. "Just forget it, lady. I'm not getting in any trouble."

"Fool, you *are* in trouble."

"I think he means in trouble with Slick Rick," Des said. "Slick Rick's connected. If Tommy crosses him he'll wind up in a pork sausage factory somewhere in Providence. The girl, too."

Gigi let out a gasp of horror.

Tommy the Pinhead said nothing. Just continued to glower. It was what he did best.

Yolie shook her head at him. "You are failing to grasp the reality of your present situation. Your problem is with us. Neither of you will make it out of this apartment alive if you do not give up everything right goddamned *now*."

Gigi started to sob, her heavy eye makeup running down her cheeks in black gobs. "Tommy, *please* . . ."

Yolie aimed her weapon at Tommy's left shoulder. "Talk."

"Lady, I got nothing for you."

She fired a shot into the wall that Des swore was less than a half-inch from his skin. "*Talk.*"

"I just told you. I got nothing."

"Okay, I'm all done playing games with this fool," huffed Yolie, who never left home without her Smith & Wesson SWAT spring-assist folding knife, size large. There are times when a combat knife can be vastly more persuasive than a SIG. This was one of those times. Yolie squeezed the knife's thumb release and its razor-sharp four-inch blade sprang open with a click. Then she flung the bedcovers from Tommy and exposed his family jewels. "Hold his legs, girl," she commanded Des. "I'm going to cut our boy Tommy down to size."

Tommy wasn't without nerve. He lay there sneering with contempt while Des grabbed his legs. And kept on sneering—right up until the moment when Yolie had that scary blade less than six inches from where he and his progeny lived. That was when he began to squirm, his eyes bulging. "*Wait,* lady!" he roared. "Are you crazy?"

"There's an honest difference of opinion about that," Yolie answered soberly. "But the state shrink cleared me for active duty. Let's do this, girl."

"I said *wait*!" he protested. "W-What do you want to know about?"

"Casey Zander," Des said. "How things went down at the Rustic."

"South in a hurry," he said, his eyes never leaving that knife. "Casey was acting all spooked, okay? Said the law was getting hip to things now that his mom's boyfriend was dead."

"Hip to what things?"

"That he was stealing meds out of the mail to pay off Slick Rick."

"*Who* was stealing them—Casey or his mom's boyfriend?"

"Don't ask me. I don't know how blubber boy's been doing it. Don't know, don't care. I just know he was into Slick Rick for big bucks and he's been paying him off with meds, iPods, anything else he can lay his hands on. He's been making good, too, until today out in the parking lot of the Rustic he starts whining like a little bitch about how the postal inspectors are grilling him and he's getting real nervous. I went back inside and told my employer. . . ."

"Slick Rick, you mean?"

Tommy nodded. "He told me we'll be toast if the feds start leaning on blubber boy. Casey would give us up in a heartbeat to save his own sorry ass. Slick Rick said to take care of it. I'd just sent Gigi to the Yankee Doodle with Casey to settle him down. Figured I'd follow them there. Except when I got outside there's some dude crouched by the woodpile watching them drive away. Same dude who was just inside the Rustic asking Steve a bunch of questions. I figured he had to be the one." He swallowed hard. "Put that thing away, will ya?"

Yolie held the knife even closer. "The one? What one?"

"The undercover cop. Slick Rick heard there might be a state narc hanging around. Word gets out."

Des felt her stomach tighten. "What did you do about him?"

"Whacked him over the head with a snow shovel and tossed him in my trunk."

"Why did you do that?"

"I couldn't just leave him lying there. People would notice him."

"No, dumb ass," Yolie growled. "Why'd you whack him over the head?"

"Because I didn't want him following me to the Yankee Doodle. I had business to take care of there. I had no personal beef with the guy but he intruded into my thing. So I did what I had to do."

Yolie raised her chin at him. "Of course you did."

"Then I drove to the Yankee Doodle, except *Gigi* had locked the bungalow door."

"I always do," she whimpered. "I told you I was sorry."

"Just shut the hell up, will you? I had to pound on the freaking door. Attract all kinds of attention to myself. That's real smart, isn't it?"

"Not here to listen to you two bicker," Yolie growled, poking at the tender flesh of Tommy's scrotum with the tip of her knife.

Tommy held up his hands, shuddering. "Okay, okay. Just take it easy, will ya? When I went in, Casey was sitting on the bed taking his boots off. Still had his clothes on which, believe me, was a good thing."

"I hated doing him," Gigi said. "He was totally fat and he had these acne scars all over his back that were disgusting."

"Yeah, like you'd know from disgusting," Yolie said.

Gigi frowned at her. "Did you just insult me?"

"Then what happened?"

"I pulled a blade and he ran into the bathroom, squealing like a little girl." Tommy's voice was eerily flat and emotionless now. "I went in there after him and stuck him until he wasn't squealing anymore."

"What did you do with him?"

"Wrapped him in the shower curtain and threw him in my trunk."

"With the other guy?"

"Yeah, with the other guy."

"Was the other guy still unconscious?"

"Don't know. I wasn't paying much attention to him."

Des's gaze flicked over to the windows, then back at the bed. "Are they still out there in your trunk?"

"No way. You think I'm stupid?"

"You don't actually want us to answer that, do you?" Yolie responded.

"What did you do after you left the Yankee Doodle?" Des asked him, struggling to maintain her calm.

"Dumped Casey's body."

"Where?"

"Breezy Point."

Breezy Point was a state park ten miles east of Dorset's Historic District. It had a nice stretch of beach and miles of bike paths and hiking trails that overlooked Long Island Sound. During the summer it was a popular destination. During the winter it was windy and desolate. Hardly anyone went there.

"Why Breezy Point?"

"It's my favorite place in the whole world," Gigi answered, brightening. "That's where Tommy and me met. Right, baby? I was wearing that little pink T-shirt and you said, 'Hey, I like pink.' Which I thought was *the* lamest line ever. But you were so cute I started talking to you anyway and . . ." She trailed off, sniffling. "I thought it would be, you know, funny."

"I don't get the joke. Yolie, do you get the joke?"

"Afraid not."

"So you drove out to Breezy Point, dumped Casey's body and then? . . ."

"Picked up a pizza and came back here," Tommy the Pinhead

said. "That's the whole story, I swear. Now put that knife away, okay?"

Yolie shook her head at him. "Not quite. The guy who you brained with the shovel . . ."

"What about him?"

"Did you gut him, too?"

"Nope. Didn't have any cause to."

Des walked around to his side of the bed and pressed the nose of her SIG against Tommy the Pinhead's forehead. "What *did* you do with him?"

CHAPTER 16

THE FIRST TIME MITCH came to he was positive he had to be on a wild ride at Disney World. It was hurtling him along incredibly fast and was bone-jarringly bouncy and everything around him was pitch-black and really, really scary. Except Mitch had never been to Disney World, which meant he had to be dreaming. Except he *wasn't* dreaming. His eyes were wide open.

Oh, God, I'm blind.

No, wait, he could see a crack of light down there by his feet. And hear the sound of tires on slushy pavement as the wild ride slowed down and came to a stop. Mitch took careful stock of himself. He seemed to be lying on his side in a fetal position. The back of his head hurt. He reached for it, fingering it. It felt sticky. . . . Okay, now he remembered. He'd been watching the parking lot of the Rustic when someone coldcocked him on the back of the head with a heavy object—like, say, a twelve-inch Lodge cast-iron skillet. Because he'd gotten his bell rung but good. Second time in less than a year, too. First time was that concussion he got at Astrid's Castle when he and Des got stranded up there with that killer who kept . . .

Focus. Try to remember what happened.

The Rustic. He'd been standing there watching, um, watching Casey and Gigi take off in Casey's Tacoma. Sure, that was it. And now?

Now I'm stuffed in the trunk of somebody's car.

It was cold and super-cramped in there. Zero headroom. And it smelled like oil and burnt rubber. Had to be an old beater of a car. Its automatic transmission was bad. As they started to pick up speed again, Mitch could feel the tranny rev and rev and rev before it lurched into second gear. He smelled more burnt rubber. Smelled something else, too. An animal smell. A *dead* animal smell. He groped around in the darkness. His fingers found the smooth roundness of a spare tire. Then, behind him, a plastic bag. Really large one. Actually, more like a tarp than a bag. Something big and heavy was wrapped inside.

Or someone.

Mitch gulped as he fought back a strong, sudden wave of nausea. Then the car went over a bump and the back of his head smacked hard against the lid of the trunk and he was out again.

The second time Mitch came to it was with a sudden yelp, as if he were awakening from an awful nightmare. He was cold. Freezing cold. He had never been so cold in his life. Shivering and shaking, his teeth chattering so violently that he was afraid he was going to shatter them.

Where am I? Why am I so cold?

He glanced around, blinking, dazed. Well, hell, he was basking on his own beach in the late-day sun. It was a nice, breezy afternoon out on Big Sister, the surf lapping against the rocks. Must have drifted off for a few minutes as he lay there in the sand in his swim trunks. Sure, that was it. He looked around for the island's familiar landmark, the old lighthouse, except it wasn't there. Wait a second, he wasn't home. This was a different beach. Someone else's beach. And this wasn't soft sand he was lying on. And he wasn't wearing swim trunks. He wasn't wearing anything at all.

I am lying stark naked in the snow.

226

He was still asleep. Had to be. This had to be a dream. Except it wasn't. He was lying naked in the snow, shaking with cold. It was, what, thirty-five degrees out? That wind off of the water was howling. His fingers and toes ached, ears and nose stung.

Where am I? How in the hell did I get here?

Someone had conked him on the head outside of the Rustic and then . . . what? Then he'd been stuffed in the trunk of that car, right? And now he was freezing his ass off on this beach. He looked around, thinking that he knew this place.

Breezy Point.

Sure, he'd come here for bike rides with Des. Breezy Point was one of the nicest places to be on a summer afternoon. In the winter? In the winter it was known as the windchill capital of the Connecticut shoreline. They didn't call it Breezy Point for nothing. The beach was deserted this time of year. Absolutely no one came here. It was also remote. Had to be a three-mile hike to Route One from here. Darkness was approaching fast. And Mitch was naked and all alone.

Except for his friend, that is. The fellow who was lying in the snow next to him with that shower curtain around him. Casey Zander. It was Casey. *He* had clothes on—a Pats hoodie sweatpants and white socks. *He* wasn't shivering. Or moving. Or-Or breathing. Just staring up at the sky, his face a winter shade of pale blue . . .

He's dead. There's blood all over that shower curtain. Blood all over his sweatshirt. Casey's dead.

The sudden realization sent Mitch scrambling to his feet to get away from Casey's body. He promptly fell right back down into the deep snow, his bare feet so frozen that they wouldn't support his weight. He felt dizzy, too. So dizzy he almost passed out again. He managed not to. Couldn't, mustn't pass out. Had to stay awake and get the hell out of here before it got dark. Because if he didn't, he would freeze to death awfully damned fast.

How did we get out here?

Slowly, it came back to him. Being lifted out of the trunk by that behemoth Tommy the Pinhead. Being forced to walk down to the beach in the snow, even though he'd been incredibly woozy and could barely maintain his balance. But the girl, Gigi, kept poking him with a gun. She was holding a gun on him. And Tommy was carrying something. A big, heavy package. Casey. He was carrying Casey's body. When they got here Tommy dropped Casey and ordered Mitch to turn around. Then the bastard beaned him again. Hit him with that gun, probably. Hit him so hard that he'd passed out for who knows how long. Long enough for them to take all of his clothes off. Damn, they'd even taken his Omega, the one that his grandfather, Sam Berger, bought for seven dollars at the Fort Dix PX before he shipped out to fight Hitler. Sam wore that watch all through the war. And Mitch had worn it since he was in high school. And now it was gone and he was shivering uncontrollably and had no feeling whatsoever in his hands or feet.

What do I do?

Think it out, calmly and rationally. He'd gotten out of tough situations before. He'd get out of this one. If he had a problem, he simply needed to solve it.

Problem One: I'm going to freeze to death.

Solution: Put some clothes on, dumb ass.

And add this to the list of 297 things that Mitch Berger, noted New York City film critic, never, ever thought he'd find himself doing—rolling a bloody dead guy out of a bloody shower curtain so that he could undress said dead guy and put his bloody clothes on. First, he wrestled the Pats hoodie off over Casey's head. Or tried to. Casey wasn't exactly cooperating and Mitch's fingers were numb and his hands were shaking. Plus his stomach kept lurching and sending hot, sour bile up into his throat. But Mitch tugged and tugged until, gasping with exhaustion, he finally managed to yank Casey's hooded sweatshirt off of him.

Mitch's stomach lurched again when he saw the deep knife wounds in Casey's abdomen. He could make out at least six of them in what was left of the afternoon sunlight. A man hadn't done that to him. Casey had been killed by a savage animal.

Teeth chattering, he pulled the dead man's sweatshirt on over his own head, snugging the hood down over his frozen ears, burying his hands in its kangaroo pouch. He didn't care that the lower half of the sweatshirt was soaked with Casey's ice-cold blood. Couldn't afford to care. He was grateful for whatever he had. It would have been nice if there'd been something tucked inside of that kangaroo pouch. Like, say, a cell phone. But that was too much to hope for. After he'd warmed his hands for a moment he removed Casey's socks and slid them on his own frozen feet. The socks were nothing more than thin cotton. And they were caked with snow. Barely any protection at all. But they were something.

His next challenge was Casey's sweatpants. As he crouched over Casey, preparing to pull the pants down his legs, Mitch's nostrils encountered some truly terrible smells. Casey's sphincters had released when he died. One of those real-life things that they never show in the movies. And, in real life, Mitch couldn't put those pants on no matter how cold he was.

That left the bloody shower curtain, which would at least work as a windbreaker. He rolled Casey off of it, folded it in half and wrapped it around the lower half of his body, tucking it at his waist like a bath towel.

Problem Two: I'm miles from nowhere.

Solution? Start walking.

Right. He had to make his way through that deep snow. Back across the beach to the path, then up the path to the parking lot. The lot had probably been plowed. Easy walking. Beyond it was a road that dipped under the Amtrak railroad trestle and then after a mile or so met up with Route 1. That wasn't so far. He could make that. And maybe he'd encounter somebody before he reached Route 1. It wasn't the middle of the night. People would be out and about. Sure, they would. He'd flag someone down and ask them to call Des on their cell phone. Not a problem. He was clothed and socked. Hands tucked inside of the kangaroo pouch. Ears covered. He could do this. All he had to do was get up and start walking.

Problem Three: I can't actually get up.

Solution: Yes, you actually can.

Slowly, Mitch got to his feet, wavering as he stood there in the gusting wind. The setting sun now was a sliver on the western horizon. Darkness was falling. He paused to say good-bye to Casey. Promised the guy he'd be back for him as soon as he could. It wasn't a long speech. This wasn't the time for words. It was the time for action. He gave Casey a jaunty wave, then snugged the shower curtain tight and started his way through the deep snow one rugged step at a time. He made it three whole strides before flashbulbs started popping in front of his eyes and he fell back down, dizzy beyond belief from those blows to his head. Everything was spinning.

Don't pass out. You can't pass out. It'll drop into the twenties once it gets dark and you'll freeze to death. Don't pass . . .

The roar of an engine brought him back. It was the Acela speeding its way across the trestle toward Boston, its passengers all warm and cozy inside, and wearing things like trousers, underwear and sweatshirts that weren't caked with someone else's blood. They were probably thinking about the hot meal they'd be having when they pulled into Boston. It would be supper time. Nothing like a scrumptious supper in Beantown on a cold, windy night. A big, hot bowl of clam chowder for starters. Then a rib eye steak, medium rare, with hash browns, creamed spinach and plenty of fresh bread slathered with sweet butter. A nice bottle of Chianti Classico. Chocolate cake for dessert. A double espresso with a jolt of Balvenie on the side. Mitch could practically taste it as the train tore past and then was gone, leaving behind the howl of the wind and the faint strumming of a guitar. Mitch recognized the tune— Leonard Cohen's "The Stranger Song" from *McCabe and Mrs. Miller*. Mitch had been downloading it yesterday, back when he was a warm, sentient film maven as opposed to a dazed oaf sitting half frozen in the snow with the winter darkness closing in on him. He had to get up. Get up and keep walking—same as Beatty had to get up and keep walking after he got shot at the end of *McCabe and Mrs. Miller*. Beatty with his bowler hat and beard and that stupid line he kept saying to people. What was that line?

"If a frog had wings he wouldn't bump his ass so much, follow me?"

Except no one ever did.

Mitch's feet ached now. He willed himself back up onto them anyway. He was standing tall. Walking tall. One foot in front of the other. He was fine—until suddenly everything seemed to be tilting at a funny angle and he realized that he wasn't walking or standing tall anymore. He'd pitched over onto his side like a mighty oak in a hurricane and lay there in the snow once again.

Get back up. Keep walking.

He wanted to. Really, he did. Except it was so hard to get up. And so easy to just settle down into the snow and stay here.

Problem Four: You're going to die.

Solution: Accept it.

They'd left him here to die. That was why they'd taken his clothing. And he was going to die—right here next to Casey. It wouldn't take long now. Mitch wished he could leave Des a goodbye note. But he had nothing to write with. Doubted his fingers would be able to hold a pen anyway, even though he had them tucked inside of Casey's sweatshirt. What were the four degrees of frostbite? He'd just been watching a special about it the other night on The Weather Channel. The first degree was frost nip, which affected only the surface skin. Second degree, the skin froze and hardened but the deep tissue wasn't affected and you were still basically okay. But once you got to degrees three and four, the blood vessels, nerves and muscles started to freeze. That was when they started talking about gangrene and amputation. And then there was the whole hypothermia thing, which occurred when your body temperature dipped below ninety-five degrees. He figured that had to be on the table soon, what with the wind-chill factor and all. Bottom line? If no one found him in the next twenty minutes Mitch Berger, noted film critic, would achieve the fifth degree, which also went by the name Certain Death.

I don't want to die. I want to live. Please, God, don't let me die. Let me live. If you let me live I-I promise you I'll take back every bad word I've ever said about Danny Kaye. I'll even watch every single one of his movies, I swear. I don't want to die.

But he knew he was going to. This was the end. As he lay there on his side Mitch drew his knees to his chest and hugged them tightly, his teeth chattering as he waited for death to come. He didn't welcome it. But he accepted it. He had to accept it. Death was the only choice left to him. And he was okay with that, because he was very, very lucky.

I became the man I wanted to be. Did the work I wanted to do. I loved a special woman. When I lost her I didn't think I'd make it— until I met a woman who was even more special and I loved her even more.

That's pretty much all a man can ask for, isn't it? What else is there? Kids? Okay, he and Des didn't get that chance. But he did pretty damned good for a shlub from Stuyvesant Town. True, maybe this fade-out scene right here was a tiny bit on the sad side. Maybe he was blinking as he fought back the tears that had started to come. Blinking as the flashbulbs started popping before his eyes again, bright as could be. But this would be over soon. He just had to surrender to it. And so he did. Mitch closed his eyes and he surrendered.

"If a frog had wings he wouldn't bump his ass so much, follow me?"

CHAPTER 17

THEY FLOORED IT TO Breezy Point, lights flashing and sirens blaring as they tore their way around the rush-hour traffic on the Post Road—Des in the lead car, Yolie on her tail with Tommy the Pinhead and Gigi Garanski handcuffed in the backseat of her cruiser. It took them ten minutes to reach the park turn-off on Route 1. When the road dipped under the Amtrak trestle, Des hit a pothole that was deep enough to rattle her spine. She slowed now as she drew nearer to the parking lot, her eyes searching the dusk for someone out walking. Someone large and Jewish who was desperately trying to find help. But she saw no one as she pulled into the deserted parking lot, her high beams sweeping the woods alongside of it.

If he's dead then I'm dead, too. I'll stop eating. I'll stop caring. I'll die. I'll just curl up and die.

She left her engine running, jumped out and threw open the back door to Yolie's cruiser. "Where are they?"

"On the beach," Tommy the Pinhead answered. "Like I told you."

"He'd better be okay. Because if he's not I swear I will shoot you both and leave you here. The coyotes will eat your remains."

"Tommy, she's *scaring* me," Gigi whimpered.

"Shut the hell up, will ya? The dude's fine," he assured Des. "I just gave him a little love pat on the head, that's all."

She slammed the door and zipped up her Gore-Tex storm

jacket. Then she and Yolie started their way down the snowy, windblown path into the park. They needed their big Maglites to show them the way in the deepening darkness. And the walking wasn't easy. Every time she put her foot down it *kerchunked* on the hard, icy surface left by last night's rain and went plunging down into two feet of soft snow. Each footstep was serious work.

"*MITCH? . . . !*" she cried out, her ears straining for a response. She heard nothing over the wind. "Damn, I hope he didn't wander off and get lost."

"If he wandered anywhere it would have been back toward Route 1. We'd have seen him. Mitch ain't dumb."

"But he got whacked on the head, Yolie. He's already had one concussion this year. And this is Mitch we're talking about. For all we know he may think he's on a lion hunt with the Ale and Quail Club."

"The Ale and Quail *who?*"

"You never saw *Palm Beach Story?* I swear, that sequence on the train has to be the funniest ten minutes I've ever . . . Will you listen to me? I'm even starting to *sound* like him. I swear, if that man's still alive I'm going to kill him."

"Okay, here we go," Yolie said as they reached the narrower path that snaked through the woods to the beach.

She could hear the surf washing up on the rocks as they made their way down the path. It was considerably windier out on the open beach. Blowing really, really hard. The windchill was something fierce. They waved their flashlight beams out along the water's edge and spotted two large shapes out there in the snow. Two large, motionless shapes.

"*MITCH?!. . . .*" Des screamed over the howling wind.

Nothing. No response.

Des broke into a mad sprint through the deep snow, her legs

straining, chest heaving as she gasped and gasped and gasped. "*MITCH?!. . . .*"

Still nothing.

The first person her flashlight beam found was Casey, who was curled up dead like a giant, frozen worm. Huddled a few feet away from him was Mitch, who lay on his side wearing only a Pats hoodie, a pair of white socks and a bloody shower curtain that had slid down around his knees. He was . . . blinking at her. Or trying to. His eyes were practically frozen shut. And he was shuddering so violently she could hear his teeth chattering. He had no pants on. Not even any underwear. The poor man's genitals were fully exposed to the howling wind.

She whipped off her parka and fell to her knees before him, tears streaming down her cheeks as she wrapped it around him. "Oh, baby, baby . . ."

"D-Do you? . . ."

"Do I what?"

"Any c-clam chowder?"

"What'd he just say?"

"He wants some clam chowder."

"Not a problem, big boy. We'll get some in you right away." Yolie took off her own jacket and put it over him.

"Can you *believe* they left him out here buck naked?"

"I can believe it."

"Would have been nice if they'd mentioned it."

"Girl, I think you need to accept that these are not nice people."

"We'll have to carry him back. I'll take him by his arms. You take his legs. Be real careful with his feet. If he's got any frostbite in those toes you don't want to squeeze them or rub them."

"Hey, I took the same lifesaving classes you did, remember?"

"Sorry, I'm just a tiny bit out of my mind right now."

"No, you're not. You're fine. We're all fine. Right, big boy?"

"K-Kids," he croaked as they secured their jackets around him. Des frowned at him. "Which kids?"

"*Our* kids."

"He must be tripping." Des shined her light on the back of his head. "Yeah, he's been bleeding. Got whacked real good."

Yolie worked the zipper of her parka up toward Mitch's exposed genitals.

"N-Not sure I'm ready for our relationship to go this f-far," he told her.

"I've seen a man's tool before," she assured him, zipping him up nice and snug. "Don't think I've ever seen one so shriveled though."

"From the c-cold. I-I don't have frostbite *there*, do I?"

"Not to worry, stud. It strikes your extremities first. And, trust me, that ain't no extremity. Girl, is it always so small?"

"We are not going to have this conversation right now. And no."

"If you p-pop it into your mouth you'll warm it right up."

"He talking to me?"

"He'd *better* be talking to *me*."

Now he was muttering something under his breath about a frog having wings.

"You following any of this?" Yolie asked her.

"Not a word. Let's lift him on two, okay? One, two . . ."

They hoisted him up. Mitch was heavy, close to two hundred pounds. But not nearly as heavy as when she'd first met him. He'd taken off a good forty pounds of man-blubber since then. Which was a mighty good thing. It wasn't easy horsing him back through that deep snow, step by step by step.

"How you doing at your end?" Yolie panted as they worked their way slowly back across the beach.

"Okay . . ." Her shoulders and back were already starting to scream. "But I think he's unconscious."

"Probably just as well. Another ten seconds and he was going to be proposing to both of us."

They made it across the beach and started their way up the narrow, twisting path. By now every single muscle in Des's body was in agony.

"Need a break?" Yolie asked her when they reached the main path.

"No, I'm good," she gasped. "Let's get him in my front seat. I've got blankets in my trunk. I'll run him straight to Shoreline Clinic. Faster than waiting for an EMT."

"Deal. I'll secure this scene, then run those two pieces of human filth in."

They could see their cars now. Just another fifty yards and they'd be there. Not so far. Not so far at all. Not when her man's life depended on it. And, hell, the last twenty feet was plowed pavement. Easy-peasy. They set him down gently on the passenger side of her front seat. Des pointed all of the heater vents in his direction and got the blankets out of the trunk and wrapped them around him. He was still unconscious. Also exceedingly pale— except for his ears and nose, which were bright red. She jumped in behind the wheel and slammed the door.

He stirred, blinking at her from inside of his blanket cocoon. "Y-You found me."

"Of course I did." She backed the cruiser up, spun it around and took off. "Think I was going to let you freeze to death out there?"

"H-How? . . ."

"Rut called from the Rustic to tell me you'd vanished. We followed your trail from there to the Yankee Doodle, where we found a whole lot of blood in Bungalow Six." She eased off of the gas as she dipped under the Amtrak trestle, not wanting to jar him, then hit the gas again. Also her siren. "I was afraid it was yours, to tell you the truth."

"It wasn't."

"After that we convinced Tommy the Pinhead to tell us where you were. Two large, angry black women with semiautomatic handguns can be very persuasive—especially if one of them is Yolie."

She made a left onto Route 1 and punched it, veering around anyone and everyone in her path.

"Why'd they take my clothes?"

"Gigi thought it would be funny."

"She needs to work on her sense of humor."

"She'll have plenty of time at York Correctional."

"They teach comedy there now?"

"That was a joke, mister."

"Sorry, I'm not . . . real with it."

In fact, he'd passed out again.

She hit ninety mph as she tore across the Baldwin Bridge and then up Route 9 to the clinic. Night was settling in as she pulled up at the ambulance entrance with a screech.

Mitch awoke with a startled yelp, his eyes wide with fright.

She put her arm around him. "You okay?"

"I-I thought I was back in that trunk again with Casey. It was like that scene in *Out of Sight* with George Clooney and Jennifer Lopez. After he escaped from prison, remember? Except it was pitch-black and he was dead. And I'd much rather have been stuffed in there with J-Lo. She was hot in that movie. Not Yvette Mimieux hot, but plenty hot."

She smiled at him. "You're jabbering. Have I told you recently how much I love it when you jabber?"

"Des, my head hurts."

"I know."

"And my toes really, really ache."

"Good. That means the nerves are still working. You won't lose them."

"*Lose* them?"

She got out, charged through the double doors to the ER and hollered, "Get some help here!"

A doctor and a nurse started toward her at once. Des had been in and out of the clinic a million times and was acquainted with the doctor, a brisk, efficient Asian woman named Cindie Tashima.

"What have we got here?" Dr. Cindie asked as Des and the nurse hoisted Mitch into a wheelchair, his eyes blinking from the entrance's bright lights.

"This man's suffered a head wound and is in and out of consciousness. He was left for dead out at Breezy Point with no clothes on. We're talking possible frostbite, especially to his feet."

"Take him into room four and start re-warming him," Dr. Cindie ordered the nurse, who promptly wheeled Mitch away. "Since they took his clothes I'm assuming he had no ID on him."

"Probably threw his wallet in a Dumpster somewhere."

"So he's a John Doe?"

"No, he's a Mitchell Berger."

Des provided an administrative aide with Mitch's address, date of birth and the name of his insurance provider. Dr. Cindie checked his body temperature and blood pressure while the nurse and an orderly unzipped the parkas Des and Yolie had covered him with and peeled off the bloody sweatshirt and shower curtain. Des watched them through the open doorway as they started re-warming his hands and feet in disposable basins filled with warm water. Not hot. Hot water could be such a shock to the system that it caused heart damage.

When the nurse handed Des the parkas Des said, "I'll need the sweatshirt and shower curtain, too. How is he?"

"Conscious. And real anxious to talk to you about something."

Des went into the room and said, "What is it, baby?"

"I-I forgot to tell you," he murmured as Dr. Cindie examined his head wound. "When I was in Tommy the Pinhead's trunk with Casey . . ."

"Is this about J-Lo again?"

"No, the tranny."

She raised an eyebrow at him. "Which tranny?"

"Tommy drives a beat-up old black Trans Am, okay? And if you're trying to find it here's what to look for—he needs a new tranny real badly."

"And you know this because? . . ."

"It kept revving and revving before it shifted into second with a real lurch. I smelled burnt rubber, too."

Des didn't bother to tell him they'd already located Tommy's Trans Am. Just nodded and said, "A beat-up old black Trans Am with a bad tranny. Got it."

"His Trans Am is toast, you know. When that tranny goes it'll cost more to replace it than the whole car's worth."

She stared at him in disbelief, her pulse quickening. "I swear, sometimes you terrify me. You've got frostbite and a possible concussion. . . ."

"Definite concussion," Dr. Cindie interjected.

"And yet you did it again."

He frowned at her, his gaze slightly out of focus. "Did what?"

"Cracked my case."

"I think I cracked a tooth. They were chattering so hard."

"I'll have a look at it in a second," Dr. Cindie promised him.

Des bent down and kissed him. "I have to leave you for a little while. I'll be back soon, okay?"

He didn't answer her. Couldn't. He was unconscious again.

The house was dark except for one light on inside. The porch light was out. Des rang the bell and stood there in the dark for a long time before she finally heard footsteps and the front door swung slowly open.

"Yes, what is it?" She peered out at Des from the darkened front hallway.

"I'm sorry to bother you again, Paulette, but I have more news for you. May I came in?"

Paulette stood there in taut silence for a moment before ushering Des inside, turning on lights as she led Des to the TV room, where Dr. Phil was in the process of stampeding his lame self into someone's life. Des had always wondered who watched Dr. Phil. Now she knew. Dorset's postmaster was still hard at work on the Carlo Rossi Chablis, a fresh gallon jug that was nearly full. The ashtray next to her recliner was crammed with cigarette butts.

"I seem to have lost track of time." Paulette muted the TV as she slumped into her chair. "My phone rang a couple of times a while ago but I didn't feel like answering it."

"Paulette, have you eaten anything today?"

"I may have," she answered vaguely, her eyes searching Des's face. "What do you want to tell me?"

"This will be hard to take right on top of Hank's loss but I'm sorry to say that we've just found Casey dead."

The color drained from Paulette's face. "Dead . . ." Her voice was a whisper. "What did . . . How did it happen?"

"He was stabbed to death at the Yankee Doodle Motor Court. We subsequently obtained information that his body had been left out on the beach at Breezy Point. We just found him there."

"Oh, lord . . ." Paulette reached for a Merit and lit it with a disposable lighter, her hand trembling. "Who would *do* such a thing?"

"Tommy Stratton. We have him in custody."

She shook her head, bewildered. "Why would he want to hurt Casey?"

"He claims that Casey's been supplying him with prescription meds, cash and whatever else he could steal from Hank's route. That Casey was our grinch."

"And you *believe* him? That's absurd. Hank was the grinch. You and I both know that."

"Do we?"

"He confessed to it last night, didn't he? I saw his confession with my own two eyes. He texted it to me before he killed himself."

"He didn't, actually," Des said. "Kill himself, I mean. We were waiting for all of the forensics results to come back before we had this conversation with you but we believe that Hank was murdered last night—by a pair of killers who staged it to look like a suicide."

"But he *apologized* to me. Sent me that text message."

"Hank didn't send it to you. His killers did."

Paulette heaved a sigh of exasperation. "Des, I don't understand what you're saying. Why would anyone want to murder Hank?"

"Because he'd discovered what was really going on. He even told me so at the Post Office. Only I was too dense to grasp it."

"Told you *what*?"

"That Casey was in a deep hole. I thought he meant a psychological hole. He meant a financial hole—a huge gambling debt.

243

Hank knew the real deal. That's why he was killed. The only thing we haven't been able to nail down is the identity of Casey's partner."

Paulette furrowed her brow. "I thought you just said Tommy the Pinhead was his partner."

"No, Tommy worked for the loan shark who Casey owed the money to. Someone else was helping Casey steal all of that stuff from Hank's route. The same someone else who helped him stage Hank's suicide scene last night. Someone who's careful and shrewd. I don't mean to cast aspersions on Casey but he was more of a follower than a leader, wouldn't you say?"

"Well, yes. I suppose that he was a . . ." The doorbell interrupted her. "I wonder who *that* is."

"I'm expecting company. Hope you don't mind." Des went to the front door and opened it. Grisky, Questa and The Aardvark were clustered out on Paulette's front porch in the frosty cold, all three of them peering at her with mystified expressions. "Come on in, gentlemen."

They came on in, Grisky's eyes swiveling to take in the surroundings. "Shmokin' hot train set," he observed. "But what is up with all of those tubas?"

"Please follow me," Des said, leading them back to the TV room, where Paulette sat, grief-stricken, staring at Dr. Phil on the muted flat-screen. "I've just informed Paulette that we found Casey. I was filling her in on what happened as best as I could."

Grisky nodded grimly. "Terrible situation."

"We're sorry for your loss," Questa said. "This must be an impossibly hard day for you."

"Thank you," Paulette said softly.

"If it's any consolation," Grisky said, "I can assure you that Lieutenant Snipes has both suspects in state police custody."

Paulette looked at him curiously. "Both suspects?"

"Tommy had a helper," Des explained. "Gigi Garanski."

Paulette made a face. "I knew she was no good. I told him and I told him. But he wouldn't listen. He just wouldn't . . ." She trailed off with a sigh. "May I offer you coffee or something?"

"No, we're good," The Aardvark told her.

Then he and the other two men stood there waiting for Des to explain why she'd summoned them.

"I was telling Paulette that we don't believe Hank committed suicide. Or that he was stealing his own mail. Hank was just an innocent bystander to this ugly mess. But he knew too much. He knew that Casey had a gambling problem. He knew that Casey owed Slick Rick Fontanella a lot of money. And he knew that to pay Slick Rick off Casey had resorted to stealing his mail. We're positive that Casey was our grinch. But we don't believe he acted alone. It's simply not credible that Casey figured out a way to raid all of the mailboxes in the Historic District in broad daylight over a period of two weeks without ever being noticed. Casey was a part-time employee. He worked on Saturdays, period. And Inspector Questa has assured us that the Dorset branch of the U.S. Postal Service is a secure, well-run branch. Am I correct so far, Inspector?"

Questa nodded his huge head. "Correct. Casey Zander couldn't have pulled this off on his own. We have too many security measures in place."

Paulette stubbed out her cigarette, considering this carefully. "Then how could he have done it?"

"I've been giving that a lot of thought," Des replied. "In my opinion the best way to steal Hank's mail would be by pulling up a few minutes behind him in a second mail truck. Who better to steal the mail than another mail carrier? It would never occur to

245

a resident or passerby that the second carrier was removing the mail as opposed to delivering it. Nor would they think twice if they noticed a second truck pulling up just after Hank went by. They'd just figure that you folks had so much volume during the holidays that you had to add an extra carrier."

Paulette poured herself some more wine and took a sip. "I suppose they would," she acknowledged.

Des shoved her heavy horn-rimmed glasses up her nose. "Casey must have had a partner on the inside, Paulette. And the only way that any of this makes sense is if that partner was you."

Paulette stared at her blankly. "Me?"

"You," she stated. "And you were awful damned clever about it, too. You and your year-end Grumman LLV fleet readiness review."

Questa frowned at her. "What readiness review?"

"Oh, it's all very official, Inspector. She even carries around a clipboard with printed forms that have to be filled out."

Questa said it louder. "*What* readiness review?"

"According to Paulette, all ten of the branch's trucks have to be road tested by the end of the year in order to qualify for the postal service's budgeted retrofitting program."

"There *is* no such program," Questa said.

"Correct, it's totally bogus. You know that. Postmaster Zander knows that. And Hank Merrill knew it, too, because he got real peeved when Paulette mentioned it to him in my presence yesterday. But her other carriers didn't know it. Didn't give it any thought either. I'm guessing from the look on your face, Inspector, that not one of them even bothered to mention it to your investigators."

"You're guessing right."

"Why would they? It was just a stupid little bureaucratic annoyance. But to Paulette it was everything. It gave her authorization to road test all of the branch's trucks while her carriers were taking their lunch breaks. No one questioned her authority. She's the boss. Casey was just a part-timer. No way he could remove a spare set of truck keys from the safe in Paulette's office. But *Paulette* could. And she did. Hank told me that three of the carriers have been going to the gym together every day on their lunch break. They leave their vehicles in the Post Office parking lot and walk to the health club at The Works. My guess? She's been taking their trucks out over and over again. Who'd pay attention to whether she took the same truck out more than once? Who'd even care?"

"I want to make sure that I'm hearing you right," Grisky said. "Are you saying that Mrs. Zander concocted a fake vehicle-readiness review so she could go out and steal the mail that Hank Merrill had just delivered?"

Des nodded her head. "No one suspected a thing. No one questioned a thing. Hell, it was such a petty matter that *I* didn't even think of it until Mitch laid something on me just now at Shoreline Clinic."

"Laid what on you?" The Aardvark asked.

"That Tommy the Pinhead's car has a bad tranny. That's when I remembered the little spat that Paulette and Hank had yesterday about the tranny on his mail truck."

Paulette sat there grim-faced, saying nothing.

"Hank got way testy when Paulette asked him about it. Unusually so for such an easygoing guy. I couldn't figure out why. Now I get why—because he knew what you two were up to, didn't he, Paulette?"

Paulette still didn't respond. Just reached for a cigarette and lit it.

"How did he know, Paulette?"

"You may as well tell us," Questa blustered at her. "Your cooperation is all you've got going for you right now."

Paulette let out a hollow laugh. "I have *nothing* going for me right now. Nothing and no one. So I'll tell you. Why the hell not?" She drank down some more wine. "Hank came home early from basketball practice the night before last and overheard us arguing in the kitchen."

"This was the night of Rut's party?" Des asked, remembering how tense Paulette had seemed. Also how reluctant she'd been to call in the postal inspectors.

"Yes, that's right."

"What did Hank overhear?"

"Me telling Casey that I couldn't keep taking the same trucks out over and over again. That people at work would start to notice. And we'd have to find another way or . . ." Paulette broke off, her chest rising and falling. "That's when Hank walked in. He got very, very upset. Told us he was going to call the postal inspectors. Have my boy arrested."

"Not to mention *you*."

"I didn't care about myself. I never have. Casey was my son. He needed me. I couldn't let those thugs hurt him, could I?"

"You didn't have any money you could give them?"

"I'd already given Casey every penny I could lay my hands on. I didn't have a cent left. So I did what any mother would do—I helped him. I *pleaded* with Hank to give us a chance. Hank could be such a Boy Scout sometimes. He said he'd have to 'think it over.' That was the best I could get out of him. He wouldn't even look at me after that. Hardly spoke to me except at Rut's party. And then, like you just said, he got real angry while you were at the Post Office yesterday."

"And you got real nervous when you saw me giving him my

card. Especially after I told you I'd be looking into the matter while you contacted the postal inspectors. You'd already done everything you could to hold them off. When the folks on Hank's route started asking where their mail was you ran straight to Rut with it, figuring he'd do his best to keep it local for you. He's fond of you and you took advantage of that. Tell me, why did you leave all of that torn-up mail on Johnny Cake?"

"Like you said, folks were starting to ask questions. I thought it created a plausible explanation—that maybe a couple of local teenagers were to blame. I was just hoping to buy some time."

"But you couldn't buy time with Hank."

"I asked him what he was going to do," Paulette recalled bitterly. "He told me that he intended to tell you people everything. He said he had no choice. Which left *me* with no choice."

"So you staged Hank's suicide and made it look like *he'd* been the grinch. You murdered him to save Casey. And Casey helped you do it. The two of you pulled it off together."

"Yes," Paulette admitted. "I got the idea after Bryce Peck took his own life. I thought that maybe we could make it look like Hank took his, too. And have him confess to stealing the mail."

"Which would wrap the whole mess up in a nice neat bow. And that would be the end of it."

"Did Bryce Peck have anything to do with stealing those prescription meds from Hank Merrill's route?" The Aardvark wanted to know.

Paulette shook her head. "Nothing at all."

Des said, "Casey was your son. You felt you had to rescue him. I get that. But you sacrificed Hank in the process. How could you do that? Didn't you love him, too?"

Paulette took a deep breath, letting it out slowly. "Hank was nice to have around. Good company, handy. But I've only been in love with one man in my life—my ex-husband Clint. After Clint left me I've never let another man into my heart. It's just been Casey and me."

"Why don't you tell us how you and Casey staged Hank's murder?"

Paulette gazed out the front window at the darkened street. "When Hank came home from work all he wanted to do was play with his train set. He didn't want to talk to me. I fetched him a beer, like usual. Only this time I added two ground-up Valiums. Within a half hour he was in la-la land. Casey and I walked him out to the garage and got him into the passenger seat of his Passat. I made sure he was slumped over when I backed out of the driveway, just in case one of our neighbors saw us leave."

"One of your neighbors did. She saw Hank's car pull out and head toward Frederick Lane. She couldn't see who was behind the wheel. Assumed it was Hank. And saw no passengers in the car."

"Casey left a few minutes later. He went in the opposite direction, like he was heading to the Rustic. He wasn't. He met me at the boat launch on Kinney Road. It's a remote spot. I figured nobody would come along for hours. I also knew that the Beckmans and the Shermans were both away."

"Wait, how did you know that?" The Aardvark wondered.

"Because they'd stopped their mail."

"Of course." He puffed out his cheeks. "You'd be in a position to know that, wouldn't you?"

"I had an unmarked prescription bottle full of Valium in my pocket. Also a pair of latex gloves. I'd already stowed the hose, the duct tape and box cutter in Hank's trunk. And a full bottle of Jack Daniels."

Des said, "When I asked if you kept any bourbon in the house you marched straight into the kitchen and came back with a half-empty bottle of Jack Daniels. Nice bit of playacting on your part. You bought yourself another bottle, didn't you?"

"Didn't have to. One of Hank's firehouse buddies gave him one for Christmas. It was under the tree in the living room."

"What'd you do after you parked at the boat launch?"

"I got out and asked him to move on over behind the wheel, which he did. He was very compliant. Or he was until I told him to drink down the bottle of Jack Daniels. He had a few sips but then he didn't want anymore. He became extremely resistant, in fact. We had to force him to drink it. Casey gripped him by the neck while I—"

"You held a gun to his head," Des said. "A Smith and Wesson .38 Special."

Paulette looked at her in surprise. "Why, yes."

"After he passed out you slipped on the latex gloves and got down to business. Tucked the Valium bottle into his jacket pocket and sent yourself that text message from his phone. Am I right?"

She nodded her head. "I left my cell phone here. I was careful to make sure I did that. Casey got the other things out of the trunk. We duct taped the hose to the tailpipe, then ran it in through the driver's window and rolled it up."

"You thought of every little detail. You even left my business card on the seat next to Hank's phone. You were very clever, Paulette. But you weren't smart. You left bruising on his neck and forehead when you forced him to drink that bourbon. You also failed to account for how Hank managed to rig up the hose to his tailpipe without ever getting out of the car. It was pouring rain out. Yet, somehow, his hair was dry. So were his shoes and his floor mat. The duct tape and box cutter were wet when I got there. The passenger seat, too. And the passenger-side floor mat was missing."

"I panicked a little," Paulette conceded. "Actually, I panicked a lot. I guess it was the . . . finality of it."

"Yeah, death is pretty damned final."

"I started shaking and couldn't stop. So I sat back down in the passenger seat to collect myself. I wanted to make sure that we'd done everything right before I turned on the engine and we left him there. When I realized I'd gotten the floor mat all wet I took it along. Figured it didn't matter if the duct tape and box cutter were wet."

"And what about the seat?"

Paulette took a small sip of her wine. "There was nothing I could do about it. I hoped you wouldn't notice. That was a mistake."

"It wasn't your only one. You also took the Jack Daniels bottle with you."

"That was Casey's doing," she acknowledged glumly. "I told him to leave it there. The poor fool thought he was being thorough. He just didn't understand."

"Where is it now?"

"He tossed it in a Dumpster this morning when he went out to buy cigarettes."

"And what about the .38 that you held to Hank's forehead?" Questa asked. "We traced an identical weapon to one of your carriers, Abe Monahan. Abe is currently on vacation with his family. How did you get the weapon out of his house? Did Tina Champlain help you?"

"*Tina?*" Paulette blinked at him. "I have no idea what you're talking about."

"Where'd you get the .38, Paulette?" Des asked.

"Casey bought it last year from some lowlife at the Rustic. It made him feel manly to have a gun."

"Where is it now?"

"In the bottom drawer of my dresser. Do you want me to get it?"

"That's okay. We'll do it."

"Whatever," Paulette said hopelessly. "It doesn't matter. Nothing matters now that he's gone. I was his mother. When you're a mother you do whatever it takes to protect your child. He was desperate. I gave him every penny I had. And when that still wasn't enough I did what I had to do. What any mother would do. None of you are mothers. You don't know what it means. Casey came from inside of me. He was connected to me. And he wasn't strong. He still needed me. He never stopped needing me."

"And now he's dead," Des pointed out. "And *you* got him killed. When you murdered Hank you wrote Casey's death sentence. There was absolutely no way Slick Rick and Tommy the Pinhead could let him stay alive. Not once they knew that the postal inspectors were grilling him about Hank's so-called suicide. Casey wasn't strong, like you said. They were positive he'd rat them out to save his own skin. They had to create some daylight between themselves and Casey. You left them no choice, Paulette. By killing your own boyfriend to protect Casey you ended up getting Casey killed."

"I did not," Paulette insisted heatedly. "Don't you dare blame me for what happened. It's Josie Cantro's fault. Every damned bit of it."

"Are you implicating his life coach in these crimes?" Grisky asked.

"I'm saying she led Casey on. He thought she was in love with him. He thought they had a future together. That's why he started betting so much money on football games. He wanted to make a fortune so that they could run away to Hawaii together. He did it for Josie. She's the one who ought to be locked up. If it hadn't been for that manipulative blond bitch, none of this would have ever happened."

"She told me she was trying to help him be more assertive," Des said.

"How?" Paulette demanded. "By filling his head with crazy fantasies? He was still a child. I should never have brought those two together. That's what I regret. But after she helped Hank quit smoking I thought that maybe, just maybe, she could help Casey, too. Biggest mistake I've ever made in my life. I'll never forgive myself. I'll never forgive *her.* She's supposed to be a professional. She should have known that he'd fall head over heels in love with her. Why, he even talked about her as if the two of them were actual lovers."

Des didn't touch that. None of them did. There was no point. Was Josie Cantro America's sweetheart? Not really. Did Des approve of her methods? Not really. Did trouble seem to have a way of following her around? Yeah, it did. So did lucrative estate settlements. But was Josie legally responsible for anything that had just gone down? No, she wasn't. Not unless the M.E. discovered that Bryce Peck's death was something other than a straight suicide. So far, he'd found no evidence of foul play and Des's gut feeling was that he never would. Bryce Peck was a burn-out case who'd taken his own life.

"Paulette, we can debate Josie Cantro's ethics all night," she said. "But it won't alter the simple truth of this matter, which is that Josie didn't steal the U.S. Mail or kill Hank. *You* did."

Paulette said nothing in response. Just stared morosely out the front window at the street.

"Well, I guess that's it then," Grisky concluded, rubbing his hands together.

"Real solid work, Master Sergeant," Sam Questa said.

Grisky nodded his jarhead in agreement. "Good job, girlfriend. If you ask me, your talents are wasted in this town."

Des looked at Paulette, who was still staring out the front window, before she said, "You couldn't be more wrong, Agent Grisky. This is where I'm needed. And I'm *still* not your girlfriend."

Epilogue

(ONE DAY LATER)

THE WORLD-CLASS PISSING CONTEST didn't stop after Paulette's arrest for the murder of Hank Merrill. Since Hank was an employee of the U.S. Postal Service his murder constituted a federal crime and the Department of Justice wanted to take the case away from Connecticut's prosecutors and try it in a U.S. Court. What with Casey Zander being a postal service employee, too, the feds also wanted their hands on Tommy the Pinhead, hoping they could persuade him to flip on Slick Rick Fontanella and the Castagno crime family.

The case got a lot of media attention in the days leading up to Christmas. Mitch followed it online when he was feeling well enough. Mostly, he stayed in bed with his two cats and his ten toes that ached beyond belief. His fingers weren't so terrific either. He also had a wicked headache, blurry vision and got so dizzy whenever he tried to stand up that he had to lean against the nearest piece of large furniture. But Dr. Cindie had assured him his head would feel a little bit better every day. Also that he'd suffered no permanent nerve damage to his fingers or toes. He just had to take it easy for a while.

Des stopped by regularly to fuss over him and to remove her yellow string bikini from his Chanukah bush. Much to Mitch's delight, she'd found his wallet and his grandfather's Omega in the trunk of Tommy's Trans Am. Tommy hadn't bothered to dispose of the stuff after he and Gigi left Mitch on the beach with Casey to die. Apparently, he'd been more interested in scoring a pizza and boinking Gigi.

They didn't call him Tommy the Pinhead for nothing.

When Mitch started to feel a bit more alert he logged on to the NOAA Web site and computed the temperature, wind velocity and windchill factor out on Breezy Point when the sun was falling that day, to determine just how long he could have survived out there. Near as he could tell, if it had taken Des and Yolie longer than twenty more minutes to find him he'd now be hobbling around with no toes—if he was lucky enough to be hobbling around at all. *If* being the operative word. *If* Rut Peck hadn't called Des from the Rustic when he had. *If* she and Yolie hadn't made a beeline to the Rustic, then the Yankee Doodle, then Tommy the Pinhead's apartment. *If* Tommy the Pinhead and Gigi hadn't been home in bed. *If* . . .

He was stretched out on the loveseat in front of a roaring fire when he got a phone call from Rut Peck, who was back in residence at Essex Meadows.

"Glad to hear that you're on the mend, young fella."

"Rut, I sure do apologize for abandoning you that way at the Rustic."

"No apology necessary. Liveliest afternoon I've had in ages."

"I also want you to know how sorry I am about Paulette."

The old postmaster fell silent, breathing heavily in and out. "Me, too."

"Did you have any idea what she was up to?" Mitch asked, recalling how uneasy the old fellow had seemed that night in his cellar, when he first told Mitch about the grinch.

"I knew that Casey was no good. I figured if things were going missing he had to be mixed up in it somehow. But I never imagined that Paulette was in on it with him. That she'd betray the job and do something so awful to Hank. No sir, not in a million years. But you never think that way about the people who you're fond of—no matter how old and wise you get. Not that I feel very wise right now. Just kind of sad."

"I guess Paulette felt she had no choice."

"We always have a choice, young fella," Rut said. "Always."

Josie stopped by a few minutes after that toting a blender full of something that looked a lot like purple diarrhea. "I'm *so* happy that you're up and about, naybs," she exclaimed, all bright eyed and pink cheeked. "I made you one of my smoothies. It's got bananas, raw kale and a bunch of Big Sister wild blackberries that I found in the freezer. Just what you need right now. Go ahead, taste it."

Mitch forced himself to take a small sip, swallowing hard. "Yum, it's as good as it looks. I'll have the rest of it later. I'm kind of full right now."

Josie tilted her blond head at him. "I'm not going to find another stash of Cocoa Puffs in your fridge am I?"

Right away, Mitch flashed back to Casey hurling his Cocoa Puffs in the parking lot of the Rustic after Tommy the Pinhead punched him in the stomach. It was one of the last things Mitch remembered before Tommy K.O.'d him with that snow shovel. "Naybs, I won't ever eat Cocoa Puffs again."

"Wow, I actually believe you." Josie perched on the edge of an overstuffed chair, clearing her throat. "So now you know everything sordid and awful about me, don't you? Des must have told you."

"She told me a bit," he acknowledged. Actually, she'd told him all about the life that Josie had led before she arrived in Dorset. Des had done so in a flat, emotionless voice. Had taken no pleasure in the telling. Des Mitry wasn't wired that way. "For starters, that your father didn't abandon you and your mother when you were twelve. He was killed in some kind of a hunting accident."

"It was no hunting accident," Josie said quietly. "My mother shot him. The police gave her a pass because they knew he'd been beating the crap out of her for years. Also that if they put her away there'd be no one to take care of me. Not that she was much good at the mothering thing. All she ever did was get loaded every night. I told you the truth, Mitch. I've been on my own since I was sixteen. I've done whatever I had to do to survive. Plenty of things that I'm not particularly proud of. But I'm not any kind of evil, scheming bitch. Just someone who's been trying to make my own way." Her big blue eyes locked on to his pleadingly. "Is that so horrible?"

"No, it's not."

She gazed into the fire now. "I know how it looks. I've lived with two older men, James and Bryce. They both killed themselves. And they both made sure I wouldn't get kicked out of the house after they died. I didn't ask either of them to do that for me. I didn't even know that they had. James and Bryce were messed up. They needed help badly. I tried to help. I failed them. I failed Casey, too. That doesn't make me a rotten person. But now everyone in Dorset thinks I am, just like they did in Castine. Because I'm an outsider. Because I'm *different*. I had to leave Castine, you know. People started spray painting the word *whore* on my car. They drove me out of there and now they'll drive me out of Dorset. Preston Peck will see to that. Glynis told me he's prepared to offer me a 'generous' cash settlement if I'll clear out. That's pretty much what I've decided to do. I'm just waiting for the medical examiner's office to release Bryce's body. I promised Bryce I'd cremate him and scatter his ashes on the beach here. I intend to

259

keep that promise. And I don't give a damn what Preston thinks."

"I'd like to be there when you do it, if you don't mind."

"I don't mind. I'd like you to be there."

"I'd also like you to reconsider your decision. Don't let him drive you away. Stay here and slug it out."

Josie looked at him curiously. "Are you serious?"

"Absolutely. I've gotten used to having you around. I'll miss you. You're not the only person in the world who's *different*, you know. I've been *different* my whole life. My idea of a good time is sitting in a dark room staring at a wall. *Normal* people think I'm completely crazy. But *normal* people are total bores. They're also the ones who're responsible for pretty much everything that goes wrong in this world. I think you should stay, Josie. You've made a home for yourself here. You have clients who need you. Don't go."

"A certain resident trooper wouldn't like it very much if I stayed."

"Who, Des? She'll be fine with it. Lots of people will. Dorset is changing fast. This isn't the same place it used to be. She's living proof of that. *We're* living proof of that. Besides, you can't keep running away your whole life. You have to put down roots."

Josie shook her head at him. "No, you don't."

"Where will you go?"

"Somewhere warm. Anywhere warm." Josie let out a mournful sigh. "Anywhere but here."

It was starting to snow again as Des eased her cruiser across the causeway, a huge bag of groceries riding on the seat next to her, along with Mitch's Christmas present. Eight inches of fresh white powder were expected overnight. Happily, Mitch's concussion symptoms were starting to ease off. Des knew this because tonight he'd placed his first highly specific dinner order—her smothered pork chops with home fries and sautéed collard greens. If Mitch had his normal appetite back then all was right in his world. And in hers, too.

He had a bottle of Chianti Classico open when she got there. A big fire blazed in the fireplace. Neil Young was on the stereo. And that wasn't all.

"Mitch, how did my little yellow bikini end up on that Christmas tree *again*?"

"I can't remember," he replied, beaming at her. "I'm still concussed."

"You know what I was thinking while I was driving over here? This is going to be my happiest Christmas ever. Would you like to know why?"

"Because I didn't freeze to death?"

"Well, yeah."

"I'm kind of happy about that, too."

As soon as they got comfy in front of the fire with their wine she handed over his present.

"Hey, I thought we were going to wait until Christmas morning to exchange gifts," he said.

"Hey, I changed my mind," she said. "Open it."

He tore open the wrapping to reveal an old book. But not just any old book. It was a signed Random House 1941 first edition of his all-time favorite Hollywood novel, *What Makes Sammy Run?* by Mr. Budd Schulberg, who also wrote the screenplays for two of his favorite films, *On the Waterfront* and *A Face in the Crowd*. It was in perfect condition, dust jacket and all.

Mitch drew in his breath, awestruck. "Do you have *any* idea how rare this is?"

"Pretty good idea."

"You shouldn't have."

"And yet I did. Nothing's too good for my boyfriend."

"Wow, girlfriend . . . Thank you large."

"You're welcome large."

Now he fetched a mailer pouch from his writing table and handed it to her. "I haven't wrapped yours yet. And it's going to seem like a dog biscuit in comparison. Promise me you won't laugh?"

"I promise." She opened it to find a navy blue wool beret inside. *A hat? He bought me a HAT?* Wait, there was something else tucked in the pouch. A letter-sized envelope containing . . . a pair of open-ended first-class tickets from JFK to CDG—as in Charles de Gaulle International Airport in Paris, France.

"We still haven't spent time together in Paris," he explained as she stared at him with her mouth open. She was not laughing. "It's something we've just got to do. And we have to do it in April. No other month's nearly as glorious. I figured we'd spend a couple of weeks there, then rent a car and get lost down in the Loire Valley until we max out your vacation time. Sound okay?"

"Sounds *incredible*. I can't wait." She tried the beret on for size, adjusting it this way and that. "How does it look?"

"Saucy," Mitch replied. "And I happen to be a major fan of saucy."

"Guess what I'd like to do tonight after we eat."

"I'm hoping I have a pretty good idea."

"No, not that. I mean, yeah. But first I want to watch *Palm Beach Story*."

"I must be drifting back into la-la land. It sounded like you just said you want to watch *Palm Beach Story*."

"Can we?"

"I'm afraid not," he answered grimly. "I have to soldier on with

262

my Danny Kaye Film Festival. I made it all of the way through *The Court Jester* this afternoon and tonight I intend to endure *The Man From the Diner's Club.*"

"Mitch, you don't like Danny Kaye."

"That's not entirely accurate. I loathe Danny Kaye."

"So why are you watching all of his movies?"

"Because I have to."

Des peered into his eyes. "You sure you're feeling okay?"

"Never better."

She gazed into the fire, sipping her wine. "You know, you were babbling about some pretty strange stuff when we found you on that beach."

"That doesn't surprise me. Like what?"

"Kids."

"*I* was talking about kids? Boy, I don't remember that at all. What did I say about them?"

"That we never had any. You seemed awful sorry about it, too."

He got up and put another log on the fire, poking at it. "Are you sure? Because that really doesn't sound like me."

"Oh, it was definitely you. The only other man there was Casey and he wasn't doing much talking."

"Des, I must have been delirious."

"So you didn't mean it?"

"Mean what?"

"That you want to have kids."

"I honestly don't know what I meant. Can't even imagine what I . . . Why, do *you* want to have kids?"

"Who, me? Maybe someday. But not right now."

Mitch nodded his head. "Not right now. I agree a hundred percent."

"Are you sure?"

He took a long time before he answered her. "Honestly? I'm not sure about much of anything anymore. But as long as I've got you and your little yellow bikini on my side I'm okay with that."

"I guess that means the bikini stays on your Christmas tree."

"Has to. Unless you want to, you know, model it before dinner."

Des looked up at him through her eyelashes. "If I do that we won't be eating dinner until ten o'clock."

"Actually, it might be after midnight. I'm still concussed. I may have forgotten some critically important moves."

"Not to worry, wow man. I'll refresh your memory."

"You'd do that for me?"

"Happy to," she assured him. "For starters, do you remember where my tattoo is?"

Mitch got that dreamy look on his face. "Oh, yeah . . ."

Des showed him her smile. "Then I think you're going to be just fine."